THE PRIME MINISTER'S SECRET AGENT

PRAISE FOR SUSAN ELIA MacNEAL'S
Maggie Hope Mysteries

"MacNeal's Maggie Hope mysteries are as addictive as a BBC miniseries, with the added attraction of a well-paced thriller. It's not just an action-packed mystery; it's also the story of a family and lovers caught in WWII and one woman's struggle to find her place in a mixed-up world." —*RT Book Reviews* (TOP PICK, 4½ stars)

"Enthralling." —*Mystery Scene Magazine*

"Compulsively readable . . . The true accomplishment of this book is the wonderfully complex Maggie. . . . With deft, empathic prose, author MacNeal creates a wholly engrossing portrait of a coming-of-age woman under fire. . . . She'll draw you in from the first page. . . . You'll be [Maggie Hope's] loyal subject, ready to follow her wherever she goes." —*Oprah.com*

"A charming book with an entertaining premise . . . a fast page-turner with several interesting plot lines keeping you on the edge using humor and playfulness to keep the story moving." —*Seattle Post-Intelligencer*

"Brave, clever Maggie's debut is an enjoyable mix of mystery, thriller and romance that captures the harrowing experiences of life in war-torn London." —*Kirkus Reviews*

"MacNeal layers the story with plenty of atmospheric, Blitz-era details and an appealing working-girl frame story as Maggie and her roommates juggle the demands of rationing and air raids with more mundane worries about boyfriends. . . . The period ambience will win the day for fans." —*Booklist*

"Maggie, a cerebral redhead, makes a smart plucky heroine." —*The Boston Globe*

"A captivating, post-feminist picture of England during its finest hour." —*The Denver Post*

BY SUSAN ELIA MacNEAL

Mr. Churchill's Secretary
Princess Elizabeth's Spy
His Majesty's Hope
The Prime Minister's Secret Agent

The Prime Minister's Secret Agent

A Maggie Hope Mystery

SUSAN ELIA MacNEAL

BANTAM BOOKS TRADE PAPERBACKS

NEW YORK

A Bantam Books Trade Paperback Original

Copyright © 2014 by Susan Elia MacNeal

Excerpt from *Mrs. Roosevelt's Confidante* by Susan Elia MacNeal copyright © 2014 by Susan Elia MacNeal

All rights reserved.

Published in the United States by Bantam Books, an imprint of Random House, a division of Random House LLC, a Penguin Random House Company, New York.

BANTAM BOOKS and the HOUSE colophon are registered trademarks of Random House LLC.

This book contains an excerpt from the forthcoming book *Mrs. Roosevelt's Confidante* by Susan Elia MacNeal. This excerpt has been set for this edition only and may not reflect the final content of the forthcoming edition.

LIBRARY OF CONGRESS CATALOGING-IN-PUBLICATION DATA
MacNeal, Susan Elia.
The Prime Minister's Secret Agent: a Maggie Hope mystery/Susan Elia MacNeal.
pages cm.—(A Maggie Hope mystery)
ISBN 978-0-345-53674-7
eBook ISBN 978-0-345-53910-6
1. Women spies—Fiction. 2. Undercover operations—Fiction. 3. World War, 1939–1945—Scotland—Fiction. 4. Mystery fiction. 5. Spy stories. I. Title.
PS3613.A2774P69 2014
813'.6—dc23
2013050770

Printed in the United States of America on acid-free paper

www.bantamdell.com

2 4 6 8 9 7 5 3

Book design by Dana Leigh Blanchette
Title-page image: © iStockphoto.com

For Kate Miciak and Victoria Skurnick,
Maggie Hope's fairy godmothers,
who sent her to the ball

Battle not with monsters, lest ye become a monster, and if you gaze into the abyss, the abyss gazes also into you.

—Friedrich Nietzsche

By the pricking of my thumbs, something wicked this way comes.

—Shakespeare, *Macbeth*, Act IV, Scene 1

THE PRIME MINISTER'S SECRET AGENT

Prologue

THERE WILL ALWAYS BE AN ENGLAND!

The graffito had been painted defiantly in blue on a brick wall in an alley off Piccadilly, near Green Park in London, during the Battle of Britain, in June 1940. Now, almost a year and a half later, it was faded, pockmarked, almost obliterated. Like London itself, like the British people, still standing alone against Hitler and bracing against imminent invasion of their island, it had seen better days.

Commander Ian Fleming walked past the scrawled sentiment with Dušan Popov, down Piccadilly to St. James's Street, then made a sharp left onto the almost-hidden St. James's Place. Their destination: Dukes Hotel, one of the Commander's favorite haunts. In Fleming's opinion, the bar at Dukes was the best place in London for a Martini, the American Bar at the Savoy notwithstanding.

Fleming was the private secretary and protégé of Rear Admiral John Godfrey, Director of Intelligence for the Royal Navy and the linchpin of all of the top-secret British intelligence agencies as well as the Prime Minister's staff. He was a handsome man, with hooded, downward-slanted eyes, a largish nose, and full lips. He'd just returned from the United States, where he'd assisted Godfrey in writing a blueprint for a new intelligence agency for the U.S.

government, in the hope that it would help the existing ones over-come the petty infighting and withholding of information.

Fleming and Popov passed through Dukes's elegant lobby with its graceful staircase to the dimly lit bar. "It's not the same," Fleming mused, shaking his head as they sat down on blue velvet chairs at a small table in the corner, where they couldn't be overheard.

"What's not the same?" Popov asked, beckoning to a waiter in a white coat. They were surrounded by the soft sounds of mur-mured conversations, punctuated by the occasional muted ring of the telephone from the front desk. "Champagne, my good man."

Popov was known as an international playboy, a lawyer with an import–export business in Belgrade that often took him to Lon-don. He was handsome, almost louche, with a rakish self-confidence that made some of the women in the bar—as well as a few of the men—glance over with interest. His receding brown hair was brushed straight back, his complexion olive, and his eyes gunpow-der gray. His hands were manicured.

"Nothing's the same," Fleming replied. "Dukes. London. All of Britain. It's sad now, worn-out, disheartened. I brought you here instead of Boodle's because I knew you'd appreciate the scen-ery." The two men looked around the small bar. A fire crackled in the fireplace, but still the room was chill. Forced white hyacinths on one of the side tables drooped; they gave off the sickly sweet aroma of decay. A few older men and their lady friends sipped drinks.

Fleming lowered his voice. "But look at these women—too thin, wearing made-over gowns, their lipstick more wax than color. Last year, they would have been laughing and flirting. Now they just look tired—"

The waiter returned with a bottle of Champagne and popped the cork. He poured the pale liquid into two coupes.

Fleming lifted his to the light and inspected it. "—and even the Champagne's flat." During the first year of the war, Londoners had delighted in defying Hitler, making it their personal battle to drink and dance as much as they could to thumb their noses at the Nazis and their bombs, which rained down nightly. In the midst of tragedy, it had been a mark of honor to attend parties and the theater, even if evenings ended in bomb shelters. Those days were now gone. London was changed, scarred, depressed, nerves stretched to the breaking point.

"I passed by a factory the other day," Fleming continued, taking a sip of Champagne. "There was all sorts of noise and banging hammers and singing—sawdust everywhere. And I thought, *How wonderful—life and industry go on.*" He grimaced at the wine's taste and set the glass down. "Then I realized they were making coffins."

Popov took a sip and, like Fleming, pushed it away. He lit a cigarette. "It's bad in Berlin, too, if it makes you feel any better."

"A bit," Fleming admitted. He looked around to make sure they couldn't be overheard. "Now, let's hear what you have for us." Popov was working for the British, as a double agent. He was Serbian by birth, born into an affluent Yugoslav family. And he was also a spy. First as agent "Ivan" for the Nazis, then as double agent "Tricycle" for the British.

Popov leaned in. "I've just returned from Lisbon," he said in a low voice. "My Abwehr handler there wants me to set up a network of Nazi spies in the U.S. They have a number of willing recruits, but they're so bumble-fingered that they were caught by the OSS. So Canaris wants me to go to the U.S. and do the job right. Specifically, the Germans want me to go to Hawaii."

"Hawaii?" This surprised the usually unflappable Fleming. "That's a bit off your usual beat, old thing."

"My handler gave me a very interesting questionnaire, from the higher-ups at the Abwehr, who are working with the Japanese. He wants me to fill it out when I go to the United States next week."

"Really."

"It has to do with Pearl Harbor, to be exact. The U.S. just moved their fleet there, from San Diego. They want me to gather information to be passed to Germany, then on to the Japanese. Detailed questions about Pearl Harbor's port facilities, fuel supply, fuel dumps, ammunition dump, ships and where they're berthed. Detailed operational planning. Looks like the British attack on Taranto proved to be an inspiration. The Royal Air Force took out more than half the Italian fleet at one go. One can only assume that Japan wants to repeat a surprise Taranto-style raid at Pearl Harbor."

Fleming shook his head. "Pearl's too shallow."

"When the RAF took out the *Regia Marina* in the harbor of Taranto they used aerial torpedoes, which took out the ships despite the shallow water."

"Bloody hell." Fleming took another sip of Champagne and grimaced again. "If the Japs attack Pearl Harbor—"

"—it might be just the thing to get Roosevelt and the Yanks into this war." Popov sighed, tapping his cigarette's ashes into a heavy crystal bowl.

"I'll set up a meeting for you with Hoover at the FBI when you arrive in Washington."

Popov leaned back in his chair, eyeing a new woman who'd entered the bar. "By the way, did you know that the Germans aren't using invisible ink anymore?" he said, finally turning his attention back to Fleming.

"No?" Fleming cocked an eyebrow. "What are the Krauts using?"

"Microdots. Pages and pages of information, stored in a period on a piece of paper. Here's a telegram with one—have your people take a look at it." He reached into the inside pocket of his dinner jacket and pulled out an innocuous-looking missive, laid it on the table. Then, "Speaking of the Abwehr, how is Clara Hess?"

Fleming sighed, then reached over and smoothly pocketed the envelope. "She's been in the country for over two months now. We haven't gotten much from her. But Churchill feels she's worth more to us alive than dead."

"Beautiful woman, Clara Hess."

Fleming once again raised an eyebrow. "Her too?"

Popov shrugged. "What can I say? I have a reputation to uphold." He smiled. "Frain says now that she's defected, she wants to spy for Britain—become a double agent."

"I don't trust her." Fleming pushed away his coupe. "However, that doesn't mean she can't be useful to us." He beckoned to one of the white-jacketed waiters.

The man walked over and bowed slightly. "Is everything all right, gentlemen?"

Fleming waved a hand. "Please take away this ghastly excuse for wine—"

The waiter bowed again. "Yes, sir. So sorry, sir—"

"—and bring us each one of your fabulous Martinis. Plymouth Gin, of course."

"Yes, sir. Right away, sir." The waiter swiftly made his way back to the bar.

Fleming called over, "And my good man—make sure they're shaken, not stirred."

As befitting his cover as a Nazi agent, Popov took a Pan American Dixie Clipper flying boat from San Ruiz, Portugal, to New York, and then traveled by train on to Washington, DC. He was carrying seventy thousand dollars in cash, four telegrams containing eleven German microdots, a hardcover copy of Virginia Woolf's *Night and Day*—which he would use for coding radio messages back to London—and a torn business card to identify himself to a German agent in New York City. He used one of the microdots to bring the Pearl Harbor questionnaire—which he intended to give to Hoover.

Popov arrived at Union Station in Washington, then took a taxi to the Beaux-Arts-designed Mayflower on Connecticut Avenue. He checked in using the U.S. dollars he'd been given by his German handler. The first thing he did after tipping the bellman for his bags was to search his penthouse suite for listening devices. He didn't trust the FBI. He didn't trust the Nazis. He didn't trust anyone except himself, really.

Placed about the rooms were vases of exquisitely made orchids in cut-glass Waterford vases. He pulled the flowers out. One by one, he checked every vase, and in every one, microphones were attached to the stems of the silk flowers—FBI-issued, from the looks of them.

Popov unzipped his suitcase and took out several boxes of medical cotton wool, kept for just such occasions. He wrapped each microphone in each vase individually, smiling as he did so. It would have been too easy just to destroy the mikes; leaving them, but keeping them from actually recording anything, was a much more elegant solution.

Despite jet lag, he had a reputation to uphold. A quick shower and shave, a bespoke dinner jacket, a splash of lavender-scented Pour un Homme de Caron, and he was ready to go to hear jazz at the Howard Theatre.

———

After days of interminable bureaucratic delays, Popov finally was able to have his audience with Hoover. The head of the FBI was an autocratic man, whose public image was that of puritanical morality. He was stocky, with a fleshy face and tightly set lips.

After a string of late nights, Popov arrived freshly shaved and lightly scented with cologne, hair slicked back with pomade. Although he'd met a number of times with Percy Foxworth, chief of the FBI's Special Intelligence Service and principal liaison with British Security Coordination, this was his first meeting with Hoover. The FBI director didn't bother to stand as Popov was ushered into his office by a stern-faced secretary.

He met Popov's eyes with a baleful glance and then a brusque "Sit down."

Popov did, looking around Hoover's office. It was spacious, but spartan and meticulously clean, with a large American flag and an enormous bronze eagle presiding. The room smelled of floor wax and window cleaner.

"I realize this meeting is unusual," Popov said, crossing his legs and taking out a cigarette, "but it's urgent. I have information you must see—a matter of the United States' national security." Popov handed over a sheaf of bills, a few telegrams, and a personal letter.

"No smoking in here," Hoover barked. Then, "What's this?"

Popov put away his unlit cigarette but gave a Cheshire-cat smile. "Information from the Abwehr. A questionnaire from the Japanese—about Pearl Harbor."

Hoover examined the bills, turning them backward and forward, holding them up to the light to check for invisible ink. He found nothing. And nothing on any of the other papers. "Don't joke with me, Popov—you'll regret it."

"Sir, I assure you that all the information from the Abwehr is contained in those documents."

"Fine, I'll have one of our cryptographers take a look at them."

Popov's smile spread over his leonine face. "No need. Is there a microscope in the building? Tweezers?"

Calls were made and when a young and cowed minion finally procured both, Popov picked up a seemingly nondescript telephone bill and held it in the slanted light from the window, showing Hoover how one of the full stops had a reflective coating. Carefully, Popov lifted the dot from the paper with the tweezers, and then put it under the microscope. He gestured to Hoover to look.

The director of the FBI stood and begrudgingly did.

Popov's smile broadened. "In that particular dot, you will find the Abwehr questionnaire, which we believe is research for Japan's Taranto-style attack on Pearl Harbor."

Hoover's face turned red. "Sit down, Popov," he snapped, starting to pace.

Popov continued, "The U.S. fleet in the Pacific operates on an inflexible schedule—at sea for certain lengths of time and at port in between. If someone is able to figure out this schedule, a sneak attack while the ships are docked at Pearl—most likely on a Sunday—is a clear possibility."

"Attack on Pearl Harbor." Hoover rounded on his desk, and pounded on it with his fist to emphasize each word. "Ridiculous! The Japs wouldn't dare! We all know that you're a rich man, a popular man, a *handsome* man—"

"I'm a spy," Popov interrupted, also standing. "I'm not a spy who turned into a playboy, I'm a man who's always lived very well who's turned into a spy. That's my cover, and it's a superb one. However, if I were undercover as a factory worker, I'd work as a factory worker."

"Why don't you, then?" Hoover spat.

"Because the Germans, who have known me for decades as an

idle playboy, would be suspicious. But please believe me, if I thought it would help our common cause, I'd live on bread and water, in the worst slum you could procure."

"With your own agendas and access, of course. You work for the Nazis, you work for MI-Six—now you're allegedly trying to help us! Where are your loyalties, man? Do you even have any?" He sat and waved one hand. "Get out."

Instead Popov took out his cigarette. This time he lit it. "I have brought you and the United States of America a serious warning, on a silver salver, indicating exactly where, when, how, and by whom your country is to be attacked."

"And even if this preposterous questionnaire points to an attack, which I doubt—looks like routine surveillance to me—what do you want in exchange?"

"I want you to pass it along to President Roosevelt, to the Secretary of State, to the Secretary of War, to the heads of the Army and Navy. To that poor bastard Kimmel, who's the Commander in Chief of the Fleet in Pearl Harbor. To any of your boys looking after Ambassador Kichisaburō Nomura in Washington and the Japanese consulate in Honolulu. They all need to know what's coming—and they'll need to coordinate their efforts."

Hoover's eyes narrowed. "What else do you want?"

"The Germans want me to go to Hawaii, to keep an eye on Pearl, to create a spy network there, to feed information to their Japanese agents there. It's the ideal position for me to send crucial information to you."

Hoover snorted. "You want to sit out the war on Waikiki Beach, Mai Tai in hand, courtesy of the U.S. government? Add a few hula girls to your roster of showgirls and movie stars and burlesque dancers, heh?"

Popov was trying valiantly to hold his temper. "We all have our areas of expertise, Mr. Hoover. Mine is the life of an international playboy. But just because of that, or even in spite of that, don't disregard me, or my message. I think a Japanese attack on Pearl Harbor is imminent. And President Roosevelt needs to be warned."

Hoover gave a braying laugh. "I do believe you're trying to teach me my job, Popov!"

Popov shook his head. "I don't think anyone could teach you anything." He stood and clicked his heels together. "Sir." He left.

"Good riddance!" Hoover called after him. He gestured through the open door to his secretary, a stern-faced plump older woman in glasses and pearls. "File this," he said, holding out the document with the tips of two fingers, as though it carried plague germs.

The secretary entered his office. "File it under what, sir?"

"Doesn't matter. Just get rid of it."

Chapter One

Maggie Hope had thought that summer in Berlin was hell, but it was nothing compared to the inferno of darkness that now raged in her own head, even as she was "safe as houses" in Arisaig on the western coast of Scotland.

A mixture of shame, anger, guilt, and grief had become a miasma of depression, which followed her everywhere, not at all helped by the lack of daylight in Scotland in November. She'd once heard Winston Churchill describe his own melancholy as his "Black Dog," but didn't understand it. She'd pictured a large black dog with long silky fur and dark, sad eyes, silently padding after his master.

But now she knew the truth: The Black Dog of depression was dirty and scarred, feral and rabid. He lurked in the night, yellow eyes gleaming, waiting for a chink in the armor, a weakness, a vulnerability, a memory. And then, jaws wide and fangs sharp, he would leap. She had trouble sleeping, and when she did finally fall unconscious, she had nightmares.

Sometimes, just sometimes, Maggie had a few moments in the morning, when she first woke up, when she didn't remember her nightmares, or any of what had happened. Those were blessed moments, innocent and sweet. Until her mind started working again, and the sharp ache returned to her heart. She remembered what had transpired in Berlin. Remembered that her contact, Gottlieb Lehrer, was dead—a devout Catholic who'd shot himself rather than be taken by the Gestapo for questioning. Remembered that she herself had killed a man.

"It was self-defense," the analyst she'd been ordered to see by Peter Frain had told her. "It's war. You don't need to torture yourself." And yet, even though he'd shot first, and she'd killed in self-defense, the man's eyes—sad and reproachful—haunted her.

As did the high-pitched voice of the little Jewish girl being pushed into a cattle car in Berlin, destined for Poland. "I'm thirsty, Mama," she'd cried, "so thirsty." *What happened to her?* Maggie often wondered. *Did she die on the train? Or later in the camp? Could she still be alive?* Because now that Maggie—and most of the rest of the world—knew that the Nazis were capable of killing their own children, calling it "Operation Compassionate Death," she didn't hold any hope at all for the children of Jews.

And as if that weren't enough burden, her mother, Clara Hess, a Nazi Abwehr agent, was imprisoned in the Tower of London—and asking to talk with her. She was also scheduled to be executed soon, if she didn't share some of the top-secret information she possessed.

And then there was John Sterling, with whom she'd worked at Number 10 for Mr. Churchill during the Battle of Britain. And had almost been engaged to marry. And who'd become an RAF pilot and been shot down near Berlin. And even though she'd managed to rescue them both and get them safe passage from Berlin to Switzerland, their return to London had been, well, less than romantic. More of a romantic disaster, really.

Maggie turned over beneath the scratchy gray wool blankets, reflexively reaching for the hard outline of the German bullet, which had just managed to miss her heart. Dumb luck was what had saved her—and allowed her to kill her attacker, instead. The doctors in Switzerland, and then in London—even one of her best friends, Chuck, a nurse—had wanted her to have the bullet re-moved, but she refused. She called it her "Berlin souvenir."

I'm dead inside, she thought, not for the first time since she'd made it to Arisaig. *Worse than dead—if I were dead at least I wouldn't have to remember everything anymore.*

On her nightstand, the black Bakelite clock ticked, and she reached over to turn it off before the alarm rang. Maggie concen-trated on breathing—in and out, in and out. Even that caused pain, as though she had a shard of ice in her heart.

Maggie had heard the expression *heartache* before, of course, but never thought it would be so literal. So much pain, physical pain in her heart. But the heart was just a muscle, an organ, made to pump blood—not to feel things. So was it stress? Adrenaline? What made it hurt so much? Of course, the brain wasn't much better—the brain could be a hellish prison of despair and pain and emptiness. Who knew that the brain could be such a traitor?

It didn't help that it was coming up on Thanksgiving—and even though she'd lived in Britain since 1938, Maggie still missed her Aunt Edith, a chemistry professor at Wellesley College. She missed the United States sometimes too, truth be told. She missed its innocence—or was it ignorance?—of war, its clear skies and untouched cities. Not to mention unlimited hot water and unra-tioned food. Although she was British by birth, she'd been raised in the U.S., and even though she'd made a choice to throw her lot in with the Brits when war started, she missed her aunt and her friends and their broad, flat, nasal accents. She missed Thanksgiv-ing. She missed turkey and cranberry sauce and pumpkin pie. She missed Boston and Cambridge. She missed America.

Maggie sighed and then rose, washed her face and brushed her teeth in the rust-tinged water in the enamel sink, and changed into her clothes, the brown twill jumpsuit all the instructors wore over layers of thermal underwear and wool socks, plus standard-issue thick-soled boots. She twisted and then pinned up her long red hair with her tortoiseshell clip. If she'd been doing office work, as she had been doing at Number 10 Downing Street, she would have put on the pearl earrings that her Aunt Edith had given to her when she'd graduated from Wellesley in '37—but not only were they inappropriate for her job as an instructor at an SOE camp, she'd lost them somewhere in London after returning from Berlin. *Not that anyone cares about anything as frivolous as earrings anymore.* But they were another symbol of everything she'd lost.

Sallow and pinched, with shadows under her eyes and a chafed red nose, Maggie shrugged into her thick wool coat and pulled on a scarf and stocking cap. She left the upstairs flat of the gardener's cottage, where she'd been assigned to live, and headed to Arisaig House, the large home that loomed above.

Although her body ached and felt as if it were made from spun glass, she jogged to warm her muscles before breaking into a run up the path of the rockery, taking the steep lichen-covered flagstone steps to the manor house at a brisk jog in the darkness. It was November and so it was light only from eight thirty in the morning to four thirty in the afternoon. But to Maggie it *always* seemed dark, not Henry Vaughan's "deep but dazzling darkness" but a sinister absence of light.

Arisaig House was the administrative heart of the War Office for Special Operations Executive—or SOE, as it was better known—in Scotland. SOE was neither MI-5 nor MI-6, but a black ops operation, training agents to be dropped into places such as France and Germany, and helping local resistance groups "set Europe ablaze," as Winston Churchill had admonished. The SOE used great houses all over Britain to train their would-be spies, sparking the joke that *SOE* really stood for "Stately 'omes of England." While training camps were preliminary schools, or specifically dedicated to parachute jumping or radio transmission, Arisaig was the place where trainees received intense training in demolition, weapons, reconnaissance, and clandestine intelligence work.

Isolated on the far western coast of Scotland, closed off by military roadblocks, the rocky mountains and stony beaches were perfect for pushing trainees to their physical and mental limits. Arisaig House was the administrative hub, with its own generator and water supply. Other great houses in the area were used for training—Traigh House, Inverailort, Camusdarrach, and Garramor, just to name a few. Maggie's lips twisted in a smile as she recalled how groups of Czech, Slovak, and Norwegian trainees had stumbled over the Scottish and Gaelic names.

But it was the perfect place for Maggie, still recovering from her wounds.

As an instructor, she trained her charges harder than Olympians—swimming in the freezing loch, navigating obstacle courses in the cold mud, and mastering rope work. From other instructors, the trainees learned field craft, demolition, Morse code, weapons training, and the Fairbairn-Sykes method of silent killing. Anything and everything they might need to know to be sent to France, or Germany, wherever a local resistance group might need aid.

Maggie hadn't always been a draconian instructor; in fact, the very idea would have made her formerly bookish and dreamy self laugh in disbelief. She'd wanted to earn her PhD in mathematics from MIT, but had instead been in London when war had broken out in 1940. She'd found a job in Winston Churchill's secretarial pool, and, after discovering secret code in an innocuous advertisement, and then foiling an IRA bomb plot, had been tapped for MI-5. She'd been sent to one of the preliminary training camps in

Scotland as a trainee in the fall of 1940. While she was excellent at Morse code and navigating by stars, she'd flamed out spectacularly at anything that required the least bit of physical fitness.

Approaching the manor house, Maggie recalled how furious she'd been when she'd washed out of the SOE program and Peter Frain of MI-5 had placed her at Windsor Castle to look after the young Princesses. But in retrospect, it had done her good. She'd grown stronger both mentally and physically, and was able to help save Princess Elizabeth from a kidnapping plot.

After her assignment at Windsor with the Royals, she'd returned to SOE training in the spring of 1941. She made it through all the various schools, and, as a newly minted agent, was sent on a secret mission to Berlin. Now she had returned once more to Arisaig House—but this time as an instructor. As she opened the thick oak door, the bells in the clock tower chimed eight times.

The vestibule of the large stone manor house led into the great hall, which SOE had turned into a lobby of sorts, with a desk for a telephone and a receptionist. Sheets protected the grand house's chestnut paneling from the government workers, while Arisaig and Traigh Houses' owner, a Miss Astley Nicholson, had been relocated to a smaller cottage up the road for the duration of the war. However, the spacious high-ceilinged entrance hall with its mullioned windows, staircase elaborately carved with birds and thistles, and views over the fields dotted with white sheep leading down to the jagged coastline made it clear this was no ordinary office.

In the vestibule, Maggie heard an ongoing discussion by some of her current charges: this time around, mostly young women bound for France. Pausing unnoticed in the doorway, she stopped to listen.

"Yes, Miss," the girl on receptionist duty said into the black telephone receiver, twisting the metal cord around her fingers. She was short, sturdy, and a bit stout, with a wide grin and eyes that crinkled when she smiled, which was often. Her name was Gwen Glyn-Jones and she was from Cardiff, Wales. But her mother was French, and she had a perfect accent from summers spent just outside Paris. She wanted to become a radio operator—if she survived the physical training at Arisaig.

In the light of an Army-issue lamp, Gwen scribbled something down on a scrap of paper, and finished with a number. "Yes, Miss—I'll make sure Miss Hope receives the message as soon as possible. Thank you, Miss." She hung up.

"Message for Lady Macbeth?" one of the other girls asked. Yvonne had been born and raised in Brixton, London, but her grandfather was French—from Normandy—and, like Gwen, she was bilingual.

"The one and only." The girls giggled. Maggie was strict. She was hard on her students. She never smiled. None of the women at Arisaig House liked her. None of the men liked her much, either, for that matter. "I loathe being in her section."

Yvonne leaned in. "Why does everyone call her Lady Macbeth?"

"Because she's a monster." Gwen lowered her plummy Welsh-inflected voice. "Rumor is, she has blood on her hands."

Yvonne's eyes opened wide. "Really?"

"I heard she killed a man in France."

Two other trainees walking down the staircase, a man and a woman, joined in the exchange. "I heard she killed three men in Munich," the woman offered.

One of the men said, "I heard she was interrogated by the Gestapo and never talked—"

"She's always nice to the gardener's dog . . ." Yvonne ventured.

"Well, Hitler loves dogs, too."

All right, that's enough. Maggie swept in, giving them what she'd come to call her "best Aunt Edith look"——cold and withering.

"Two, Five, and Eight—aren't you supposed to be out running?" Maggie had given her trainees numbers instead of names.

There was an uncomfortable silence, punctured only by the ticking of a great mahogany long-case clock. Then, "I'm on desk duty . . ." sputtered Gwen.

"And I was waiting . . ." Yvonne tried.

Maggie held up one hand. "Stop making excuses."

"I'm—I'm sorry, Miss Hope," Gwen stuttered.

"Stop apologizing." Maggie looked them all up and down. "You—Twelve—stay here and do your job. You others—go run on the beach. Relay races on the stony part of the shore—they're good for your ankles and knees and will help your parachute jumps. I'll be there shortly."

They stared, frozen in place.

Maggie glared. "I said, *go.* Go! *Gae own wi' it,* as they say around here!"

The trainees nearly fell over themselves in their haste to get away from her. Gwen became very busy at the reception desk.

Harold Burns, a fit man with smile lines etched around his eyes and rough skin dotted with liver spots, walked in from one of the other huge rooms of the house, now used as administrative offices. He favored Maggie with a wintry grin from around the billiard pipe clenched between his teeth. The tobacco smoke smelled sweet in the frigid air.

He removed the pipe to speak. "Impressive, Miss Hope. I remember a time when you could barely run a mile without passing out. Or twisting your ankle. Or dropping your fellow trainees in the mud."

Maggie put a finger to her lips. "Shhhhh, Mr. Burns. That's our little secret."

Burns fell into step beside her. They entered what used to be the great house's dining room. "When you first came here, you were god-awful. One of the worst trainees I ever had. But you persevered. And you came back. You worked hard. I've heard of some of the things you've accomplished, Miss Hope, and I must say I'm proud." Mr. Burns was a survivor of the Great War. Maggie could see in his eyes that, like her, he had seen things. Things he wished he hadn't.

The grandfather clock chimed, sending out a loud metallic *gong*. Maggie started, breathing fast, pupils dilated.

"It's all right," Mr. Burns murmured as if to a lost lamb, nearly putting a hand on her arm—and then withdrawing it. "You're safe here, Miss Hope."

Safe. Who's safe, really? Certainly not children with any sort of illness in Germany. Certainly not the Jews. Certainly not young men who just happen to be on the wrong side of a gun. But Maggie liked Mr. Burns, she did, even though he'd been hard on her when she'd been in his section. In fact, much of what he taught her had helped keep her alive in Berlin.

She looked out the window, to the sheep grazing in the neighboring fields, in the shadow of mountains. Maggie watched them until she felt calmer.

"Thank you, Mr. Burns." She reached for the letter in her marked mail cubby and opened it. She frowned as she read the contents.

"Everything all right, Miss Hope?"

She didn't receive that many letters. Occasionally a postcard from David, Mr. Churchill's chief private secretary at Number 10—with funny pen-and-ink cartoons illustrating his favorite expressions: *Merciful Minerva* and *Jumping Jupiter.* Sarah sent letters in loopy scrawl on hotel stationery from around Britain, on tour with the Vic-Wells Ballet. And Chuck wrote less now that her husband, Nigel, was stationed in the Mideast and she was taking care of their baby, Griffin, almost three months old. And of course there was RAF pilot Captain John Sterling, now working once again for Mr. Churchill. But after what had happened between them in London last summer, after their return from Berlin, Maggie didn't expect any letters from him.

But in fact, everything was *not* all right. The letter was regarding Maggie's house—the house on Portland Place in Marylebone that she'd inherited from her Grandmother Hope and moved to in '38. The house she'd lived in with flatmates Paige, Sarah, Chuck, and the twins. The house that, after everything that had happened with the attempted assassination of Mr. Churchill, the planned bombing of St. Paul's, and Paige's death, she'd wanted nothing to do with. She'd let out to a lovely couple—he a high-level muckety-muck at the Treasury and she a young wife with the Wrens.

According to the letter, the house had sustained significant bomb damage. Her tenants—who had survived—had moved.

"Fine, fine, Mr. Burns," Maggie murmured. "Everything's just fine."

But her face said otherwise. She hadn't been to the house in over a year, yes—but it was still a part of her, part of her family, part of her past, a past that had grown ever more complicated and confusing the more she learned about it. And now it had been bombed. Was she sad? Angry at the Luftwaffe? Maybe even just a little bit relieved to be free of the responsibility of it and forced to move on? *It doesn't matter anyway,* she decided. *Probably all for the best.* She crumpled the letter and threw it into the waste bin.

Burns shifted his weight from side to side. "You know, Miss Hope, I served, too—over in France, in the trenches. I was a soldier then. Oh, you wouldn't know it now, but once I was young—almost handsome, too. We all were, back then. Saw a lot of my friends killed, better men than I ever was, and killed any number myself."

"Mr. Burns—no one died. Truly. It's just a house—my house—that was bombed. But no one was hurt. And houses can—perhaps someday—be rebuilt."

Mr. Burns didn't seem to hear her, lost in his own memories. "I don't remember their faces, but I still think of them. What I try to remember is the Christmas truce—Christmas of '14, we had a cease-fire over in France. We sang songs, if you can believe—us with 'Silent Night,' and them with 'Stille Nacht.' Same melody, though. We even had a game of football, that afternoon, the 'Huns' versus the 'Island Apes.' Then, the next day, back to the killing business . . ."

He shook his head. "I'll leave you to read your telephone message, Miss Hope."

"Thank you, Mr. Burns." Maggie turned her attention to the message Gwen had written out:

Sarah Sanderson called to say that the Vic-Wells Ballet is performing La Sylphide *at the Royal Lyceum Theatre in Edinburgh. She may be going on as the Sylph (and she specified, "the* lead *sylph, not one of the idiot fairies fluttering uselessly in the background"). She'll put house seats on hold for you and truly hopes you'll make it!*

Long-legged and high-cheekboned, Sarah was one of Maggie's closest friends. At first Maggie had found her intimidating—Sarah was so worldly, after all, so beautiful and glamorous, with the slim figure of a runway model, dark sparkling eyes, and long dark hair. But she had an irresistible sense of humor and was given to witty retorts in a decidedly Liverpudlian accent.

Maggie had only seen Sarah a few times since they'd parted ways in London the summer of the attempted bombing of St. Paul's Cathedral, and missed her. If it was at all possible, she'd make it to Sarah's performance. The trouble was the Black Dog. Would the Black Dog let her? Sometimes it was hard to know. He was always ready to strike, but would he go for her throat? She walked back to the entrance hall, Mr. Burns not far behind.

"Miss Hope?" Gwen asked from her seat at the reception desk.

Maggie blinked. "Yes, Twelve."

"Are you—are you going to go to Edinburgh to see your friend dance in the ballet? Because that sounds so very exciting and glamorous—and, quite frankly, fun."

Fun. What's fun anymore? The Black Dog growled low in his throat and bared his teeth. But he didn't strike.

"Miss Hope?" Mr. Burns said. "I'll arrange for the time off, if you'd like to go."

Maggie crumpled the message and threw it into the trash bin. "Thank you, but I won't be needing it, Mr. Burns."

She turned back to the girl. "Carry on, Twelve!"

Then she pivoted on her heel to make her way to the back garden and down to her trainees, whom she'd sent to run on the beach.

I can't, Sarah, I just can't do it, she thought. *I'm sorry, so very sorry.*

Take it up with the Black Dog.

Chapter Two

As the winter sun was rising in Arisaig, Scotland, it was setting over Kagoshima Bay in Japan—a deep inlet on the south coast of the island of Kyūshū, Japan's southwesternmost island and the port for the city of Kagoshima. The bay was shallow and well protected, just like Pearl Harbor, which made it ideal for Admiral Yamamoto's war games.

Isoroku Yamamoto was the newly appointed and highly decorated Admiral of the *rengo kantai*—the combined fleet of Japan's Imperial Navy. He was in his midfifties, short and slim, with cropped graying hair cut so short that his skull showed white beneath the bristles. White gloves hid the loss of his two fingers at the Battle of Tsushima. The Admiral wasn't what anyone would call handsome, but he had a certain wry charm, and when he smiled his face lit up.

Yamamoto excelled at all games of strategy, including poker, mah-jongg, and *shogi*—Japanese chess—and loved to gamble. He was also the man behind the questionnaire Dušan Popov's Nazi handler wanted to take with him to Pearl Harbor, Hawaii.

But Yamamoto didn't want to fight. And certainly not with the United States of America, earning him the nickname "the Reluctant Admiral." He didn't believe Japan should have withdrawn from the League of Nations or that Japan should have signed the Tripartite Pact with Nazi Germany and Fascist Italy.

But when the United States had placed an embargo on scrap metal shipments to Japan, closed the Panama Canal to Japanese shipping, and stopped oil and gasoline exports, relations between Japan and the U.S. grew ever more strained. Japan would have to either agree to Washington's demands or use force to gain access to the resources it needed.

Yamamoto stood on the deck of his ship in the cold wind, his breath visible, watching the long-range fighter planes with red suns painted on their wings engage in a mock attack of the ships in port. He held binoculars and looked through, muttering, "Perfect." As Yamamoto gazed at the Mitsubishi Zeros silhouetted against a leaden sky, the wind changed direction.

Behind him, an officer cleared his throat. "Here's the latest intel, sir." The young naval officer saluted, then handed him decrypts from Consul Nagai Kita in Pearl Harbor. "And Kita and Yoshikawa also sent these."

The officer handed over a packet of postcards, which Yamamoto flipped through. *Greetings from Pearl Harbor!* read one. *Aloha!* exclaimed another. *Wish you were here!* Yamamoto's lip twitched at the irony. All the postcards had glossy color photographs showing a clear aerial view of Pearl Harbor.

"I want every pilot to have one of these," Yamamoto ordered, raising his voice to carry over the wind. "They should all have one taped to the dashboard of their planes." He looked at the young man. "Tell Kita we'll need more."

The officer saluted, his cheeks flushed from the cold. "Yes, sir!"

Yamamoto looked through the binoculars again. "I wish the General Staff could see this," he muttered.

"Sir?" The young officer hesitated, unsure whether to stay or go.

"They think that naval engagements are won by whoever has the most battleships. The war in Europe is being fought by the

Luftwaffe against the RAF. Ships have nothing to do with it any-more."

"They won't have a chance against our pilots at Pearl Harbor, sir."

Yamamoto lowered the binoculars. The young man's ears turned red; he knew he'd spoken out of turn.

"I hope our differences may be resolved through diplomacy—peace is always better than war. Always. And anyone ignorant enough to want to go to war with the United States should think about that—especially General Tōjō and his Army hotheads!"

The young man cringed. "Yes, sir."

"It's the Army leaders who are at fault—a bloodthirsty lot." The Admiral looked at the young sailor. "Take a message from me to Commander Fuchida when he lands, saying congratulations on a brilliant drill."

"Yes, sir."

The young man left and once again Yamamoto peered through his binoculars. "Genda's mad plan is a gamble," he muttered, watching the planes. "Six aircraft carriers, planes with modified shallow-water torpedoes, an attack on a Sunday at dawn . . . Refueling, weather . . . If we achieve a surprise attack . . ."

The Admiral shook his head. "No, it is up to the diplomats to prevent all this. They *must* prevent this."

What Yamamoto didn't know was that the reports they were send-ing from Honolulu to Tokyo were being decoded in Washington, DC. And not just by the Japanese Embassy, but by the Americans, as well. The Americans had broken the Japanese diplomatic code, which they called "Purple."

At the U.S. Navy headquarters, an anonymous limestone office building on DC's National Mall, Lieutenant Commander Alvin D.

Kramer was also reading Kita's reports, sometimes decrypting them faster than the Japanese Embassy did. A tall, thin man with the gaunt face of an ascetic, he was responsible for evaluating the intercepts and distributing them to the Navy's higher-ups. His dark-blue uniform was spotless, the white of his collar matched the white of his hair, and the gold bars and stars of his epaulets glinted under the office's fluorescent ceiling lights.

Kramer's fiefdom was in the Main Navy and Munitions Buildings on B Street: a large airless, windowless room where men translated intercepted messages and women typed, the clatter of keys punctuated by the occasional shrill ring of one of the many telephones. The scent of ink and correction fluid hung in the stale air. The walls were lined with shelf upon shelf of files containing untranslated Japanese diplomatic decrypts, stacked so high that some could only be accessed by ladder. There just wasn't enough interest, or enough manpower, to translate all of them as they poured in.

And so most of the messages from Consul Kita in Honolulu waited to be translated, often for weeks, sometimes for months. Above the heads of the workers was a line of clocks with black hands, ticking away the hours, minutes, and seconds in Tokyo, Washington, London, Moscow, Berlin, and Rome.

Colonel Rufus Bratton was two minutes late for his meeting with Kramer. In a sea of blue naval uniforms, Bratton stood out in his Army-issue brown coat and khakis, and the brown hat he carried under his arm. He was short and stocky, with an earnest face and balding pate. His buttons strained under the bulge of his stomach. The men who worked for him had nicknamed him "Grumpy," after the dwarf in *Snow White*.

"Good morning, Colonel Bratton." Kramer's secretary looked up from her typewriter. Dorothy Edgars was new, but she'd made it her business to learn the names and faces of the key players in the office. She was in her late thirties, with dark hair streaked with gray pulled back into a severe bun. She'd landed the job because she'd spent over seven years in Tokyo, and was certified to teach Japanese at the high school level. "Would you like coffee, sir? Or tea?"

Bratton did his best to smile—but from him it looked more like a grimace. "No, thank you, Mrs. Edgars." There was just the hint of a South Carolina twang in his voice.

Dorothy walked to a door marked ABSOLUTELY NO ADMITTANCE TO THIS ROOM with a brass letter slot marked CLASSIFIED MATERIAL ONLY and knocked.

"What?" barked an irritated voice from inside.

"Colonel Bratton is here to see you, Lieutenant Kramer," she called, unruffled.

There was a pause, then the door swung open. "Come in, come in," Kramer snapped to Bratton. "You're late."

Bratton glanced up at the clocks lining the walls of the inner sanctum. "Not by Japanese time," he remarked. The men were a study in contrasts—one in blue, one in brown. One tall and one short, one lean and one stout. They were an unlikely pair, but had been forced to work together. For there was no central authority when it came to reading all the Japanese intercepts collected from the Army, Navy, and SIS, no clear-cut point of responsibility.

The political struggles between the two U.S. military branches had become so divisive that the Navy was charged with handling the decryption of Japanese Purple messages on the odd-numbered days of the month and the Army on the even. They would each then distribute the information on the opposite. And while Kramer and Bratton had been ordered to work together on the decrypts, neither was pleased with his assignment.

Bratton took off his overcoat and hung it with his hat on a brass hook on the back of the door. The room was small, with maps of the Pacific tacked up to the walls, pushpins indicating different battles. In the center was a long wooden table, with a complex, three-part machine.

"I've been working with you for months now," Bratton said, rubbing his hands together to warm them, "but I still can't get over how you make your Magic." Magic was the name that had been given to the decoding and translating project, while Purple was the name of the diplomatic code.

Kramer allowed himself a pinched, proud smile. "Thank you, Colonel Bratton." The first machine, which looked like a typewriter, intercepted all diplomatic correspondence between Japanese embassies and Tokyo. The correspondence, in the code named Purple, was typed in, then fed into the next machine, which looked like a wooden box with wires, buttons, and switches, connected by wires to the first. The messages were deciphered in there, and then came out from the third machine, another typewriter, connected by still more wires to the decryptor, decoded and in Japanese. Then skilled personnel had to be found to translate them—which was difficult, since few Americans were proficient at Japanese.

There was a knock at the door. "The latest intercept, sir," an intelligence officer said, holding a sheaf of papers.

"Might as well get on it, even if there's no one around to translate."

"Yes, sir." The young officer sat at the first typewriter, the coded documents in front of him. He began typing. As he did, lights began to wink and blink on the deciphering machine in the middle. On the far end, the typewriter began typing automatically, like a player piano.

Slowly, as if by supernatural forces, a document in Japanese was being typed out by the last machine—a coded message from Kita at the Japanese Consulate in Hawaii to the Japanese Navy.

"At least the President's back on the distribution list now," Kramer said. He walked to a chalkboard against the far wall and gestured to a list of twelve names: "the twelve apostles," the only men authorized to see the decrypts. The list read:

ULTRAS

THE PRESIDENT

SEC. OF STATE

SEC. OF WAR

SEC. OF THE NAVY

ARMY

GEN. G. C. MARSHALL

BRIG. GEN. L. T. GEROW

BRIG. GEN. S. MILES

NAVY

ADM. H. R. STARK

RADM. R. K. TURNER

CAPT. R. E. INGERSOLL

CMDR. A. H. MCCOLLUM

LT. CMDR. E. WATTS

The words THE PRESIDENT had been crossed out in chalk when decrypts had been found in the White House wastebasket and Roosevelt stopped receiving them because of security concerns. Now he was back on, the yellow chalk line erased but still visible.

"I'm glad the President's reading them again, but I'm concerned that the Chief of the Air Corps isn't on the list. And what about our overseas commanders? What about Admiral Kimmel in Hawaii, for Pete's sake?" Bratton asked. "He's head of the whole Pacific Fleet!"

"We're lucky that even the President's getting them these days—these are *extremely* sensitive documents," Kramer admonished, heading back to the typewriter with the decrypted message. "Not so much for their content, but if the Japanese ever found out we'd broken their diplomatic code . . ."

He pulled out the typed piece of paper. "Since the Navy and Army are sharing these now, for 'information, evaluation and dissemination'—here you go. I don't read Japanese—can't make out a damn thing without the translator."

Bratton accepted the paper. He had basic knowledge of Japanese characters and could make out the gist of the memo. This particular memo, from Consul Kita in Honolulu to Admiral Yamamoto at sea, divided Pearl Harbor into five distinct zones, with the locations and numbers of U.S. warships indicated on a grid. It read:

THE WARSHIPS AT ANCHOR AT PEARL HARBOR ON NOVEMBER 27, 1941, ARE:

1. Alongside Ford Island East—one *Texas*-class battleship, total one.
2. Alongside Ford Island West—one *Indianapolis*-class, one unidentified-type heavy cruiser, total two.
3. Vicinity of Ford Island, East and West—seven light cruisers of *Honolulu*- and *Omaha*-class, 26 destroyers.
4. Repair dock in Navy Yard—one *Omaha*-class light cruiser.
5. Also, six submarines, one troopship, and two destroyers off Waikiki.

"My God," Bratton whispered. "They're mapping out which ships are in Pearl Harbor and where. Is it possible that they're . . . ?" He left the rest hanging.

"Of course not!" Kramer snapped. "They'd be fools to attack Pearl—and besides, the water's too shallow for torpedoes. No," he said decisively, turning away, "this is just Japanese research at its most exacting. The Japs are fussy that way, you know."

"How long does it usually take to get these decrypts translated?"

Kramer pulled at his collar. "We're short-staffed here. These are diplomatic messages—of very little consequence as far as we're concerned. We have piles of them. Not enough linguists on staff to translate them fast enough. The diplomatic messages are of the lowest priority and are worked on when there's nothing else to do. Which is never."

Bratton held fast to the decrypt. "Do you mind if I take this? Get a proper version?"

"Suit yourself." Kramer pointed to the shelves and shelves of untranslated decrypts. "We have about twenty thousand more, waiting to be translated, if your boys in brown would like to lend a hand."

Back in his own office, in the Intelligence Section of the War Department, Bratton put down the decrypt. "So they're dividing Pearl Harbor into a grid . . ."

He looked to the map of the Pacific he had mounted on the wall. It bristled with yellow pushpins, signifying Japanese ships on various sections of the blue paper.

He went to his desk drawer and selected a larger tack. This one was red.

With it, he pierced the black dot over Pearl Harbor.

———

Clara Hess had been up since before the sunrise and was pacing the length of her room in the Tower of London, back and forth, back and forth, like a caged jungle cat.

Occasionally, she'd stop to do a few sets of push-ups or sit-ups or jack-knives, but then resumed pacing. Despite the fact that her platinum-blond hair was growing in and showing gray and dirty-blond roots—and despite her one wandering eye—she was still as beautiful as Marlene Dietrich.

It had been more than three months since she'd arrived in London from Berlin, as evidenced by the scratch marks on the wall by her bed she'd made with her fingernails. While Clara had once been a high-level Abwehr officer, she had failed at a series of missions. To escape punishment by the SS, she'd staged the ultimate ploy—she defected to Britain in Switzerland and turned herself over to SOE. Her line was that she wanted to negotiate peace between Germany and England. Of course that wasn't possible and she knew it, but it was her story and she stood by it, telling anyone who would listen.

She'd hoped her insider's knowledge of the Abwehr, and the Nazi party itself, would prove irresistible to the British. She'd also hoped to work with her daughter, Margaret Hope, to disseminate the information. She wouldn't share information without Maggie.

And so all she did each day was exercise on the hard stone floor, the tedium relieved only by the arrival of plain meals on trays, brought by silent guards.

Sometimes, overcome by frustration and boredom, she would scream, and hurl herself at the thick wooden door. Her voice, unused to vocalization of any kind in her solitary confinement, quickly grew raw, and her body bruised. Outside, the two yeomen of the guard would glance at each other and shrug. They were under strict orders not to open the door, not to interact with her, not to speak with her, not to be manipulated by her.

Clara had only one visitor, her first husband and Maggie's father, Edmund Hope. He'd seen her when she'd first arrived. Now
he was encouraging her to cooperate with MI-5, regardless of
Maggie's involvement.

"She's not going to talk to you. Forget about her," he said
about their daughter as they walked the length of the Tower Green
outside the Queen's House under the watchful eye of yeoman
guards—an unexpected privilege for Clara.

"I can't," she insisted. "I won't."

"Because she brought you down—or because she's your
daughter?" Then, "Or both?"

"She's the one who wants to hurt me. She wants to see me *executed*!"

Edmund frowned. "She can't hurt you. And all you have to do
to remain alive is talk to someone. Anyone. Even me, for that matter. There's no reason you need Maggie involved."

"She won't talk to me—and I'm stuck here, like some sort of
zoo animal. I'm *Clara Hess*, for God's sake! And she's an ungrate-
ful bitch of a daughter and it's all her fault.

"And for that I'm going to make her pay."

Chapter Three

The coastline of Arisaig, even in November—perhaps especially in November—was stunning. Snow-covered mountain peaks poked into heavy leaden clouds, while the stony shoreline melted into the icy waters of Loch nan Ceall. The purple islands of Rhum, Eigg, and Muck peeked through the mist in the distance, as well as a few smaller, unnamed islands, home to gray seals and a few bare, forlorn trees. A golden eagle circled above; Maggie could make out the faint warning clucks of chickens from the nearby henhouse.

She ran at a brisk pace from the main house to the shore, her feet crunching on paths of frosted leaves and grass. The trails were lined with garish green moss on stones and tree trunks, and as she ran, she could hear the sound of rushing streams, and smell salt water and wood smoke. Overhead, the sky was gray, and swollen clouds threatened rain.

The trainees were on a different part of the shore, still hidden from Maggie's view. Exhausted by her driving pace, she leaned against a lichen-covered rock, taking a moment to gulp in burning breaths. The cold, damp air tasted of seaweed.

Since she'd arrived in Arisaig, she'd often found herself on the jagged shore in her free hours, sitting on one of the larger rocks, watching the water as the tide rushed in or out. It was a still-peaceful part of the world, if you could ignore the occasional loud bang from SOE training groups learning to use explosives on various parts of the grounds, and the pops of gunfire. The neighboring sheep had become accustomed to the noise, grazing placidly despite the explosions, but the racket still startled the birds, who would twitter in alarm from the branches of ancient oaks.

Looking out over the gray-green water, Maggie remembered one of the American literature classes she'd taken at college. They'd read Kate Chopin's novel *The Awakening*. In the end, the heroine, Edna Pontellier, walked straight into the Gulf of Mexico.

She'd written a paper for that class on the ending, years ago—did Edna really commit suicide? Or did she swim back to shore? Most people assumed Edna actually killed herself, despite the fact Miss Chopin had left her ending vague.

Maggie remembered how, in her paper, she'd argued for Edna's metaphoric, not literal, death—the clues the author left were the allusions to Walt Whitman's poem "Out of the Cradle Endlessly Rocking." The ocean, a background chorus in Whitman's poem, was like the wise mother who reveals the word that awakened Whitman's own songs: *"And the word was 'death, death, death, death' . . . Creeping steadily up to my ears and laving me softly over."*

Death, but then rebirth. Edna had confronted death and walked out of the Gulf of Mexico a different woman, at least in Maggie's paper. Now that she herself contemplated the Loch nan Ceall, however, she wasn't so certain.

Looking out over the cold water, Maggie thought about death. How easy it would be to load up her pockets with stones—like Virginia Woolf—and walk into those icy waves never to come back, putting an end to the pain. No more heartache, no more guilt, no more sleepless nights . . . No more Black Dog. If she died, he would die along with her. And, she had to admit, there was a certain satisfaction in that.

Out of the corner of her eye, she spotted a young man, in his midtwenties, who'd arrived at Arisaig only a few days earlier. He was leaning against a lichen-stained boulder. *What's Three doing here? And why isn't he running?*

She rose and strode over, her eyes narrowing as she approached the young man, who was trying to light a cigarette in the wind. *Damn trainees,* Maggie thought. *They're everywhere. I can't even contemplate my own suicide in peace.*

"You're supposed to be running."

Seagulls screeched in the distance. "I'm a fast runner, so I have time for a smoke." His eyes twinkled. "And to look for mermaids. Although we're more likely to see seals. That's what the sailors of yore mistook for mermaids, you know."

His accent was posh, she noted. He was handsome. She looked at his hands: They were white and soft. *A gentleman,* she thought. *Let's see if he makes it through to the end.*

"Yes, seals, most likely." Maggie had no energy left to admonish him; keeping the Black Dog at bay was using it all. She watched the waves crest and break over the rocky shore. An explosion sounded in the distance.

He kicked at a thick rotting rope left behind by the family when the beach had been used as a launch, the wind ruffling his golden hair. "They're blowing up bridges today."

"So I've heard." Then, when he gave up and dropped the cigarettes and lighter back into his pocket: "It's not good to run and smoke."

"Who says?"

"I do. When I came back here, I quit. Smoking was affecting my time. I'm much faster now."

The man gazed at her through thick eyelashes. "You don't recognize me, do you?"

"Of course I do, Three. Decent at Morse code, always at the front of the pack in any race—but a terrible shot."

He laughed. "No, I mean, you don't recognize *me*."

Who is this arrogant twit? "Should I?"

"Most people around here do, or at least think they do. Although I always thought—who better to be a spy than an actor?"

"You're an actor, then." Maggie was not impressed. She knew the type—handsome, charming, self-absorbed. Strong jaw—check. Dimples—check. Full red lips—check. "Sorry, but I don't think I've seen anything you've done."

"Really?" His face drooped in child-like disappointment. "*Home Away from Home? Dead Men Are Dangerous? The Girl Must Live?*" He rubbed the back of his neck. "Well, how about theater, then—played Jack Favell, the first Mrs. De Winter's lover, in *Rebecca*. It was the West End, summer of '40, during the worst of the Blitz. Any number of times we had to finish the production down in the air-raid shelter in the cellar of the Queen's Theatre."

"Right," Maggie said, remembering. Her twin flatmates had been the stage manager and costume assistant for *Rebecca,* and of course she and the rest of the group had gone to see the production. She remembered him, too, now: handsome with a mustache and slick Brylcreemed hair. Decent rapport with Mrs. Danvers. "Yes, I saw that."

She realized that, puppy-like, he was waiting for more, so she added, "You were quite good." She decided against patting his head.

The young man pushed away from the rock and bowed. "At your service, Lady Macbeth."

Maggie gave a broken smile. "The last group called me Nessie." He looked blank. "Nessie? You know—the Loch Ness Monster?"

Three did his best to stifle a grin behind a hand. "Ahem, I'm afraid so. But it's better to be feared than to be loved, isn't it?"

"If you're Machiavelli. Or a Prince." Her smile turned grim. "Or a spy, for that matter."

"I think being an actor will make me a very good spy."

"You do, do you?"

"Oh, I've been ready for ages. I wish they'd just drop me in France already."

"Really." Maggie's sarcasm was lost on him.

"Oh yes, I might as well just skip the so-called finishing school. Piece of cake."

I used to say that . . . Not anymore.

"My actual name is Charles Campbell, by the way. The press calls me Good Time Charlie."

"Hello, Charles." She tilted her head. "Where are you from?"

"Glasgow, actually." Maggie must have looked surprised, for he didn't have a Glaswegian's distinctive accent. "Aye, wee lassie—ye pro'ly think we all wear kilts, eat haggis with tatties and neeps, an' get drunk on whiskey ev'ry day!" He switched back to his upper-crust enunciation. "It's true—but only on Sundays."

"How——?"

Charles smiled. "I watched films, imitated the actors. When I started to make some real money, I hired an accent coach, a regular Henry Higgins of a fellow. Trained all my bad habits out of me. Now I can speak with almost any accent—used them in plenty of films, some even in Hollywood."

"The ability to switch accents—that's useful, for a spy."

Charles looked deep into her eyes. Maggie looked back, coolly.

"You're *not* in love with me, are you?" he asked, sounding just a touch disappointed.

Despite the razor in her heart, Maggie choked out a laugh. *Love?* Love was the last thing on her mind these days. "In *love* with you? I just met you!"

"Most of the girls here are madly in love with me." He said it factually. "Or at least the *image* of me they have from my films. It can be annoying."

My goodness, he reeks of youth. "Well," Maggie managed, "never fear. Not only have I never seen your films, but I have no interest in romance, whatsoever."

"What's your type?"

"Tall, dark, and damaged. Or tall, fair, and damaged. And Charles, you're not nearly tall enough, nor damaged enough, even to be in the running. Plus, I've sworn off men. I'm celibate now. Like the goddess Diana."

Charles draped an arm over her shoulder and grinned. Maggie could see how he could easily be a matinee idol. "Then we shall get along very well," he said.

She shot him a warning look. "First, don't do that."

He removed his arm.

"Second, don't *ever* do that again."

He had the grace to redden.

"And third—" She pushed back her sleeve to take a look at her watch. "—start running. Or you'll be late."

Charles stood on a mound of slippery seaweed and gave a crisp salute. "Yes, Ma'am!"

The trainees had assembled in a line on the beach, in the gray shadows of snowcapped mountains. "Well, it's not exactly Waikiki, but it will do," Maggie deadpanned. The dark skies began to weep sleet; several trainees shivered and brushed the icy water from their faces.

The weather reminded Maggie of a boy from Harvard she once dated. From Buffalo, New York, he'd sworn that, like the Eskimos, Buffalonians had hundreds of different words to describe snow—although that was after a fair amount of rum punch at a Porcellian Club party. Maggie wondered where he was now, and if he'd registered for the draft. Then she shook her head and focused on her trainees.

She stalked up and down the line of young men and women. "I see some of you didn't bother to wear your hat. Always wear it! You lose ninety percent of body heat from your head!"

There were assorted mumbles of "Yes, Ma'am."

"What? I didn't hear you?"

"Yes, Ma'am!" they shouted.

"Now, there's a boat in a boathouse on the shore not too far north. In teams of two, you will commandeer the boat and practice silent landings. Five and Seven—you're up first!"

The pair saluted and began to make their way over the seaweed-draped stones. "The Nazis are after you!" Maggie called into the wind. "Hurry!"

"And what should the rest of us do, Miss Hope?" asked one of the sturdier women, older and often slower, but in many ways far more advanced than the younger trainees.

"We're going to do relay races over the stones and then up and down those hills," Maggie answered. "Remember—when you're coming up or down a steep hill, bend your knees and angle your feet—you'll have more traction that way. And you'll need it in this slippery muck. Evens, you stay here, odd numbers, *go!*"

Half the trainees began scrambling over the rocky shore. One slipped and fell; when he pulled his foot out of the mud, there was a loud sucking sound. "Keep going!" Maggie yelled, saying a silent prayer for the poor nuns in Glasgow who did all of the trainees' laundry. "And you—Nine—don't wipe your nose—let it drip! You can wipe it off later—if and when you've outrun the Nazis!"

As the agents-in-training began climbing the rocky hills that led to the boathouse, the sleet turned to rain, falling in ever-heavier drops. The trainees knew better than to complain.

But Yvonne took a moment to muse to Gwen, "I wonder if you'd get wetter walking in the rain or running? If you walk, you'll spend more time in the rain—but if you run, you'll be hitting more raindrops from the side . . ."

Basic physics, Maggie thought, crossing her arms. They could see the trainees racing, skidding, and sliding down the muddy hill, making their way back.

Gwen answered, "You probably hit more raindrops when you're running."

Maggie bit her lip.

"Well, that makes sense," Yvonne mused.

"Total wetness equals wetness per second times number of seconds spent in rain plus wetness per meter times meters traveled," Maggie muttered.

"What was that? Ma'am?"

"In other words, it's better to run in the rain—so get moving!"

When the second group sprinted off, Maggie took a few moments to look out over the roiling water. Then she spotted something by the shore, where the waves were crashing in. A gray seal? A large stone? Driftwood?

She walked closer. It was a sheep, or rather the carcass of a sheep—dead some time from the look of the body. *Poor thing must have wandered away from the flock and fallen into the water* . . . She examined the body more closely. She saw the clips in its ear, two notches, not one, and a dyed red dot on its rump, indicating it didn't belong to the local farmer's flock. Those sheep had just one ear notch and a blue stripe on the shoulders.

Maggie also noted that its body was encrusted with open, oozing black sores.

———

After the day's training sessions were completed, Maggie shed her damp clothes, washed, changed into clean clothes, then walked in the dark over the deserted road to the village of Arisaig, to see the town veterinarian, Angus McNeil. It was still early evening, but overhead the winter-night sky was black and dripped rain.

The office was small, with a low ceiling and a yellowing print of a Cameron landscape tacked up on the wall. The veterinarian was an older man, tall—well over six feet—with a tuft of white hair sprouting from each ear. He might have started out the day with what was left of his hair neatly combed, but now the red and white strands—pink, almost—were standing up straight, like prawn antennae. His features were large, like an ancient Lewis chess piece. Where his long legs were thin, his midsection was full, and he moved like a great circus bear on its hind legs.

"What do you want, lass?" he demanded, scowling, as Maggie entered the office dripping wet, her large black umbrella no help. His words were spoken with a thick burr, his voice low and rumbling.

"I found a dead sheep on the beach near Arisaig House—" she began, folding her umbrella.

"Well, if it's dead, lass—you don't need a veterinarian."

Score one for the ginger-haired brute from Barra. "At first I thought it was one of the neighboring flock that had somehow slipped through a fence and accidentally fallen in and drowned," Maggie continued, undeterred, "but it's from a different flock."

"So? Could have fallen in somewhere else, then washed ashore near Arisaig House."

"Then I noticed it was covered with sores."

The vet's face creased. "What kind of sores?"

"About an inch or two across, looked like blisters. They were black."

"And this sheep—you didn't happen to notice any other markings on it?"

I'm a bloody spy, you addlepated giant, she thought. *Of course I noticed everything.* "There were two triangular-shaped notches in his right ear, and a dot of red paint on his rump."

The vet ran his hands through his hair. "That sheep belongs to Fergus Macnab, then." He rubbed the back of his neck. "But his flock doesn't graze anywhere near the coast . . ."

"I just thought someone should know."

"Yes, yes . . ." growled the vet, lost in thought. "You didn't touch the beast, did ye, Doreen?"

"No, I most assuredly did not." Maggie was cold and wet. And her feet in heavy, muddy boots were numb. "And my name's not Doreen."

"*Doreen*'s Gaelic for a sourpuss—and your puss is a sour one. Sour and sallow."

From the back room came a mewing sound. "What's that?" Maggie asked.

"Stray cat."

"Is he all right?"

"It's a cat, Miss." The vet's voice betrayed annoyance. "I'm a vet—I deal with sheep and cows and horses. Farm animals. Great beasts of the field. *Not* cats. Especially cats that won't quiet down."

The mewing continued. "What's he doing here, then?"

"Pub owner brought him in, didn't want him hanging around, beggin' for food. He's an older cat, not a great mouser. I'd guess he was an indoor cat for most of his life—maybe when his owner died, no one wanted him, so they dumped him in the country. Probably doesn't have much time left anyway."

"But why's he here then? Are *you* taking him in?"

The doctor looked down at her from his immense height with a mixture of annoyance and pity. "I'm going to euthanize him, Miss. Can't fend for himself, since he's a pampered indoor cat. It's kinder this way."

"What?" Maggie exclaimed. "No!" She pushed past the doctor and opened the door to his office. Two eyes glowed phosphorescent in the darkness. Maggie switched on the light. There, on the vet's pinewood desk, sat a tabby cat. He was painfully thin, with rough reddish fur and bald patches and a torn ear. He looked up at Maggie with green eyes, pupils narrowing to slits. *Goodness gracious, you look as bad as I feel,* she thought.

"Meh," the tabby proclaimed. The disdainful sound was expressed in a peculiar nasal tone.

" *'Meh'*?" Maggie looked up at the doctor, who'd followed her in. "I thought cats said *meow.*"

The vet shrugged. "He's a talker, that one is. Talk your ear off. I think whoever he belonged to lived alone and talked to him. Talked to him day and night, and fed him from her plate. That's why he's no good as a mouser. Thinks he's human, he does. A wee man in a cat suit."

Maggie went up to the cat and held out her hand. She knew cats from the Prime Minister's office, where they roamed freely, along with a few of the Churchills' dogs.

The cat acquiesced to sniff her hand, then stepped closer. Raising himself on his haunches, he put one paw on her left shoulder and one paw on her right, holding her in place as he looked into her eyes with laser-like intensity. Maggie looked back, disconcerted by the scrutiny.

"Meh," he said finally, then dropped back down to all fours and rubbed against her, beginning to purr. Something was communicated between them; she had passed his test. Although no words had been spoken, Maggie knew, as clear as she knew her name or the day of the week, that she and this animal belonged together.

Or at least he had chosen her, for whatever reason, and she was powerless to say no.

"Bold as brass, that one," Dr. McNeil said. "Looks like he's decided on you. Whether you fancy him or no. What are you going to do, then?"

"I'll take him," Maggie said, scooping him up in her arms without hesitation. "My little Schrödinger."

"Don't know his name, lass." The cat settled in, purring. Then he opened his mouth and hissed at Dr. McNeil.

"I just meant—" Maggie wasn't up to explaining the paradox of Schrödinger's cat. "Never mind."

"Suit yourself, Miss," the vet said as Maggie turned to leave, cat in her arms. "But don't think he'll be catching any mice for you."

"Come on," she whispered to the cat, unbuttoning her coat and slipping him inside, where he clung to her. "We're going home."

As the door closed behind her, Dr. McNeil reached for the telephone. "Put me through to the Ministry of Agriculture and Fisheries. It's urgent—someone found another dead one."

Chapter Four

In his office in the Intelligence Section of the War Department, Colonel Bratton sat at his desk, going over Purple decrypts. His forehead was sweating; the top button of his shirt was open and his tie askew. He mopped his grim face with his handkerchief and re-read the papers in front of him.

His secretary showed in Lieutenant Commander Kramer.

"Are you all right?" Kramer said, taking in the shorter man's disarray.

Bratton didn't look up. "I've been reading these intercepts over and over again. Things are looking bad. Ambassadors Nomura and Kurusu recently asked their government to extend the deadline suspending negotiations between Japan and the United States."

Kramer sat down opposite Bratton, his long legs at angles, a pull in his sock exposed. "Yes, I know. We *all* know."

"But according to this latest decrypt, Tokyo wants to conclude negotiations, and I quote, 'no later than November twenty-ninth.' After which 'things are automatically going to happen.'"

He looked up at Kramer, who met his gaze. "Yes, we've all read it," the Lieutenant said.

Bratton was undeterred. "But look at this intelligence report from the British—five Japanese troop transports with naval escort were sighted off China's coast, near Formosa, heading south."

"That must be a mistake." Kramer crossed his legs. "You know we've been monitoring the Japanese fleet. And most of their ships are in home waters."

Bratton shook his head. "We have intelligence that the Japanese are on the move," he said, standing and walking to the map. "One of their expeditionary forces is embarking in Shanghai on as many as forty or fifty ships." He pointed at the map. "And a number of ships have left Japan and are sailing toward the Pescadores. And now a cruiser division, a destroyer squadron, and a number of aircraft carriers have been spotted in the harbor of Samah on Hainan Island. Everything we have indicates that Admiral Yamamoto's forces are set to sail in a matter of days. If not hours."

The pieces came together and clicked in Bratton's brain. "I bet you they're going to attack us." His voice rising in both pitch and intensity, he finally spoke his worst fears aloud: "I bet that Japan is going to attack the United States of America—most likely on a Sunday, when the fleet is in. This Sunday is November thirtieth."

Bratton's eyes met Kramer's in an unwavering gaze. "The goddamn Japs are going to attack us on Sunday, the thirtieth of November!"

Prime Minister Winston Churchill had seen the film *That Hamilton Woman* so many times that he would often unconsciously mouth the words along with the actors on-screen. On this night, it was playing at the library at Chequers, set up as a makeshift movie theater. All of the oil paintings had been rolled up and put away for safekeeping, leaving the ornate gold frames empty, like blank eyes. The film viewing was after a long and rich dinner, with bottles of wine and spirits, and a few of the guests and staff had settled in, preparing for a nap. But Churchill, a wine stain on the lapel of his velvet siren suit (which the staff referred to, behind his back, as his "rompers"), was on the edge of his seat.

In his own plush armchair, while the rest sat behind, in metal folding chairs, the Prime Minister growled, unlit cigar clenched between his teeth, "Mr. Greene, please start the projector. Mr. Sterling, turn off the lights."

His two private secretaries did his bidding, and soon the room was dark, filled with the noise of the whirring projector and then the black-and-white images projected onto a screen.

When Lord Nelson, played by Laurence Olivier, said, *"Gentlemen, you will never make peace with Napoleon . . . Napoleon cannot be master of the world until he has smashed us up, and believe me, gentlemen, he means to be master of the world! You cannot make peace with dictators. You have to destroy them—wipe them out!"* the P.M. rose and shook his fist at the screen.

He turned toward the audience, who did their best to rouse themselves and look attentive. "I'll have you know I wrote that line—and several others of Nelson's! Just fill in 'Hitler' wherever 'Napoleon' appears and have done with it!" he barked, stabbing the air with his cigar for emphasis.

"Winston . . ." his wife, Clementine Churchill, said from a brocade settee behind the P.M.'s armchair.

But Churchill paced in front of the screen, mouthing Nelson's words. "Yes, things were different when we were here five years ago, weren't they? Our braid was shining in those days. Today they won't even let us anchor in the harbor. It's as though we had the plague. They're so scared of Bonaparte they daren't lift a finger to help those who are still fighting him . . ."

Then he stopped his pacing. "Turn off the damn projector! Mr. Greene! Mr. Greene!" David Greene jumped to his feet to do the P.M.'s bidding.

"And Mr. Sterling—let there be light!" John Sterling switched on the lights. The two private secretaries exchanged a knowing glance. They knew from experience that whether the film was done or not, movie time was over.

David Greene was the shorter and slighter of the two, with light hair and silver-rimmed spectacles. He and his friend, John Sterling, had worked for Winston Churchill during his so-called Wilderness Years, when no one in the House took his warnings of Nazi armament seriously. Now that he was almost thirty, his former impish charm had become somewhat subdued, yet another casualty of the war.

John was taller, with curly brown hair and dark eyes and a grim smile. He wore his RAF uniform well, his body not betraying, at least to the casual observer, the injuries he'd survived in Berlin.

The enormous bookcase-lined Long Gallery was chilly, even though a fire burned in the grate and the floor was covered in Kazakh rugs. The room smelled of book restorer and wood smoke. Churchill began to pace, his round face pink from the prodigious quantities of Pol Roger Champagne and red Burgundy he'd put away during dinner. "Do you know that that damn isolationist group, the so-called America First Committee, calls *That Hamilton Woman* 'wartime propaganda'? And has called on the U.S. public to boycott it? Apparently, the AFC sees them as 'preparing Americans for war.'"

He kicked a metal wastebasket, and Nelson, the P.M.'s black cat, who'd been curled up on one of the folding chairs, started, then scurried away. "No one named Nelson—man or cat—ever runs from a fight!" Churchill shouted after the feline, shaking his fist. "And of course we're trying to rouse the damn Americans. They've sat on their fat—"

Clementine shot her husband a warning look.

"—*posteriors* long enough. The Nazzies have sunk the USS *Robin Moor*, the *Kearny*, and the *Reuben James*. Do they have to invade the East Coast and march on Washington before President Roosevelt will declare war?

"Meanwhile," Churchill continued, his voice rising in power, as if addressing the back benches of the House of Commons, "they're wasting time rounding up filmmakers when they should be after the bl—"

He shot a look at Clementine, who arched one eyebrow in warning. ". . . the Nazzies," he amended, in a gentler tone, using his usual and distinctive sibilant pronunciation.

"Winston, darling," his wife said, rising, "if you're done with the film, I think I'll retire for the evening. Good night, love. Good night, all." The gentlemen stood as Mrs. Churchill, with her fine posture and impeccably cut silk dress, walked out in a trail of Arpège. The rest of the women, including Churchill's daughter Mary, also excused themselves.

When they were gone, Churchill gave a fierce battle cry: "Gentlemen," he thundered, rallying the troops, "to the Hawtree Room!" As he stalked out, he called over his shoulder to his beleaguered manservant, "And Inces! We shall require both port and Stilton!"

Churchill led the way through a secret door, camouflaged in the library's books, to the Cromwell Passage, and then to the Hawtree Room, which he'd commandeered as his study. There the Prime Minister threw himself into one of the leather club chairs. Nelson rubbed up against his shins.

The P.M. reached down to scratch Nelson under the chin, and the cat started purring—but then froze at the rumble of German planes flying overhead, flattening his ears. "Don't worry, darling Nelson," murmured the Prime Minister, continuing his chin scratches, "just remember what those brave boys in the RAF are doing." Nelson, named after the venerable Lord Horatio, was prone to hiding under beds during air raids.

"Come, dearest Nelson," the P.M. crooned, patting his lap. "Up!" The cat jumped up, kneaded a bit, then settled in, wrapping his tail around his compact body and closing his eyes.

There were five men in the Hawtree Room at Chequers Court: Sir John Dill, Chief of the Imperial General Staff; General Ismay, chief staff officer and military adviser; and Churchill and his two private secretaries.

Since the P.M. was known to say, "A change is as good as a rest!" and resting wasn't possible, Churchill often decided—at the last minute, to the consternation of his detectives and staff, not to mention his wife—to travel.

Although a fire crackled in the room's fireplace behind bronze fenders, behind the blackout curtains the windows were loose and rattled in the wind, a damp chill in the air. The men sat on chairs with faded petit-point seats at the enormous mahogany pedestal table, under the watchful eyes of a painting of Cromwell's General, John Lambert. All waited for the meat of the discussion to begin. There was a globe on a stand in the corner, with territories marked from the midthirties, now hopelessly out of date.

Mr. Inces, his footsteps muffled by the Ochark carpet, carried in blue-veined Stilton and plum bread on Frankenthal dishes, and a cut-crystal decanter filled with amber liquid that glowed in the firelight.

"Stilton and port are like man and wife," the P.M. intoned. "Whom God has joined together, let no man tear asunder." Then, "Damn it, Inces, pour the port!"

Churchill took a greedy sip and swallowed. "I hear Popov made it to the U.S. Told that Hoover chap at the FBI about the

Pearl Harbor survey from the Germans. Didn't seem to make much of an impression, though, according to my sources at MI-Six."

"The Yanks are disorganized, sir," David said, pushing up his wire-rimmed glasses. "The Army doesn't talk to the Navy and the Navy doesn't talk to the Army. On any given day, neither of them may be talking to the President. And Hoover's supposed to be the worst of them, in terms of cronyism and iron-fisted control over information. Controlling, petty—"

"That's enough, Mr. Greene!" the P.M. said, taking another gulp of port and slipping a tiny sliver of Stilton to Nelson. "But I did hear that when Mr. Hoover discovered our man Popov had taken a woman from New York to Florida, he threatened to have him arrested under some ancient American blue law if he didn't leave the U.S. immediately." He shook his head in mock despair. "Yanks—often licentious, and yet suspect of pleasure. It's their beginnings, you know. No matter where they come from, they're all affected by America's Puritan beginnings. And what about the Orient? Granted, Herr Hitler is keeping us more than occupied in the Atlantic, but the Japanese have now bound themselves to him and Mussolini. And their atrocities in the Far East are just as savage as the Nazzies'."

"Just in China, though," said Dill.

"'Just in China'?" the P.M. boomed. "They're *starting* with China, an *amuse-bouche,* just as Hitler started with Austria and the Sudetenland. First China, then French Indo-China? The Dutch West Indies? Our own Hong Kong and Singapore? If they went after our colonies, we couldn't take them. Not with all of our manpower needed in the Atlantic. I asked Roosevelt for a few ships from his Pacific Fleet, do you know what he said? No!"

The booming voice had grown thunderous. "He said, and I quote, 'It's not the job of the United States to steam around the world, shoring up other people's empires. We don't like empires, no matter whose flag they fly.'" He gestured with his glass of port, spilling some on the linen tablecloth. "Damn Yanks!"

"Well, as a former British colony themselves . . ." David began. John gave him a swift kick under the table.

The P.M. didn't notice. "It would serve them right if the Japanese attacked them in the Far East—they might not have 'colonies,' but they do have territories. Guam, the Philippines, Samoa. Even their Hawaiian Islands are territories, not a state of their Union . . ."

Miss Stewart, one of Mr. Churchill's long-suffering typists, entered the room. "Excuse me, Mr. Churchill, gentlemen," she said, her white chignon glistening in the firelight. "But this Friday's list of figures has just arrived by courier from Porton Down."

"Yes, yes, Miss Stewart, thank you—just leave it here." The plump older woman did so and departed.

The Prime Minister put on his gold-framed glasses and read over the document, the typed figures sent by the War Cabinet every Friday, detailing the progress made on chemical and biological weapons. His forehead creased with concern.

"Not enough," he muttered, "not nearly enough." To the room he growled, "Those concerned should be beaten soundly, by Jove!"

"Sir?" David said.

"Still—we must KBO! Mr. Greene, please make sure a memo goes out to Beaverbrook—Miss Stewart can type it for you—that the absolute maximum effort must be used with priority to make, store, and fill into containers the largest possible quantities of gas. Largest possible quantities! It says here, mustard is running at only one hundred and thirty tons per week, a third of the full capacity. Tell Brookie we damn well need to ginger things up.

"And be sure to ask him who exactly is responsible for this failure. I will not tolerate ineptitude, especially with something so important!" The P.M. took out one of his Romeo y Julieta cigars from his breast pocket and began to gnaw on it. "At any moment, peril may be upon us."

"Yes, sir." David took the memo and left the room to find Miss Stewart.

The Prime Minister turned his attention back to the other men. "Dilly! Why the long face?"

Dill swallowed his sip of port, then replied, "Sir, I would like to discuss N, our new biological weapon. I know you're keen on developing it, but I want you to think seriously about the moral implications of our using it. I wouldn't want it in play unless it could be shown either that it was life or death for us, or that it would shorten the war by a year or more."

"What?" Churchill growled, finally clipping, then igniting his cigar with a heavy silver lighter. "Moral qualms getting the better of you? Angels and devils on your shoulders? Won't mean much when there are Nazzies on our doorstep."

Dill smoothed his mustache. "It's absurd to consider morality on the topic of mustard gas when everybody used it in the last war without a word of complaint from the moralists of the Church. On the other hand, the bombing of open cities was once forbidden. Now everyone does it as a matter of course. It is simply a matter of the fashions of war changing, as long and short skirts for women. However, N . . ."

The Prime Minister chewed harder on his cigar, then banged his fist on the table, making Nelson jump. Nelson pretended to groom himself to restore his dignity, then slunk off.

"When your back is up against the wall, do you play by the rules of the Geneva Conventions?" The P.M. poked the air with his cigar. "Do you consult the International Committee of the Red

Cross? Hitler's not playing by those rules, and I don't believe we need to, either. Mr. Sterling, I want a cold-blooded calculation made as to how it would benefit us to use this new N that my warlocks and wizards at Porton Down are creating in their cauldrons."

"Sir, if I may—" John ventured.

"Well, speak up, Mr. Sterling! That's why I keep you around!" Then, remembering the man had served as an RAF pilot and had been shot down over Nazi territory, the P.M.'s voice softened. "Go on."

"I don't have any qualm about our using every weapon in our arsenal to stop a Nazi invasion, but it is nonetheless true that chemical weapons and gas have a particular . . . unpleasantness . . . about them. Part of that is because they're really not that easy to control in a tactical way—their sole purpose is to kill and incapacitate people downwind. That makes them much more indiscriminate. It's the equivalent of the weaker party in a fight resorting to throwing a fistful of sand in the stronger party's face."

"I meant it when I said we would fight on the beaches, and that includes throwing sand—or anything else my wizards at Porton Down conjure—in the faces of Nazzi invaders."

John didn't flinch. "Nevertheless, sir, to use chemical and biological weapons is to cross a dangerous threshold, especially when used with civilians. The Americans would be horrified to learn of our research."

"The Americans don't need to know everything we're thinking," the P.M. rumbled, "especially when they're sitting pretty and don't seem to be bothered much by Britons killed by Nazzi bombs."

Dill interjected, "Our experiments with N include putting them into cakes of grain, which would be dropped for livestock to eat."

"So starvation's better than gas or poison?" John asked.

"Mr. Sterling, you are certainly correct—the dead are dead in any case, and it's unclear that having someone choke to death while convulsing is somehow worse than burning them to death with jellied gasoline, or causing a firestorm, or blowing them up, or shooting them in the head, or even instituting a blockade that denies them access to food and medicine."

The P.M. puffed on his cigar; he looked tired, his eyes were ringed with red. "War is a terrible, terrible thing. Robert E. Lee allegedly said that it is well that war is so terrible, or we should grow too fond of it. And now we have witchcraft and magic added to the mix. *'Double, double, toil and trouble,'*" he quoted, "*'Fire burn, and cauldron bubble.'* Find out what progress there is on our hell-broth boiling and broiling in Porton Down, Mr. Sterling!"

John rose. "Yes, sir." He left the room.

Only Dill and Ismay remained with Churchill. "And these developments are *not* something we will share with the Americans," Churchill decided, rising and pacing, jabbing at the air with his cigar. Blue smoke wove tendrils around his head like the tentacles of a man-of-war.

"Understood, sir," Dill said.

"Yes, sir," chimed in Ismay.

Abruptly, Churchill changed the subject. "Odds of Russia falling?"

"I should be inclined to put it even at this point, sir, with Old Man Winter giving Mother Russia the edge," Dill replied.

"The Balkans are a sticking point—but if Hitler invaded hell, I would make at least a favorable reference to the Devil in the House of Commons. If we're still standing alone by the end of '41 . . ."

Churchill bellowed, "Fetch me the women!" referring to his typists. "I'm going to dictate another letter to President Roosevelt," the Prime Minister stated. "Let's meet up again later—at one, back here, to discuss these matters further, once Greene and

Sterling have procured more information." He left the room, muttering,

Swelter'd venom sleeping got,
Boil thou first i' the charmed pot!
For a charm of powerful trouble,
Like a hell-broth boil and bubble.

Chapter Five

By Clara's calculations, it was 3 A.M. on November twenty-sixth—three months to the day since she'd been taken into British custody. None of her many overtures at brokering a peace treaty had been taken seriously. Her daughter wouldn't meet with her. She'd continued to refuse to offer British Intelligence anything without her daughter's intervention. And so, like the German spy Josef Jakobs before her, she was to be executed. The date of her death had been set: Sunday, December 7, 1941.

Clara stood at one of the barred windows overlooking the Thames and began to sing, her once golden voice now breathy and raspy. What she chose for her debut at the Tower of London was Olympia's aria, *"Les oiseaux dans la charmille,"* from Offenbach's opera *Les contes d'Hoffmann,* her voice gaining in strength, and she went along, muscle memory stirring. Olympia was a mechanical doll with whom Hoffmann fell in love and so Clara accompanied her singing with stiff, robotic, doll-like movements, as though in performance. As she sang, her voice steadied, returning to its former glory.

Les oiseaux dans la charmille
Dans les cieux l'astre du jour,
Tout parle à la jeune fille d'amour!

Ah! Voilà la chanson gentille
La chanson d'Olympia! Ah!

Tout ce qui chante et résonne
Et soupire, tour à tour,
Emeut son coeur qui frissonne d'amour!
Ah! Voilà la chanson mignonne
La chanson d'Olympia! Ah!

When she had finished, the last sweet notes dying in her cell, she fell to the cold stone floor.

Maggie's screams woke her.

It was a different nightmare every night—variations and permutations of her time in Berlin. There was the one where she saw Gottlieb Lehrer, part of the German Resistance and ardent Catholic, shoot himself in the head rather than be taken alive by the Gestapo. There was the one where she saw the small Jewish girl cry for water. And the one where her sister Elise looked at her as if she were a monster, after she had killed a young German man, really no more than a boy.

This night, however, there was a cat in her bed. She'd made him his own place to sleep—a wicker basket lined with fabric scraps, near the radiator. But at some point during the night he'd crawled in with her, curling up into a tight furry ball encircled by her torso. Now he was purring, and rose to pad over to her head and try to lick her hair.

"What the—?" Maggie said, still disoriented. "No, I don't need a bath—no, thank you!" The cat's tongue was starting to catch on the long red strands, and he couldn't get them out of his mouth.

He shook his head repeatedly. She pulled out the offending hairs from his mouth and sat up. "Are you trying to *groom* me?" she demanded of her small companion. She had to admit it was pleasant to have company; no more Sister Anne in the Tower.

The cat regarded her with concerned eyes. *"Meh."*

She scratched him under his chin and he leaned into her, purring. "Look at us," Maggie said, unsure of what to say to him. She'd never had a pet before. "Two broken-down and battered creatures. Red-haired strays. Kindred spirits?"

The creature blinked, not at all impressed with her self-pity or sentimentality.

"Oh, so it's stiff-upper-lip then, I see. Good, you're a proper British moggie through and through—I like that." Maggie reached for her tattered flannel robe. It was freezing in her small bedroom. She stood up and put on heavy slippers, then pulled the blackout curtains open.

It didn't make much difference to the way the room looked: It was bare as a nun's cell, with only a postcard of Robert Burns's *Diana and Her Nymphs* that the previous occupant had left, and E. T. Bell's *Men of Mathematics*, an old battered volume of Frances Hodgson Burnett's *The Secret Garden*, and a borrowed copy of T. H. White's *The Sword in the Stone*. On the floor next to the bed was a bag full of the knitting Maggie had started since she'd returned from Berlin—socks for soldiers, which she knitted with the Morse code for "victory" around the cuff.

The clock on the night table said it was just before 6 A.M., but it would be at least two more hours until the sun rose. *This perpetual darkness of winter in Scotland isn't helping things . . .* Her fingers found the hard outline of the bullet. It was still there, becoming even more prominent as it worked itself closer to the surface of her skin.

The higher-ups at Arisaig House said that she'd earned having a private flat in the gardener's dwelling, as opposed to rooming with the other instructors in the main house, because she was the only female. But Maggie knew it was also because of the nightmares.

And the screaming.

The rooms were over the gardener's flat, but had its own entrance. Maggie had three rooms: a bedroom, an efficiency kitchen and small table with two chairs, and a W.C. During the short winter daylight hours, she could look out mullioned windows for a view of one of the sheep-dotted fields, as well as the snow-covered mountains in the distance. If she craned her neck a bit, she could see the blue-gray waves and rocky shore of the loch.

The tabby peered at Maggie with large green eyes. "Hmm," she said to him, peering back. "I suppose you'd like your breakfast now?"

The cat blinked, and rubbed against her. "You know that word, don't you?" Maggie asked, petting his coarse fur. He was rough to the touch, unkempt, but warm. No wonder Mr. Churchill so often slept with Nelson.

She remembered how the Prime Minister had once barked at her, when she was being slow: "This feline does more for the war effort than you do! He acts as a hot-water bottle and saves fuel and power!" She now saw the P.M.'s point. She gathered the cat in her arms and pressed her cheek against his furry back. He had a faint scent, but it wasn't unpleasant. Like freshly washed sheets hung outside to dry in the summer sun.

She set him down and headed for the loo, closing the door firmly behind her. "Excuse me, I do need at least a moment of privacy, if you don't mind." But apparently, the cat *did* mind, for he scratched at the door until she was finished. When she was washing her hands, he jumped up on the toilet seat and squatted over the bowl.

Maggie was speechless. She stared, and he stared right back with his glowing eyes, as if saying, *Woman, did you actually think I was going to use a box? Like an . . . animal?* Maggie shook her head in disbelief, then—giving him the privacy he'd denied her— went down the narrow hallway to the kitchen.

She turned on the kettle and looked through the icebox. There was some leftover stew she'd saved; it would have to do.

The cat trotted out to meet her, proud as could be. *"Meh."*

"Here," she said, putting a saucer of it on the worn wooden floor. "It's cold, and the cook wouldn't know what to do with a clove of garlic if one magically appeared in front of her. But—" Maggie turned on the wireless on the kitchen counter. BBC. "—in case you hadn't noticed, there's a war on, Cat."

The cat blinked a few times, as if to say, *Cat? Woman, you denigrate me.* Then he tucked into the stew, eating ravenously.

"Well, I don't know your name." She crouched down to address him. There was only the sound of the cat lapping at the food in his bowl. He was obviously going to leave this up to her. "Schrödinger, perhaps? Things were rather touch and go there for a bit with the vet."

He raised his head to glare at her before returning to his breakfast.

"Not Schrödinger," she decided, "as you are very much alive and not in a state of quantum flux anymore. And so, your name henceforth shall be—Kitty."

The cat flicked his tail in annoyance. *No, not Kitty either, apparently.*

"Well then, what *is* your name, Jellicle cat? Macavity the Mystery Cat? The Hidden Paw, perhaps?"

The cat left his food bowl and stalked over to Maggie. He rose up onto his haunches, putting one paw on either side of her neck. He looked into her eyes and touched his pink nose to hers. "All right, all right," she relented. "I'll call you K. How's that? K for Kitty. K will be your secret-agent name—after all, you're at a spy training camp. And Mr. K for the veterinarian and on Sundays, when more formality is needed."

Satisfied, K gave another *"Meh,"* then dropped down to the floor and began to groom himself.

"Well, glad that's settled," Maggie said, getting up to wash and dress. Then she had her tea and a bannock that she'd saved. K was prowling by the door, keen to be let out. "I thought you were an indoor cat?"

K took a running leap at the doorknob, grabbing it with his front paw, and with the skill of an Olympic gymnast managed to fling his small body round the knob. A moment later he had opened the door by himself. *"Meh!"* he cried in triumph.

"Well, I suppose if you're smart enough to open the door, you're smart enough to look after yourself outside, aren't you?" Maggie reached for her coat and hat.

K paused at the doorway. He touched one paw to the stair landing, then drew it back, as if stung. *"Meh,"* he complained. The stone was cold and damp, like all of Scotland in November. *"Meeeeeeeeeeh!"*

"Sorry, I know I may seem all-powerful, but I can't heat the outdoors for you. In or out, then?"

Hesitating only briefly, K chose out, picking his way over the chill lichen-spotted flagstones of the walk.

Maggie had a self-defense class to teach at nine on the main house's grass badminton lawn, just past the walled formal garden. Even though it *was* November in Scotland, the warmer Gulf Stream currents kept the weather in Arisaig more temperate. So the grass was a vivid shade of green and relatively soft to land on, if cold and wet. The sky above turned from darkness to a heavy gray, and the wind whipped about them.

The class was taught by a young American man of Japanese descent, Satoshi Nagoka, who specialized in jujitsu. Maggie had taken his classes, twice, and was on her way to becoming an expert. She was now considered proficient enough to teach the France-bound group while the sensei was off for a special session with the Czech and Slovak trainees.

Arisaig was no-man's-land during the war, international, without a class system, with women training alongside men. It wasn't Scotland per se anymore, because it had been taken over by the military, and was "out of bounds" to all locals and civilian travelers. To obtain entrance, one had to show special identification. The instructors and staff of Arisaig and the various houses co-opted by the military for training weren't necessarily Scottish; like Maggie and Satoshi, they came from the four corners of the earth.

The families who owned the houses had been found lodging elsewhere, and the "stately 'omes" had been taken over by the military—mostly English men of the upper class and a certain age, although there were certainly a number of men in the "thieving" class as well, who provided instruction in lock picking, jumping off moving trains, and other activities considered unsavory in peacetime.

It was a respite from England's usual creaky and claustrophobic class- and gender-bound society—a bizarre democracy of the brave, resourceful, and perhaps slightly suicidal, where a Glaswegian arsonist might train next to a Duke's daughter. But the truth was, at a certain point in the training, especially the intensely physical paramilitary training they did in Scotland, they all started to look alike: hollow-eyed, damp, shivering in their uniforms, and miserable. By this point in their journey, they had thin, athletic bodies with ropy muscles, yet their faces were often still round and

quick to smile or laugh. While Maggie didn't resent their easy ca-
maraderie and banter, she felt a bit lonely to be left out of it; she'd
been the same way with her group, a long, long time ago.

In the shadow of Arisaig House, on the croquet lawn, Maggie
could see them sizing her up. She was fit, but she was still female,
and somewhat petite at that. "Who wants to go first?" she called,
her breath forming clouds in the chill air. *It's probably wrong how
much I enjoy this part,* she thought. The women all held back,
squeamish at the thought of hand-to-hand combat. *That's all right,
I'll get to them next.* Maggie had her routine down cold—the first
task was to select the alpha male of the group. "Come on, light the
blue torch paper!" She recognized Charlie. "You!" She pointed at
him. "Three! You're up!"

Charlie gave his most appealing movie-star smile and ambled
over to where Maggie stood in the grass. He pulled a face and the
other trainees laughed. *Oh, this will be fun.* Charlie was almost a
foot taller than her, and about eighty pounds heavier. She seemed
to be no match for him.

He blushed, his cheeks staining pink, afraid to make the first
move.

"Come on," Maggie goaded, "pretend I'm a Nazi sympathizer
who's going to blow your cover in France. What're you going to
do?"

Charlie tried to grab Maggie's slender wrists with his large
hands. Maggie could feel the mood of the students shift—they
were afraid for her, afraid she'd be hurt. Afraid, but also just a little
excited. Those who knew her didn't like her. Those who didn't
know her yet had heard the stories. Whatever Charlie was going to
do, all of them believed she'd asked for it.

As an explosion boomed in the distance, Maggie stepped aside.
She seemed to merely touch Charlie's wrist with her delicate
hands—and then he lurched forward, rose up in the air, and som-

ersaulted over, coming down hard on his back in the grass about six feet away. Her expression never changed.

Charlie groaned in agony, but scrambled to his feet, brushing off dirt and glass. "Ouch" was all he could come up with. He limped back to the rest of the trainees, rubbing one elbow. Some of the men laughed at him, for being thrown by a woman. There were whispers of "Lady Macbeth."

"This is no joke," Maggie said, hands on hips. "I want you to take this seriously. What you learn here, your skills—may save your life someday. I'm not hard on you because I enjoy it, I'm hard on you because I want you to come back alive."

"Because you'd miss us, Ma'am?" Charlie put a hand to his heart in mock sentiment.

"Because we would have wasted our time and effort on your training," Maggie retorted. "Now, who's next?"

Later that day, the trainees were taken to another grand manor house not far from Arisaig. K jumped up onto Maggie's shoulder and perched there, as if to say, *Well, of course I'm going with you!*

The trainees had been practicing with their British Stens and Brens and different foreign guns using stationary, close-range targets in the pistol practice room at Arisaig House—formerly the servants' dining hall. They'd learned the Fairbairn-Sykes method of shooting, created by William Fairbairn and Eric Sykes, inspired by the gun crime they'd witnessed as police officers on the Shanghai waterfront.

In the army and traditional police, officers would extend their arm, raise the weapon to eye level, take aim, and then shoot. Fairbairn and Sykes thought this wasted precious seconds—their practice was to draw and fire from hip level, with a crooked arm, using two shots called a double tap. This could be managed from a crouched or running position.

Now it was time to try for practice with something less static.

As they approached the abandoned house on the shore, Mr. Burns gestured for them to stop. "We've been practicing on pictures of Hitler on the firing range, and you've improved," he said, his voice fading in the chill wind. "But it's unlikely that Herr Hitler, or any other enemy combatant, will be so obliging as to sit still while you take aim and shoot. And so we've created a moving training exercise for you that will test your instincts and reaction times."

Maggie looked at the house. She remembered her own experiences shooting there, at mocked-up dummies that danced on ropes and pulleys, controlled by a technician in the front garden. Back then, she'd thought of it as a kind of fairground shooting gallery, with targets popping out from cupboards, or flying in on fishing line. Back then, it had seemed like nothing more than fun and games. *What a little fool I was.*

K jumped down to check under the house's front steps for prey.

Mr. Burns eyed the group. "All right, then. Who wants to go first?"

Charlie raised his hand, perhaps eager to make up for his poor showing in jujitsu earlier.

"Fine." Mr. Burns nodded. "I'll give you the countdown, and then in you go."

Charlie drew his pistol, his jaw set. Maggie wondered if, in his mind, he was playing the role of war hero. She could picture him someday repeating the same grimace for a movie camera. *If the boy survives this damn war . . .*

"And five, four, three, two . . ."

Charlie approached the front door of the house as they'd all been taught, pistol cocked and held at his side, ready for action. On an angle, he snuck up the porch to the door and waited there, listening, before signaling the all-clear. He kicked in the door.

Mr. Burns, Maggie, and the students waited outside the open door as he made his way inside. There he saw an old, warped mirror and took in his reflection, posing just a bit with the gun.

Mr. Burns nodded to the technician, who pulled a lever. A cardboard figure of a man appeared at the top of the staircase and, through use of rope and pulleys, drifted, ghost-like, down the stairs.

Charlie shot. And missed. And missed again and again and again. "Damn thing keeps moving!"

"That's the point, lad," Mr. Burns said drily. He turned to the technician. "Stop." Then, *"Stop!"* he called to Charlie, who was still trying to hit the target. Mr. Burns shook his head in disgust. "That's enough. God help you and your team if you even make it to France."

He scanned the group, his eyes lighting upon Maggie. "Miss Hope, this was always one of your favorite exercises. Come and show Charlie and the rest how it's done."

Maggie hadn't touched a gun since she'd returned from Berlin. She had no desire to, ever again. "Mr. Burns, I would prefer not to." But apparently Mr. Burns wasn't a Melville aficionado.

"Miss Hope," Mr. Burns said, his voice kind but firm. She knew that he knew why she didn't want to touch a gun. And he wasn't going to let her get away with it any longer.

"All right." There was a rustle of whispers from the trainees. They were eager to see what she could do.

She took Charlie's gun from him, weighing it in her hand. It was a Sten, not a Luger, the weapon she'd used in Germany. Feeling sick, she inspected it, then walked to the front of the house.

Doing as she'd been trained, she stood, back to the door frame, and listened. Nothing. She reached out and turned the knob. The door swung inward, groaning on its hinge.

Maggie kicked it all the way open, gun shifting in her sweating palm. She gripped it tighter. Nothing. No one.

She made her way into the dim light of the room; a few floorboards gave way and creaked underfoot. Dust motes floated in the air, illuminated the slanting sunlight from a high window. A chill lurked around the corners of the room.

Out of the corner of her eye, Maggie spotted movement. She shot once at a plywood cutout of a man painted to look as if he was wearing a Nazi uniform moving at the top of the stairs, the bullet piercing the cross over his heart. She then spun around to shoot another cutout, this time of a Nazi officer emerging from an armoire. From behind a door, there was a movement. Maggie whirled, her heartbeat exploding in her chest, her weapon raised to shoot. The cutout this time was of a mother, holding a baby in her arms.

Maggie fell to her knees. And stayed there, paralyzed.

Mr. Burns came through the door. He was saying something. Maggie turned the gun on him, eyes wild.

She couldn't hear him, but she could see he'd put his hands up. She kept the Sten trained on his chest. There was an interminable moment before she could make out who he was, and what he was saying.

"Put the gun down, Miss Hope," Mr. Burns said, walking to her slowly.

She backed away on her knees, keeping the gun on him, eyes darting, every nerve alert.

"Stop!" she called. "Stop—or I'll shoot!"

"It is only I—Mr. Burns," the older man said. He continued to walk toward her, as one would approach a wild animal with teeth bared. "It's all right, Miss Hope. Everything is all right now. You're safe—you're fine. Everything is fine."

Maggie's eyes were still glassy with terror, and the hand holding the gun was shaking, but she let Mr. Burns approach her, and then allowed him to take her gun, put on the safety, and pocket it. It was the scent of pipe tobacco clinging to his sweater that calmed her, finally.

"It's all right." He extended a callused hand and she grabbed on to it, letting herself be pulled up.

"It's all right," he whispered to her as she sank into the cushions of the dusty sofa. "Get out!" he yelled at the faces peering in the doorway. "Go away! There's nothing to see here!"

The trainees dispersed.

Burns sat down next to Maggie.

"Shooting triggered a bad memory," he stated. It was not a question.

"Yes," Maggie managed.

"Happens to all of us," he said gruffly, pulling out a cambric handkerchief from his jacket pocket and handing it to her. She accepted it and wiped at her eyes, then blew her nose.

"That message you received, Miss Hope—what was it for?"

"What?"

"The telephone message you received yesterday morning."

"It—" Maggie concentrated on her breathing. "It was a message from my friend Sarah. She's performing with the Vic-Wells Ballet in Edinburgh. She wants me to come and see her perform."

"And you binned it and didn't get back to her. Not even to say that you weren't coming."

"Yes," Maggie whispered.

"Why?"

She turned her eyes up to his. "You know why."

"And that's why I'm ordering you to go."

"Sir?"

"Go to Edinburgh. Spend some time with your friend. Take the weekend."

"No, no—I couldn't possibly . . ."

"It's an order, Miss Hope."

"I can't—"

He patted her hand awkwardly. "I repeat, it's an order, Miss Hope. You're going to Edinburgh. No arguing."

"But—" Maggie gave a faint smile and nodded. "Yes, sir."

It looked as if she was going to Edinburgh—Black Dog or no Black Dog.

During the training exercises, K had found a place on a stone wall in the weak winter sun, and kept watch through slit eyes. When Maggie and Mr. Burns left Traigh House, K leapt from the wall and trotted after them.

But then the wind had picked up, and the cat became distracted, chasing after a papery brown leaf. "K! Mr. K! Naughty kitty!" Maggie shouted, her voice blown away.

"I'll leave you to your chase," Mr. Burns said, tipping his hat. "Enjoy the ballet."

"Thank you, sir," Maggie said as she began running after the tabby.

K had turned and trotted off over the dead grass to a path in the surrounding forest, which led down to the rocky shore. Maggie scrambled after him. "Wait, come back here!" she called, her voice lost in the blustery weather. *Cats are not like dogs,* she had to remind herself, more used to Churchill's dog Rufus and Princess Elizabeth's menagerie of corgis. Even Nelson, the P.M.'s cat, would at least *pretend* to listen every once in a while.

K darted over the moss-covered stones, tail low, as if on the trail of something. He slunk under a rusty metal gate, which Maggie then had to climb, wire biting into her hands.

Stupid cat, she thought as she pushed loose hair out of her eyes. *Why did I ever think I could take care of an animal?* She trailed him through thorny underbrush, then found herself on the rocks of a different cove, on the property next to Arisaig House. The beach was stonier, harder to walk on. K jumped up onto a boulder and sat, watching.

There were men on the shore, leading a line of docile sheep down a worn path, then loading them into a waiting boat. Some of the sheep were white, or cream, or gray; some had black patches. Each had two notches cut into one ear and a red dot on its rump. Maggie could hear their *baa*s carried off in the wind.

K jumped down, then walked back to Maggie, pawing her knee, wanting to be lifted. Absently, still watching the men, she bent and scooped him up into her arms. He purred and settled himself on her shoulder, like a pirate's parrot. "And what do you suppose we have here?" she muttered as the boats drifted farther and farther from the shore, toward a small island, whose name she didn't know. "Maybe they're taking them to another island to graze?"

"*Meh.*"

"Yes, *meh* indeed," Maggie replied, scratching him under the chin. "But now I need to pack for Edinburgh."

When her next meal was brought in, Clara was found unconscious and she was rushed to the Tower of London's infirmary. There Dr. Clive Carroll, a fifty-something man with gray-blond hair and narrow shoulders, was called to examine her. By the time Dr. Carroll had finished, Peter Frain, Director of MI-5, was on the telephone.

Carroll sat down behind his wooden desk to take the call.

"What do you think it is?" Frain asked without preamble. "What's wrong with Hess?"

The doctor fidgeted with the coiled telephone cord. "Physically, Frau Hess is fine, Mr. Frain. Robust health. Good muscle tone, strong pulse, normal blood pressure, even breathing . . ."

"So, what the devil's wrong with her?"

Dr. Carroll pushed up horn-rimmed glasses. "Well, she is—in a word—catatonic."

"Catatonic?" Frain didn't sound convinced. "What does that mean, exactly? Medically speaking?"

"Well, we still need to rule out stroke—but I believe Frau Hess is experiencing what we call catatonic stupor. She's in an apathetic state and nonreactive to external stimuli. Right now, motor activity is nearly nonexistent. She's not making eye contact and appears to be mute."

The telephone lines hissed and crackled. "And . . . how do you know she's not faking?"

"I don't. However, I'm going to proceed as if she is indeed catatonic, and for that I suggest electroshock therapy. We've had some good results with it in the past. It's a new technology—only been around a few years."

"What is—what did you call it? Electroshock therapy?"

Dr. Carroll took off his glasses and put them in his jacket pocket. "It's a psychiatric treatment where we electronically induce seizures in patients for therapeutic effect."

Frain's bark was so loud that Carroll had to pull the receiver away from his ear. "You *electrocute* them? Why?"

"Well, we don't really know why it works."

Frain gave a dry laugh. "Well, that's not very reassuring." Then, "And if she's faking?"

"The procedure is . . . most uncomfortable. No one in her right mind would voluntarily go through with it."

"My dear doctor," Frain said, "let me assure you—you've never met anyone like Clara Hess before. And her state of mind has always been up for question." In his large office at MI-5, Frain lit a cigarette and leaned back in his leather chair. "She's playing you, Dr. Carroll. Like the proverbial violin."

"Mr. Frain, I suggest you come here, to see Frau Hess's condition with your own eyes."

"I've seen her act many times, back in the day. Her portrayal of Konstanze in Mozart's *Die Entführung aus dem Serail* was sublime. But I don't need to see her do it again." Then, "And as far as I'm concerned, her execution proceeds on schedule. December seventh at twelve noon."

Before the doctor at the Tower of London could take Clara for her electroshock therapy, however, something happened.

"Wo bin ich?" said a little girl's voice. Where am I?

"Frau Hess," Dr. Carroll said, also in German, "you are safe, you're—"

"I'm going to play by the lake today!" Clara said in the same little girl's voice, sitting up in bed with evident glee.

"The lake?" the doctor said, taken aback. "Frau Hess—"

"Who is Frau Hess?" the little girl asked, giggling. "Not I, certainly."

The doctor tilted his head. "Who are you?"

She smiled. "Don't you know?"

"Why don't you tell me?"

"Agna, of course," Clara said, with a hint of impatience. "Agna Frei."

Dr. Carroll was on his guard, but willing to play along. "And you are going to play by the lake today, *gnädiges Fräulein?* Where do you play?"

"The lake!" she said. When he didn't react, she said, "Lake Wannsee?"

"Who will go with you?"

Clara's mouth turned down. "No one. I don't have any friends. My mother won't let me have any friends."

"She won't? Why?"

"I'm not allowed to say," she whispered, hunching over and wrapping her arms around herself. "Don't tell *Mutti* I said anything."

"No, no, I won't," answered the doctor. He thought a moment. "What month is it?"

"June!" she exclaimed and jumped up a bit. Then she rubbed her head. "Ouch!"

"What happened?"

"I bumped my head." She giggled.

"On what?"

"A bookshelf." Then, "Sometimes I pray. I pray to God."

"What do you pray for?"

"That *Papa* and *Mutti* will stop fighting. That I'll be allowed to have a friend. That *Mutti* will be nicer to me." Clara whispered confidentially, "She doesn't like me very much, you know."

"Why doesn't your mother like you?"

Clara yawned, then lay back down, curling inward like a child. She began sucking on her thumb, and within moments was fast asleep.

Chapter Six

Before Maggie could leave Arisaig House for Edinburgh the next morning, she realized she was now responsible for someone else—a very vocal, very spoiled, very opinionated ginger tabby. And she couldn't just leave him alone.

With K in what was becoming his usual perch on her shoulder, she approached Arisaig House's head gardener. He was a wizened gnome of a man, with gnarled hands, who took care of large plots of the kitchen gardens, a small apple orchard, rows of berry bushes, and several greenhouses. Maggie had nicknamed him—if only to herself—Ben Weatherstaff, after the crusty gardener in *The Secret Garden*.

Although that would make me Mary, Mary Quite Contrary, she mused, as her boots crunched on the road's gravel. But his real name was Angus Fraser, and the golden Labrador who followed Angus faithfully was Riska, named after one of the western isles. Maggie could only hope that he—and his dog—liked cats.

"Mr. Fraser?" Maggie called, coming upon him as he was digging in the black earth. The smell was rich and loamy. Overhead, the sky remained leaden.

"What's that, lassie?" he said, giving a perfunctory tip of his tweed cap.

"I'm, well—" Maggie spoke up to make herself heard over the rush of cold damp wind. "I'm going to be in Edinburgh for the weekend, and I was wondering—if you wouldn't mind, that is—keeping an eye on my cat? Just while I'm away?"

Fraser kept digging. "Don't like cats."

"Please?"

He shrugged. "A dinna ken—it's up to Riska, not to me. What d'ye think, girl?" he said, addressing the dog.

As if he understood the conversation, K jumped down from Maggie's shoulder and passed by Riska with head and tail held high, until he reached a dog bed of sorts. It was made from an old plaid cushion and covered in golden fur. Fraser had put it out for Riska against one of the stone walls, for outdoor naps during clement days.

K hopped onto the cushion and turned around three times before settling in and wrapping his tail around himself. His eyes slitted as if to say, *This will do. This will do nicely—that is, until The Woman returns.*

Riska looked up at Fraser with anxious eyes and whined.

"Well, I'm not going to fight your battles for ye, lassie," he said to the dog, a slow smile creeping over his face.

K had the indecency to look smug from his perch on the cushion.

Although the golden Lab probably outweighed K by at least sixty pounds, she slunk away to the gnarled apple trees, trying to find a squirrel to chase to cheer herself up.

"Well, glad that's settled, then," Maggie said. "Thank you ever so much, Mr. Fraser. Really, thank you."

"Nae problem, Miss."

Maggie was about to leave when she caught sight of one of the large shrubs that dotted the grounds of Arisaig. Their leaves were glossy and green and they sported large yellow buds, even in cold weather. She'd always been bothered by them, not understanding why in early winter, something would be getting ready to bloom.

Wouldn't they just wither and die in the cold? Was there any way to save them?

"I've been meaning to ask you, Mr. Fraser—are these rhododendron all right?" She'd seen banks of rhododendron at Wellesley College and they were dormant all winter, bursting into gorgeous hot pink blooms usually just as the senior class graduated in May.

Fraser threw his head back and laughed, a loud hearty bray. "Yes, lassie." He took out a square of flannel and wiped at his eyes. "Ya see, we're on the shore and affected by the Gulf Stream current, comin' from the Caribbean. So what you're seein' is flowers getting ready to bloom."

"Flowers that bloom in winter . . ." Such things didn't happen in Boston or London, and she certainly never pictured them happening in western Scotland.

"Well, they're alive the whole time—only takes a bit o' warmth to make 'em come out. Sometimes they bloom in time for Advent— look nice on the altar there, with the pink an' purple candles. Spring is comin', lass, even in the bleak midwinter. That's why the pagans put evergreens in their homes in the darkest day of the year—and why we now have Christmas trees. Light in the darkness. The promise of new life."

Maggie felt an almost inexplicable sense of relief knowing it was the natural order of things, not an anomaly. "Thank you, Mr. Fraser," she said, turning to go. "Thank you so very much for telling me that."

Washington was different from London. The faces of the people were plump and well fed. Their eyes weren't shadowed by sleepless nights of Luftwaffe bombing. Lights burned all night, unhampered by blackout regulations. And the stores were full of food and clothing—everything one could possibly need. To anyone from Britain, it would have seemed a veritable paradise. But for Washingtonians, it was just another day, overcast, with sullen gray clouds hanging above and a sharp wind blowing.

Secretary of State Cordell Hull was meeting once again with Ambassador Kichisaburō Nomura, this time near the Lincoln Memorial—away from both the State Department and the Japanese Embassy.

The two men were visual opposites. Hull was tall, slim, and white-haired—the very picture of an American aristocrat, even though he'd been born in a log cabin in Tennessee. Now in his sixties, Nomura had come up through the Japanese Navy and Japanese politics, and had been chosen for the position of Japanese Ambassador to the United States for the number of his American connections, including having known President Roosevelt when FDR had been Assistant Secretary of the Navy in the Wilson Administration, while he had been the naval attaché. Nomura was short, plump, and jolly looking, with etched smile lines. But he wasn't smiling today, and hadn't been for some time.

The year 1941 had been long and difficult for the two men, and it wasn't over yet. Nomura had arrived in Washington, DC, in March, charged with improving the increasingly strained diplomatic relationship between the United States and Japan. In the eight months he'd spent in the U.S., he looked as if he had aged at least a decade. He'd repeatedly offered his resignation to his higher-ups in Japan to no avail—they would not let him leave Washington.

To say negotiations between the two countries were not going well would be an understatement.

Ambassador Nomura was trying his best. Hull was not an unreasonable man, nor was President Roosevelt. Nomura and Hull had spent countless hours in meetings, attempting to resolve sticky diplomatic points such as the Japanese conflict with China, the Japanese occupation of French Indo-China, and the U.S. oil embargo against Japan. Hull could do little, as the President was convinced that any compromises with Japan would be seen by most Americans as "appeasement."

And Nomura's own requests to his superiors in Tokyo to offer the Americans meaningful concessions were summarily rejected. Diplomacy had stalled and tensions were rising. Still the two men met, as they always did, with open minds—both desperate to avert war.

"Well, Mr. Ambassador," Hull said, sitting down on their usual bench with a sigh, "here we are again." The wind had died down, but the air remained chill. They were surrounded by small and delicate newly planted maple trees, their branches leafless, their trunks the color of bruises.

"Yes, Mr. Secretary, here we are again." The two men's voices betrayed the exhaustion at the diplomatic dance they had been engaged in for so long—one step forward, two steps back.

"I like your President Lincoln," Nomura continued, looking up at the oversized marble statue. "*All men created equal.* What would he have made of this Japanese man, in his own nation's capital?"

"I believe he would have been honored," Hull replied, reaching into his coat pocket. He had a brown bag full of doughnuts. "My secretary brought them in this morning," he said. "Hope the pigeons don't mind cinnamon." He took a doughnut from the bag, then broke it in half, handing part to Nomura. Hull threw a few crumbs onto the path, hoping to attract birds.

"As always, Japan wishes America nothing but harmony."

"But—as your own Emperor said—'If all men are brethren, then why are the winds and waves so restless?' "

Nomura gave a nervous smile as he, too, sprinkled crumbs onto the path in front of him. "Mr. Secretary, as we have said—if

America could find her way toward lifting some of the embargoes on oil and other resources Japan needs . . ."

Hull shook his head. "President Roosevelt will not budge." He threw out a few more crumbs.

Nomura tried again. "As you know, our goal is to create the Greater East Asia Co-Prosperity Sphere—"

Hull lifted one eyebrow. "Your goal is to colonize China."

Nomura smiled apologetically, his wide face creasing. "Many Western powers—including the United States and Britain, of course—have colonies in Asia. We consider the situation inequitable. The British have colonized the planet and America doesn't say anything—"

"Well, we had a *little* something to say about it, back in 1776—"

"But not if it's far away and has nothing to do with you. The European countries have taken territory in Asia—France, Portugal . . . We are only doing what they have done for many centuries. And we took Singapore and Malaysia from the British, not fellow Asians. America took the Philippines, who took it from the Spanish. Why should only we be punished? Why not the British, French, Dutch, Italians, Spanish, Portuguese . . . and the Americans, as well, who set the example?" He took a piece of the doughnut and popped it in his mouth. "It's not a black-and-white issue."

Hull's violent exhale misted in the cold air. He sidestepped the issue, like a do-si-do in a square dance. "Look, Mr. Ambassador, we don't want war with Japan. And we don't believe your Emperor truly wants war with us."

A few pigeons landed by the men's feet, flapping their dun-colored wings before tucking them under. They began to peck for crumbs. Looking down, Hull smiled.

Nomura smiled, too. "If, Secretary Hull, you would make a concession—even a small one—one I can give to General

Tōjō . . . Even if we can't get what we want, we Japanese need to—how do you say?—save face."

"I know this is very hard for you, Mr. Ambassador. I know you've offered your resignation many times."

"Tokyo won't let me quit." Nomura watched as the plump pigeons pecked away, squabbling over the biggest pieces. "And today a second ambassador to the U.S. will arrive—Saburō Kurusu. A *'special envoy.'"* Nomura's tone conveyed his distaste.

"Kurusu—he's the one who signed the Axis Treaty with Italy and Germany." Hull raised a bushy white eyebrow. "Not a great choice for a country that allegedly wants to avoid war."

The two men continued to drop crumbs, watching even more birds arrive. "Do you think Kurusu can offer us anything new?" Hull asked.

"I would like to say yes."

"Always trying to look on the bright side, eh?"

"Sometimes it seems as if it is all that I can do."

The men sat in silence, each lost in his own thoughts. As the pigeons pecked at the crumbs, tiny black-masked sparrows landed, stealing crumbs out from under the larger, slower birds. Hull chuckled at the pigeons' indignation.

Nomura stood, brushing crumbs from his coat. "I will see you this afternoon, Mr. Secretary—for the arrival of 'Special Envoy' Kurusu?"

Hull rose as well and nodded. "See you this afternoon, Mr. Ambassador." He smiled and held out a gloved hand. Nomura bowed deeply, then extended his hand. The men shook.

A cold wind picked up, causing the bare tree branches to rustle. Both men pulled down on their hats as they walked away.

Hull turned, calling over his shoulder, "Next time *you* bring the doughnuts!"

———

Ambassador Nomura returned directly to his office after his out-door meeting with Secretary Hull and was drinking tea in his office at the Japanese Embassy—Darjeeling, with both milk and sugar, from a porcelain cup and saucer. He'd eaten most of the still-warm cookies that had also been sent up—chocolate chip, his favorite American sweet.

Although the building was a lavish mansion, furnished with dark, sturdy Victorian furnishings, and the entire staff wore Western-style clothing, there were nods here and there to Japan: paintings, ceremonial swords, and ceramics. There was even a carved wooden turtle from the fifteenth century that Namura kept on his desk and had named Masayoshi—meaning "righteous government and shining goodness."

Teatime was something he loved—one of the only things in his day he looked forward to anymore—but today he was displeased. The portly man usually had sparkling eyes and a quick grin. But today his eyes were weary; there was no life in his expression.

He took off his round black glasses and pinched the bridge of his nose as he leaned in to the wireless radio—according to the announcer, his countryman Saburō Kurusu had left San Francisco and would soon be arriving in Washington. The "Special Envoy" mission was seen as a last-ditch chance for peace between the two countries. Nomura turned the wireless off with a loud *click*.

He picked up the decrypted message that had been sent to him by General Tōjō. He'd read it so many times, the paper had become worn and creased, with a grease stain from a dropped chocolate chip cookie crumb. *Conditions both within and without Japan are so tense that no longer is procrastination possible. This is our final ef-*

fort. The success or failure of the pending discussions will have an immense effect on the destiny of our Empire.

This missive had been followed immediately by two others: *Our internal situation makes it impossible for us to make any further compromise . . .* And: *Because of various circumstances, it is imperative that all arrangements for the signing of this agreement be completed as soon as possible.*

Nomura looked at the calendar on his desk; it was already the end of November. He finished reading the communiqué. *I realize that this is a difficult order, but it is unavoidable under the circumstances. Please understand this fully and do your utmost to save Japanese-American relations from falling into a chaotic condition. Do so with great resolve and unstinted labor, I beg of you. This information is to be kept strictly to yourself.*

Nomura pushed the decrypts away and finished his tea and cookies, keeping an eye on the bronze mantel clock. It was almost time to meet with Kurusu. He sighed, resigned to his fate, and pressed a button on his telephone. "Please bring my hat and coat, Miss Ito," he said in approximation of his usual jovial, gentle tones. "We must prepare to welcome Special Envoy Kurusu."

At the press conference, held outside the Japanese Embassy in Washington, cold winds blew, making it difficult for the sound technicians to set up the microphones. Finally, the platform was arranged, with a lectern and the various radio stations' microphones surrounding, like a wall of thorns. All they needed now was the "Special Envoy."

Ambassador Nomura pulled out his pocket watch. Kurusu was late. The Japanese were never late. Everything was always timed perfectly, down to the second.

Finally, finally, the long black limousine pulled up and Kurusu emerged to applause from various Japanese diplomats and their staff, who had been allowed to attend.

He was a short man, even shorter than Ambassador Nomura, and slighter, with an almost delicate appearance. He wore an impeccable gray suit, a black wool overcoat, black hat, and black round glasses. Over the frames, his eyebrows turned up almost comically, like upended commas, and he had a faint mustache.

He walked to the podium, took a breath, and began to speak. "I am indeed glad to be here, in your nation's capital," he said in a clear but thin voice, his English accented but still understandable. "I extend greetings to all from the bottom of my heart.

"You all know how difficult my mission is," he continued, the wind dispersing his words. "But I will do all I can to make it a successful one, for the sake of two countries, Japan and the United States of America."

With that he lifted his hat to the audience and made his way down the reception line to Ambassador Nomura. Both men bowed, then reached out their hands for a Western-style handshake. "Welcome to Washington, Special Envoy Kurusu."

"Thank you," the shorter man replied. "We have much work to do."

"Indeed," Ambassador Nomura responded, noticing Hull's tall shadow. "And now," he said, with his most charming smile, "I would like to introduce you to the United States' Secretary of State Hull."

Kurusu bowed deeply, then extended his hand to Hull. Hull did not return the bow, but shook the envoy's hand. "Welcome to America, Special Envoy Kurusu," he said, cigarette clenched between his teeth. "You certainly have your work cut out for you."

Then he clapped the Japanese man on the back. Kurusu tried not to flinch at being touched in such a familiar way during formal introductions.

But Hull didn't notice. "Come on, let's shake a leg!" he said to the two Japanese ambassadors, looking at his wristwatch, then turning to stride down Massachusetts Avenue toward the White House, still chewing on his cigarette. "The President's waiting for you boys."

Still walking, Hull looked back toward the Japanese diplomats, his voice rising against the icy wind: "I know you must be hungry, so we'll have some nice chop suey waiting for you when you're done."

Kurusu and Nomura met with Hull and President Roosevelt. Kurusu presented Japan's proposal: that the United States should stop sending aid to China and resume trade relations with Japan.

Hull countered with President Roosevelt's demands for Japan to withdraw its troops from China, and, just as important if not more so, to sever its Axis ties with Germany and Italy.

The meeting was polite, but when it was over, Kurusu turned to Nomura as they waited for their car to be brought around to the front door of the White House. "If this is the attitude of the American government, I don't see how an agreement is possible."

"The Americans won't budge, and Tokyo will throw up its hands at their demands. And that," Nomura said, his voice breaking with barely contained frustration, "is what I've been dealing with."

"It's all right—it's not as if any great change can be effected now. Even an extension won't affect the ultimate outcome."

Nomura's eyes widened behind his round spectacles. "What do you mean?"

"We're only here for show. We are just part of the three-ring circus."

Nomura shook his head. "There is still a chance for peace," he insisted. "I believe that to be true."

Kurusu tapped his foot, clad in black leather Rohde shoes he'd picked up in Berlin, as their limousine approached. "If that's what helps you sleep at night, my friend."

Leaving the relative comfort and safety of Arisaig House for the Beasdale train station felt a bit like picking her way barefoot over glass shards, but Maggie was determined not to let Sarah down. The Black Dog was napping, but for how long?

It was an uphill walk over dirt roads and under pewter skies to the tiny station, where she waited for the one and only train of the morning. It pulled in with a shrieking whistle and a billow of steam. The cold and drafty train took her to nearby Fort William, where it stood and waited for more passengers to board, then wended east through the mountains.

Maggie had brought her knitting, but she couldn't help staring at the vistas outside the train's dirty window. It was as if Scotland's history were flashing before her eyes. Snowcapped mountains cut by the ancient glaciers. Giant oaks, with the dark tangle of birds' nests in the bare branches. Sheep and horses grazing in frozen fields, dotted with white farmhouses.

She transferred trains at Glasgow's Queen Street, waiting under the curved-glass Victorian glass ceiling, and continued east. There were graveyards on the curve of hills, older men on brown and patchy golf courses, small towns with lonely church spires beside blue lochs. Unconsciously, as the sun began to set, she began to hum the tune of "Scots Wha Hæ," which she'd heard many times at the pub in the town of Arisaig. She loved the sound of the bagpipes and the cadences of Robert Burns's lyrics:

Scots, wha hæ wi Wallace bled,
Scots, wham Bruce has aften led,

Walcome tæ yer gory bed,
Or tæ victorie.

Lay the proud usurpers low,
Tyrants fall in every foe,
Libertie's in every blow!—
Let us do or dee.

Maggie's feet and hands were aching with cold by the time she finally arrived at Princes Street Station in Edinburgh. She wrestled her valise from an overhead bin, and then made her way toward a great red sandstone building with Victorian carved figures and Corinthian columns, illuminated by moonlight.

Maggie snorted, remembering how David had once called the Langham Hotel "a Victorian train station." Well, now she knew exactly what he meant. The Caledonian was one of Britain's great railroad hotels. Made of red brick, it was as Victorian as the Queen herself—heavy, stately, and not quite fashionable. Angels and a sphinx overlooked doormen in livery who held large black umbrellas to shelter the hotel's guests.

On the street corner a Salvation Army worker in her navy-blue uniform rang a brass bell. "Advent is coming!" she called in a Scots accent. "Advent is coming! Give to the poor!"

Maggie dropped a few coins into the woman's basket and made her way up the steps to the lobby. There were marble floors and a great chandelier, pillars and a grand staircase. Upstairs, a dignified sign announced, was The Pompadour restaurant, but Maggie didn't have the time or money for that. She checked in and then took the creaky elevator upstairs.

Her room might have been small, but it afforded an excellent view of Edinburgh Castle. The furniture was handsome, the duvet rose silk, and on the wall was a reproduction of George Henry's oil painting *Geisha Girl,* her smile as mysterious as the Mona Lisa's.

Maggie looked at the small silver bedside clock. It was time to get ready. She washed up and rolled her hair, dabbing on a touch of red lipstick. *Wish I could find my pearl earrings,* she thought absently, as she put on her hat and gloves, making sure to drop the wrought-iron key in her handbag.

She just had time for a quick cup of tea and roll with margarine at a restaurant across the street. As she sat, watching the other patrons talk and smile, she felt out of place. *I shouldn't have come,* she thought, imagining her Black Dog flick his tail and bare his fangs in his sleep. *What am I doing here?*

Edinburgh boasted the same signs from the Ministry of War as London—BRITISHERS: ENLIST TODAY! and IT CAN HAPPEN HERE! Someone had used a finger to write in the dust on the back window of a vehicle: IF YOU THINK THE VAN'S DIRTY, YOU SHOULD SEE THE DRIVER.

Well, I suppose it could "happen here," but it really hasn't, Maggie thought. Yes, Edinburgh had the same sandbags and barbed wire as London, its metal fences and railings taken to be melted down for planes and tanks. It had the same black taxis and red telephone booths. But unlike London, Edinburgh had sustained no serious bomb damage. Maggie knew that some of the outlying areas had been hit and lay in rubble. But the city itself looked unscathed.

The people walked a different way, too, she noted—they were still confident and untouched, certain their families and homes would still be there when they returned. Edinburgh might have been a city at war, but it was not, like London, a warrior city. *And there's a big difference,* Maggie realized, looking at the people:

mothers pushing infants in prams, old men with tweed hats and goose-headed walking sticks, a pair of teenagers ducking into a door frame to get out of the wind long enough to light their cigarettes. They were able to sleep through the night in their beds, unmolested, not required to crawl off to Anderson shelters. She both resented their innocence of the brute reality of war, and also desperately wanted to protect it.

Her feet, usually in thick wool socks and boots, hurt. They weren't used to stockings and pumps anymore. And her head, accustomed to a knit cap, was cold in her feather-festooned pinwheel. *Why don't ladies' hats cover ears?* Maggie thought as she sidestepped several puddles. Around her, she could hear the clang of a trolley and the clip-clop of horses' hooves.

She walked through the streets past soot-stained buildings with fan windows and glossy black-painted doors to the Royal Lyceum Theatre on Grindlay Street. She was just in time for the curtain, sliding into her velvet seat just before the cleft-chinned conductor made his entrance, bowed to the audience, and raised his baton. Herman Severin Løvenskiold's delicate, wistful overture began.

The Vic-Wells, Britain's fledgling ballet company under the direction of Ninette de Valois, was dancing *La Sylphide*. A Romantic ballet in two acts, choreographed by August Bournonville, it was, fittingly, set in the Scottish Highlands. There was polite applause, and then the heavy curtains parted.

The spotlight centered on the dancer playing James Ruben, in traditional Highland dress, sleeping in an oversized velvet wing chair in a Scottish great house. A sylph entered, lit in blue, dancing in an unearthly, weightless way. She wasn't Sarah. *Wait, I thought she was dancing the lead?*

Maggie looked down at her program, squinting to read it in the dim light. The role of the lead sylph was being danced by Estelle Crawford, a new company member, who looked every inch a fairy queen. *Still,* Maggie thought, *if the idiots in charge of casting had any sense, Sarah would dance it.*

The blond ballerina danced with delicate flourishes of phrasing, costumed as the ideal fairy: gossamer wings, a long white tutu, and a crown of pale pink roses. She kissed James. When he woke, she magically disappeared.

In the next scene, Maggie watched raven-haired Sarah, radiant as ever, enter as one of the friends of James's fiancée Effie. Sarah jumped and twirled in her red velvet bodice and tartan skirt, as beautiful as the woman playing the sylph, but stronger, and glowing with passion.

The crone, Old Madge, entered the farmhouse, with more than a touch of the sinister about her. She pantomimed to James: *Let's see if you're* truly *in love.* Maggie looked down at her program again. Madge was being played by a dancer named Mildred Petrie. Maggie remembered meeting Mildred, back in London. Sarah had always loathed her, and Maggie could see why. Mildred was an aging dancer—still in the corps, left behind as generation after generation of dancers had been promoted over her. And as she'd aged, she'd grown increasingly bitter.

Nature gives you the face you have at twenty. Life shapes the face you have at thirty. But at fifty you get the face you deserve. Mildred, who must have been close to fifty, certainly had the face she deserved: pale and puffy, with small eyes like tiny black currants in white batter, her thin lips pursed and cynical. Or it might just have been her facial expression, a perpetual sneer of disgust at life for daring to pass her by. *Although,* Maggie noted, *she* does *make a decent witch. Perhaps it's her true calling?*

During intermission, Maggie went to use the ladies' loo. The lounge's walls were covered in ivory silk. There, the grande dames of Edinburgh touched up their vibrant lipstick at the mirrors. Most were older ballet aficionados and society matrons. As Maggie washed her hands, she studied her reflection, then shook her head. She seemed more wax figure than flesh and blood.

Next to her, a fat woman drew a matte red bow on her lips. "Mildred Petrie would have done anything to play the Sylph, you know. It must be *killing* her to dance character roles now."

"Well, darling, I heard she has even more reason to hate Estelle," a tall thin woman said, smoothing flyaway hairs from her gray chignon. "*I* heard that Mildred's been in love with the company's orchestra conductor for years, and he's never paid her any attention. But when Estelle joined the company, she and the conductor began a mad love affair. People say his wife is devastated. And Mildred is, too."

"I remember when dear Diana was still Diana Angius. Such a beauty she was, back in the day. And from a respected family in Whitshire."

Hmmm, Maggie thought as she returned to her seat. *Mr. Cleft Chin's quite popular.* After living with Sarah in London, and hearing daily reports, she knew quite well how the goings-on in a dance company could sometimes be far more dramatic than anything onstage.

The lights dimmed and the conductor once again strode out. He was indeed handsome in his black tie and jacket, she had to admit, with his winning smile and shaggy hair. An electricity crackled from him, and Maggie could see how the dancers would fall under his spell. Idly, she wondered if he really was having an affair with Estelle, and if he'd really broken Mildred's heart. *Oh stop it, Hope,* she chided herself. *No gossip! Don't let yourself be dragged in, too.* She looked down at the program—the conductor's name was Richard Atholl.

As she watched act two, Madge and the witches danced around a cauldron as the witch plotted the Sylph's demise, creating a magic veil that would kill her. Mildred as Madge gave it to James, who was delighted, believing that it would bind the Sylph to him forever. In the forest, James and his Sylph danced. Maggie watched Sarah, now in the corps of sylphs, her technique flawless as always.

When James caught the Sylph around her waist and bound her hands as Madge showed him, the Sylph died, wilting in his arms like the last white rose of autumn, delicate and impossibly fragile. Madge had her victory, and James was heartbroken.

The curtain closed.

Really? Maggie thought as she applauded with all her heart. She'd loved seeing Sarah dance, but found it all too sad to bear. *Really, in the midst of war, can't we please have a happy ending? If only on the stage? Curse the witches of the world . . .*

The curtain reopened and the corps took their curtseys. Maggie applauded so hard for Sarah her gloved palms stung. The lead dancers all took their turn. Finally, it was Estelle's time in the spotlight. Smiling, she floated to the front of the stage. The dancer playing James presented her with a bouquet of red roses, which she took in her arms, plucking out one and giving it back to him.

Then she pulled out another blossom. She threw it at Richard Atholl, down in the orchestra pit. The crowd went wild as the conductor caught the rose and blew her a kiss. Estelle stood completely still in the center of the stage as the applause continued to thunder, and a few voices in the first ring cried, *"Brava! Bravissima!"*

As Maggie watched, a shadow passed over Atholl's face. He spun around on the conductor's podium and held out the flower. A stocky older woman with a round face in a black silk dress took it, unsmiling. Maggie guessed she was his wife.

And then, as the applause continued to build and the roars of *Brava!* began in earnest, Estelle crumpled to the stage floor in a heap of satin and tulle.

Chapter Seven

As the theater's curtain closed with a billow of red velvet, the audience erupted: *My goodness, what happened? Do you think she's ill? Poor thing—much too thin, you know . . .*

Maggie grabbed her pocketbook and made her way to a door at the side of the stage. She walked up a flight of stairs to the backstage area, dark and cramped, filled with ballet barres covered in hastily thrown-off sweaters and leg warmers, a broken mirror, and a box of rosin in the corner. The air was pungent with sweat and perfume.

When she reached the stage, it was clear the company was in complete chaos. Estelle was still lying on the floor. A tall man in tweeds, who seemed to be a doctor, was taking her pulse and shouting, "She needs an ambulance! An ambulance, damn you!" Burly stagehands in black hung back awkwardly in the wings, glancing at one another, unsure what to do. The atmosphere, charged with adrenaline from the performance, was now tinged with fear.

Atholl had also made his way backstage. The conductor went to Estelle and knelt beside her, pressing her limp white hand to his cheek, oblivious to the dancers and stagehands swirling around them.

Maggie tried to find Sarah among the throng of sylphs. *Throng of sylphs? Exaltation of sylphs? Murder of sylphs?* she wondered, scanning the dancers. They were all slim, graceful, and wearing white tulle and gossamer fairy wings, their faces painted in Kabuki-like exaggerated makeup. Maggie couldn't tell one from the other.

Then one called her name, in a low voice of whiskey and honey. "Maggie!"

She knew the voice. Only it was lower and huskier than usual, followed by a deep, rattling cough. Yes! That sylph was Sarah—Maggie recognized her dark eyes immediately. But while they were lovely as always, they were also strained and frightened. Maggie ran to her and they embraced. Sarah smelled of her usual clove cigarettes and L'Heure Bleue.

"My goodness," Maggie exclaimed. "I do hope she's all right."

"I'm so glad you're here, kitten." Sarah was thinner, even thinner than the last time they had seen each other, in London. While the outline of the delicate bones of Sarah's sternum were visible up close, her arms were still wiry with visible tendons and strong muscles.

"For heaven's sake, when is the ambulance going to arrive?" Sarah muttered, starting to unpin her flowered headpiece. Estelle still had not moved. "Our stage manager said he'd called for one!"

"Has she been sick?"

"Yes," Sarah answered, putting one graceful hand to her bony chest and coughing softly. "But then again, it's late autumn in Scotland—with the cold and damp in the theater and the hotel, who isn't sick these days? I never thought she'd dance tonight. Which is why I invited you."

"I wouldn't have missed seeing you for the world," Maggie said, squeezing her friend's waist. "Lead or corps." She knew it wasn't her friend. She knew it was none of her business. And yet, she just couldn't stay away. "Wait here," she told Sarah.

Maggie made her way over to the ballerina's body. "How is she?" she asked the man in tweed kneeling beside her. Atholl was holding vigil next to him. Maggie could see the woman in black—the wife—looming over his shoulder.

"Thready pulse, weak heartbeat, I'm afraid," the doctor said. "Everyone thinks of these girls as sprites and sylphs, but they're athletes. They push just as hard as Jesse Owens did in the Olympics."

Estelle's already-pale skin was covered in white pancake makeup. But Maggie noticed some black spots, blister-like sores that had come through on Estelle's collarbones, where the makeup had sweated off. Her eyes narrowed. "What are those?"

"I've been a pediatrician for nearly forty years," the doctor said, looking up at Maggie, "and I've never seen anything like them in my life."

He put his fingers to the carotid artery at the ballerina's throat and listened for breath. His eyes met Maggie's; he shook his head.

The conductor stood. He shrugged off his wife's concern, heading out to one of the fire doors and opening it with a reverberating echo. "Richard," his wife called, her heels clattering, "you're making a spectacle of yourself!"

The doctor gently closed Estelle's eyelids, then rose. "Cancel the ambulance. Someone will need to call the police, too." He cleared his throat and lowered his head. "I'm afraid she's dead."

Oh, dear God. Maggie looked at Sarah. Her eyes were blank with shock. One of the other sylphs staggered and nearly fell, but was held up by her fellow dancers.

Madame de Valois emerged from the wings and clapped her hands together. Everyone stopped and turned to her, a vision in violet. Madame walked forward from the shadows of the wings to Estelle's body. She bent to her knees and kissed the dead girl's cheek. Then, slowly, she stood.

"Girls and boys of the ballet," she began in a plummy voice. "Of course all of our prayers are with Estelle and her family at this time. Estelle died doing what she loved to do most—dance. Let us have a moment of silence."

Her dark eyes scanned the lines of dancers. "Where is Sarah Sanderson?"

Sarah took a small step forward. "Yes, Madame?"

"As understudy, you will be performing the role of the Sylph until further notice." Madame clapped her hands again. "That is all." And she strode off the stage.

The dancers erupted into fits of whispers. The officials arrived with a stretcher for Estelle's body, looking even tinier and more delicate in death than it had in motion on the stage. The dancers stood wide-eyed and mute now, unable to comprehend what had just happened.

Sarah put her hand on Maggie's arm. "I need to get out of here."

Together they climbed the back stairs to the corps dressing room. It was narrow and windowless, lined with lighted mirrors, the counters littered with pans of eye shadow and tubes of lipstick. There was a pincushion on the counter, a porcelain Hitler, bent over, with straight pins bristling in his fabric bottom. And in the corner, an enormous bouquet—white roses, yellow laburnum, and purple carnations. It was arranged in the Victorian tussy-mussy style, petals just beginning to fall, water turning brackish.

Maggie had learned the symbolism of flowers in literature from an English class at Wellesley. She had even written a paper on flower imagery in Oscar Wilde's *Picture of Dorian Gray*. She'd never liked writing papers, but was enthralled by the idea of sending coded messages through flowers, called floriography. The New England college classroom seemed very long ago and far away—certainly a world away from Edinburgh at war.

"These are—were—Estelle's," Sarah said, walking to the flowers and bending down to sniff. "Ouch!" she cried.

"Are you all right?"

"Damn thorns," Sarah mumbled, sucking at her finger.

"*'But he who dares not grasp the thorn, should never crave the rose,'*" Maggie quoted. It was easier to quote from novels than think about Estelle.

"Honestly, I have no idea what you're talking about half the time." Sarah gave a crooked smile and sat down to wipe off her makeup. "I wish I'd gone to university, like you, kitten."

"It's a quote from Anne Brontë—and I wish I could go *en pointe*, like you. I'm so clumsy most of the time." Maggie remembered seeing John in Berlin and almost falling before they could embrace. She wished that she could tell Sarah all about Berlin, and John, and even the Black Dog—but she couldn't.

Lithe dancers began to filter in, uncharacteristically silent and somber, slipping into silk robes and taking off their thick makeup. Sarah was pulling off spidery false eyelashes when there was a sharp knock on the dressing room door. "Open up!"

The dancer closest, huddled into a robe, opened it. "Nobody leaves!" a tall policeman shouted in a thick Scottish burr. "This is a crime scene!

"You!" he said, jabbing a finger at the dancer who'd opened the door, one of the youngest of the corps.

"Yes?" she whispered, shrinking back. "Sir?"

"We're looking for a Miss Mildred Petrie. And a Miss Sarah Sanderson. Are they here?"

Sarah stood. "I'm Sarah Sanderson."

The witch rose, too. "And I'm Mildred Petrie." She still had on her prosthetic warty nose and green makeup, looking like the Wicked Witch of the West from *The Wizard of Oz*. Sarah's eyes were large and frightened. Mildred looked to be in shock as well—although her small eyes were far less expressive.

"I'm afraid, ladies, that we're taking you in for questioning."

"May I at least put on some clothes?" Sarah asked.

"Yes, of course," said the shorter officer, recoiling from Mildred and her nose. "Please do."

Maggie went outside with the police officers. "What sort of questioning?" she demanded, stepping forward.

"Sorry, Miss. Police business."

"Well then, which station are you taking them to?"

"St. Leonard's."

Sarah and Mildred both emerged a few minutes later, their faces pale without makeup, wearing street clothes. Maggie trotted alongside as they exited the theater by the stage door. The dancers were guided into the backseat of a shiny black police car. "Why do you need to question them?" Maggie insisted.

"I can't say anything, Miss," answered the shorter police officer. "I'm sorry."

Sarah and Mildred settled into the seat. "Maggie . . ." Sarah put her fingers against the glass.

"I'll get to the bottom of this, I swear," Maggie promised.

She turned to the taller officer. "Are you charging them with a crime?" Maggie wasn't an expert in the laws of Britain, but she was pretty sure people had to be informed. "You *do* have to tell them!"

The bobby looked Maggie straight in the eye. "We're bringing them both in for questioning—regarding the murder of Miss Estelle Crawford."

St. Leonard's Police Station, on St. Leonard's Lane, was a yellow-brick building dwarfed by the cliffs of Castle Rock and then the imposing fortress itself. Maggie entered and took a seat in the waiting room, watching the clock and worrying at an unraveling seam at the fingertips of her gloves. "Cuppa tea, Miss?" the woman at the reception desk asked.

"No," Maggie managed. "No, thank you."

Sarah was in another room, being questioned. The taller police officer, Herbert Craig, sat down in a battered metal chair across the small wooden table from Sarah. The legs scraped at the worn gray linoleum. "I want to reiterate, for the record, Miss Sanderson, that you've waived your right to a solicitor."

"Yes," Sarah said softly. "I have nothing to hide."

"All right." Craig uncapped his pen and scribbled on the margin of his notepad, to encourage the ink flowing. "You're Miss Estelle Crawford's understudy?" He was youngish, maybe in his late twenties, with a long, thin face that matched his long, thin body. An empty pinned-up left sleeve explained why he wasn't serving in the military.

"Yes," Sarah answered. She was pale from shock.

"So, if she didn't go on, you would dance the leading role in her place."

"Yes."

Craig made a note on his pad. "And that would mean extra money?"

"Well . . . yes. But you can't imagine . . ."

"Just answer the questions, please, Miss Sanderson."

"Yes."

"And I understand this was a special night? Opening night? And there would be critics in attendance?"

"Yes." Sarah blinked back tears. "But I adored Estelle—we all did—you can't imagine I'd ever—"

"Again, please just answer the questions, Miss," he commanded, but he took out a cambric handkerchief from his breast pocket and handed it to her.

She dabbed at her eyes. "Yes, it was opening night, and yes, there were several critics in attendance."

He made another note. "Do you know a Mr. Richard Atholl?"

"Of course. He's our conductor."

"How would you characterize your relationship with him?"

"Relationship?" Sarah looked puzzled and blew her nose. Another coughing jag, this one even more violent, from down deep in her lungs, shook her slender body.

The officer's eyes softened. "Are you all right, Miss?"

"Fine," Sarah said dismissively, raising her chin. "And my relationship with Mr. Atholl is professional." She lowered the handkerchief and twisted it in her lap. "I am a dancer. Mr. Atholl is a conductor. The orchestra under his direction that accompanies us is excellent."

"Did you and he ever have a relationship that was closer? More . . ." Officer Craig looked almost embarrassed to have to ask. The tips of his oversized ears glowed red. ". . . *intimate?*"

"No!" Sarah cried. "He's married, for heaven's sake!" Then, realizing how naïve that sounded, she amended, "No, we were never intimate, we're not even what you'd call friends. It's a professional relationship. That's all."

"Were you aware of his having any extramarital relationships with any of the other dancers?"

Sarah folded the handkerchief in her lap and sat up straight, posture impeccable. She radiated dignity. "Officer Craig, I am a professional dancer in Britain's finest ballet company. We work together, we travel together, we perform together, and, yes, sometimes people do sleep together." She lifted her chin. "But I'm focused on my dancing. And pay no mind to gossip."

Craig made another note, then set down his pen and stood. "Thank you, Miss Sanderson."

Sarah breathed a sigh of relief. "May I go now?"

He shook his head and had the decency to look shamefaced. "We're going to keep you in custody for a little while longer, I'm afraid."

Sarah's long, graceful hand went to her mouth, smothering another cough. "Are you—are you charging me with—" She couldn't say the word *murder*, so she amended to "—a crime?"

"Since you're under suspicion of murder, we can keep you, without arresting you, for three days." Craig added, in gentler tones: "But no, for the time being, we're not charging you with anything."

"Three days?" Sarah whispered.

"If you'd like to confess something . . ."

"No," she said, setting her jaw and standing, her spine ramrod-straight. "No. I have nothing further to say."

A meeting had been called to discuss Bratton's theory about a possible Japanese strike.

As Secretary of Defense General George C. Marshall was out of town, overseeing maneuvers in North Carolina, Bratton took his decrypts and his analysis for presentation to Secretary of War Henry L. Stimson.

The meeting was held at Stimson's overheated smoke-filled office, with Secretary of State Hull in attendance. Stimson was unconvinced. "But do you have any actual *facts*, Colonel Bratton?" In the background, the radiator clanked and a French mantel clock ticked, then chimed seven.

Hull looked up from copies of Bratton's memos and put down his pince-nez on the glossy wooden table. "Bratton's analysis is on the nose," he said.

Bratton's usually sour expression lightened for a moment.

But Hull continued. "Henry, I'm washing my hands of the whole matter. From now on, it's up to you and the Navy."

Stimson crushed out his black cigarillo in a heavy aluminum

Navy ashtray bearing the insignia of the USS *Arizona* and nodded. "I'll call the President."

Bratton was shocked, first that Hull was relinquishing all responsibility and also that Stimson wasn't going to do more. "But what *else* can we do? Sir?" he added.

"The President will be informed, Colonel Bratton," Stimson shot back. "But I know just what he's going to say—he's adamant that we maneuver the Japanese into firing the first shot. You'll keep me appraised of any new developments?"

Bratton looked as if he were about to say something—then closed his mouth. "Yes, sir. I'll keep you appraised."

To pass the time, Maggie was knitting dark-blue soldiers' socks she had stashed in her handbag, metal needles clicking in the silence. She nearly pounced on Craig when he appeared in the waiting room of the St. Leonard's Police Station. "Is Sarah Sanderson under arrest?" she asked, slipping the half-finished sock in her handbag.

"I'm sorry, I can't comment, Miss."

"How long are you going to hold her?"

"I really can't say, Miss."

Maggie sensed he was a decent fellow, just doing his job. "Is she . . . all right?"

"As all right as anyone can be in a situation like this, Miss." He looked at the black-and-white clock on the cement wall: According to the black Roman numerals, it was three in the morning. "Miss Sanderson's being taken to a cell now, where she can get some sleep, while we question the other dancer. Why don't you go and get some rest, too? Come back in the morning. Maybe there will be more information then."

"I'll stay," Maggie said resolutely, not wanting to leave her friend.

In an even gentler voice, Officer Craig said, "I'm afraid you can't, Miss. I must insist you leave. It's policy—no overnight guests."

Reluctantly, Maggie returned to the Caledonian Hotel, rows of chimneys black against the starry indigo sky. Up in her tiny room, she tugged off her coat and gloves, unpinned her hat, kicked off her shoes, then threw herself on the bed. In her mind's eye, images spun—Estelle as the Sylph, Mildred as the witch, making her poisonous brew . . . Estelle's collapse . . . Sarah's face as the officer called her name . . . The little Jewish girl in the Berlin train station, asking for water . . . Gottlieb killing himself before the Gestapo could get to him . . . The young German train attendant, her bullet piercing his chest . . .

The Black Dog bared his fangs and circled.

"No!" Maggie called out aloud, knowing she sounded foolish, but well past the point of caring. "Sarah's going to be fine. I will do everything I can to see to that, you hear me? Now, *go*! Off with you! That's right, *shoo*!"

This time, the Black Dog backed down—and Maggie fell into a restless sleep.

Chapter Eight

It was morning, and still Clara seemed to be in a catatonic state. She'd been moved to a cage in Dr. Carroll's office. Behind the bars, she lay on a metal bed with a thin mattress, her wrists and ankles bound with leather restraints. Her glassy eyes stared up at the ceiling.

"The emergence of the Agna Frei personality seems to have been spontaneous," said Dr. Carroll to Peter Frain. "Frau Hess is able to slip into a spontaneous hypnotic trance that's deep enough to allow age regression. But with hypnosis, we can also induce the emergence of Agna."

"We'll see," Frain said skeptically.

Dr. Carroll sat on a chair positioned next to the bed. Frain remained in the door frame, neither in nor out of the room, hat in hand, coat over his arm. Behind him lurked the two omnipresent guards.

"I want you to close your eyes and relax," Dr. Carroll said in a soothing voice. Clara's eyes closed. "You are going into a deep sleep. I want you to relax the muscles in your forehead, in your cheeks, around your mouth. I want you to relax your eyes . . ."

On and on, Dr. Carroll spoke, until Clara's breathing became deep and regular.

When he was finished, she woke.

She immediately began to cry. "My *Oma* is sick! They told me she was on holiday, but really she's in hospital."

"Agna?" Dr. Carroll wanted to make sure who it was.

"Yes?" The voice was thin and childish.

"How do you know your *Oma* is sick?"

"I heard *Mutti* talking to the doctor on the telephone when she thought I was outside, playing."

"Is *Mutti* with you now?"

"No, I'm alone in the house." Clara struggled against her restraints, then quieted. "I'm always alone."

"Do you know where your mother is?"

"I don't know. I don't know where *Mutti* goes." Then, "She doesn't love me, you know."

"Why do you think she doesn't love you?"

"She says I make her nervous. She doesn't like it when I'm around." Clara's eyes brimmed with tears. "I try to be good," she insisted. "I try hard. So hard."

"You try hard, yes," the doctor said, making notes in Clara's chart.

"My *Oma* loves me, though. I can tell. She doesn't mind my being around. Even if I spill something, or break something."

"What does your mother do if you spill or break something?"

Clara's gaze blurred. "I'm a doll!" she said, giggling. It was as if someone had changed the wireless station.

"You're a doll? What kind of doll?"

"A doll—like the one my *Oma* made me. She's beautiful, with a painted china face and real silk for her dress."

"What's her name?"

"Clara."

The doctor looked to Frain, who gestured for him to continue. "Clara is your doll?"

"Clara is my friend. I don't have any other friends. Real friends."

"Doesn't your mother want you to have friends?"

"No, just Clara. And my books. And I like to sing. I have that." She smiled, an utterly guileless smile. She began to sing, not in an operatic soprano's voice, but in the dulcet tones of a child, the traditional song *"Eins, zwei, Polizei":*

> *One, two, police*
> *three, four, officer*
> *five, six, old witch*
> *seven, eight, good night!*
> *nine, ten, good-bye!*

And with that, she fell back down to the pillow, breathing heavily, eyes closed—as if asleep.

After a restless night, Maggie woke. She slipped from the bed and pulled back the blackout curtains. Outside she could see, in the gray just before the breaking of the dawn, the dark outline of Edinburgh Castle, perched atop the sheer Castle Rock. *Ha—I'd like to see any invading Nazis try and climb that!* For this was where Edinburgh's last stand would take place—if it came to that.

She had breakfast at the hotel's dining room, and then started out for St. Leonard's Police Station. As the sun rose in a pearly lavender sky, she had a chance to actually see Edinburgh, which had been blacked out the night before.

It was quieter and the streets were less crowded than London. Chimneys in a row belched thick black smoke, while a lone seagull flew high overhead, giving a faint cry. The architecture felt heavier, darker, more Victorian; most buildings were made from porous sandstone, which absorbed the soot and smog carried back down by the rain before it could drift away.

The gray sky began to snow, big lacy flakes that melted as soon as they hit the dark wet pavement. Maggie did her best to avoid the slushy puddles, bird droppings, and burned-out cigarette butts as the flakes flew thicker and faster. She saw a young boy and girl tucked into an alley to huddle together for warmth, sneaking a few kisses. *How long will it be until he volunteers or is called up?* Maggie wondered. In Princes Street Gardens, in the shadows of the castle, boys threw snowballs through the twisted trees. *And how long before they'll be throwing bombs?*

At St. Leonard's she opened the main door and heard raised voices coming from the front desk. "And I don't care if you're the Pope of Rome," a deep, booming voice shouted, "MI-Five is taking over this case!"

Maggie could only see the man from the back. He was wearing a black coat and hat, his shoulders wide and sturdy.

"It's a murder, it happened in Edinburgh, and so it's our jurisdiction!" she heard Officer Craig snap back.

"It may have started out as a local crime, but *now* it's a matter of national security," the man in the black hat retorted. "And I've instructed the Director General of MI-Five, Peter Frain, to take over the case of the murder of Estelle Crawford."

Maggie was sure she recognized the man's voice. And he'd mentioned Peter Frain and MI-5 . . . She took a few steps closer. "Agent Standish? Agent Mark Standish?"

The man spun around to face her. His eyes widened in recognition and shock. "Miss Hope?" Then, "What on God's green earth are *you* doing here?"

"I'd ask you the same thing, except I just overheard most of your conversation with Officer Craig."

"You two—know each other?" Officer Craig had a bewildered look on his face.

"We've met," Mark Standish said tersely.

"We were colleagues," Maggie corrected.

Craig's eyebrows rose with surprise and respect.

Mark glared. "And, Miss Hope, I'll ask you again—what are you doing here?"

"I came to Edinburgh to see Sarah Sanderson perform in the Vic-Wells's *La Sylphide*."

"Sarah Sanderson?"

Maggie felt a hot wave of impatience wash over her. He should remember Sarah. After all, she'd nearly died helping them catch the IRA thugs trying to assassinate Winston Churchill in the summer of 1940.

"Sarah," Maggie repeated. "Sarah Sanderson." She enunciated clearly, as though to a small child. "Remember? Ballet dancer?" She tried not to pull a face. "The ballet dancer who's being held here on suspicion of murder?"

Mark looked confused. "How on earth do you know her?"

"May we have a moment in private?" Maggie asked Officer Craig.

"Of course," he replied, turning on his heel to walk down one of the corridors.

When he was out of earshot, Maggie turned back to Mark. "Sarah Sanderson," she hissed. "Nearly killed by Paige Claire Kelly? Helped save St. Paul's Cathedral from being bombed? Helped save the Prime Minister from being murdered? *That* Sarah Sanderson?" Maggie gave him a hard look. "When I was working as Mr. Churchill's secretary?" She tried very hard not to roll her eyes. "Really, Mark, it's only been—what—a year and a half."

"*That* Sarah Sanderson?" he said, unwinding his scarf and

scratching his neck. "She's the same Sarah Sanderson who's being held here?"

What wizard powers of deduction you have. No wonder you're still an entry-level flunky. "Yes, she's being held as a suspect in Estelle Crawford's alleged murder. Although, as of last night, she hasn't been charged." Maggie cocked her head and narrowed her eyes. "But why is MI-Five involved? Since when does the death of a ballerina become a matter of British national security?" *And how is one of my best friends involved?*

"I'm afraid I can't tell you that, Miss Hope." His smile was patronizing. "For obvious reasons."

Maggie inhaled sharply. This case was personal. And she didn't like to be condescended to by anyone, let alone a former MI-5 colleague.

Peter Frain from MI-5 owes me one—and I think it's time to collect. "I'm going to make a telephone call, Mr. Standish," she said with the same Aunt Edith look and tone she used on her Arisaig trainees, "and then we'll have a little chat."

For the moment, the Black Dog was held at bay.

"I'm not happy about this." Mark shook his head as they made their way down slippery snow-covered streets to the morgue. "Not happy at all."

Maggie, however, was flush from her victory, and not about to let him spoil her rare good mood. "You're British, Mark. It's always difficult to tell when you're experiencing any emotion at all—let alone which one it may be."

Maggie had convinced Frain that Sarah deserved to be released on bail. And so Maggie knew Sarah was back at the Caledonian, having a bath and scrubbing off the stink of the jail cell. Maggie was also pleased because she'd persuaded Frain that she should partner with Mark Standish on the investigation into the murder of Estelle Crawford.

And working on the investigation was keeping the Black Dog at bay.

"Regardless of anything personal," she'd said into the green Bakelite receiver, "whether this is a straightforward murder or a national threat, whoever's responsible *must* be stopped."

Then, "You owe me, Peter. First, you owe Sarah, for her self-less act of patriotism that nearly killed her. But you also owe me. Since Berlin, I'm a ghost of a human being. But seeing Sarah through this and clearing her name gives me a purpose. And when I'm thinking about clearing her name and finding the real killer, I'm not thinking about filling my pockets with rocks and walking into a Scottish loch. You owe Sarah this. You owe *me* this."

He'd been convinced.

Maggie looked over at Mark. "I realize you're not pleased," she said, trying not to look as delighted as she felt. "But we're professionals. I'm sure we can work together on this case well and solve it quickly."

"Not everyone thinks you're professional, you know." Mark stopped suddenly and grabbed her arm, causing her to stop, too. Overhead, seagulls shrieked. "Not everyone likes you, Maggie Hope."

If you set out to be liked, you'll achieve nothing. "I do understand that, Mr. Standish," she replied, shaking off his grip. "Winning Miss Congeniality is not, and has never been, my goal."

"*I,*" he added with emphasis, kicking at an empty packet of cigarettes that littered the pavement, "do not like you."

Maggie had never worked closely with Mark Standish; in fact, she'd rarely interacted with him. But they'd crossed paths on two

MI-5 cases and Maggie had, for a time, stepped out with his partner, Hugh Thompson, the "tall, fair, and damaged" man of Maggie's past.

"Because of Hugh?"

Red splotches dotted his pale face. "No, *not* because of Hugh, although that would be enough in itself. I never understood what he saw in you, quite frankly. No, I don't like you because you didn't pay your dues. You didn't come up through the ranks. And because of that, you're willful. You refuse to follow the rules. And you're stubborn to the point of endangering yourself and others." He walked forward, leaving her behind.

Maggie was shocked. She'd never seen herself in this light. "What?" she asked, racing to keep up.

"Take the bombing at St. Paul's—you should have come to MI-Five directly when you suspected a threat—"

Maggie had caught up with him, sidestepping being splashed by a bus. She raised one gloved finger. "First of all, when I saw the code in the newspaper advertisement, no one at the Prime Minister's office took me seriously. Do you really think I could have just marched into MI-Five?" She shook her head. "You never would have given any of my theories credence."

Mark was not deterred. "Then there's the Windsor matter. You were distracted by your personal biases—spent valuable time going after the wrong suspect, leaving the actual kidnappers time to nearly carry out their plans."

"Nearly," Maggie retorted. "That's the key word. Because the King was *not* killed and the Princess was *not* kidnapped."

"But Hugh was shot." Mark affected a girlish American voice. "'Oh, come on, Hugh, as we say in the good ol' U. S. of A.—let's *wing* it!'" His voice deepened again. "You almost had him killed, you silly git."

Maggie's breath began to come faster. *Who is he to judge me?*

He wasn't there, he wasn't at St. Paul's, he wasn't in Berlin . . . All he does is sit at a desk all day and look at photographs of suspects through a loupe . . . How easy it is to criticize the soldiers when you're not actually in the trenches! What was it Teddy Roosevelt said? "It is not the critic who counts; not the man who points out how the strong man stumbles, or where the doer of deeds could have done them better. The credit belongs to the man who is actually in the arena . . ."

Maggie chose her words carefully. "The objective was never to put Hugh in harm's way, but to rescue the Princess. If the tables had been turned, I would have understood—"

"And then you had him sacked."

This, Maggie was not expecting. "I, responsible for Hugh's being fired?" She shook her head. "No, I was out of the country at the time—and working for SOE, not MI-Five, if you recall. I had nothing to do with Hugh's mission *or* with his being sacked."

Mark stopped and cocked his head to one side, taking in her expression. "You really don't know, do you?"

Maggie was mystified. "Know *what?*"

"He didn't tell you? A gentleman to the end, poor blighter . . ."

"Tell me!"

"Later." Mark eyed her. "Now, Miss Hope—let's trot along." He turned and strode into what looked like a soot-covered Victorian prison.

Chapter Nine

"I'm Mr. Standish and I'm here to speak with the procurator fiscal," he said, flashing his MI-5 identity card.

The woman behind the desk was tiny with bright eyes, like a sparrow. "That's Mr. Findlay," she said, nodding. "Down that corridor and first office on the right." She glanced at Maggie. "You're not going, too, are you, dear?"

Mark appraised Maggie with something approaching amusement. "Yes, Miss Hope, will you be accompanying me? We're going to talk to the procurator fiscal about Estelle Crawford's death—and examine her corpse." He said it as though it were a dare.

Maggie had never been to a morgue, and the smell of decay and disinfectant was already starting to turn her stomach. But she refused to give Mark the satisfaction of sitting it out.

She squared her shoulders. "Of course I'm coming, too," she said.

In a small, windowless office, going through a stack of paperwork, Mr. Findlay was at his desk. The only relief on the white-painted cement walls was a loudly ticking clock and the framed flag of Scotland. He looked up with bleary brown eyes, not at all pleased to be disturbed. Maggie realized that while his haggard, sun-spotted face and full head of chestnut curls was average-sized, as were his hands, the rest of his body was disproportionately small. *Dwarfism*, she thought.

"I'm Mr. Standish, and this is Miss Hope. We're here for the autopsy of Estelle Crawford."

"Too late!" Findlay barked. "Can a body no get any peace aroun' here? Only the dead, it seems . . ."

"Too late?" Mark echoed. "I'm with MI-Five. There's been a murder. You were under explicit instructions to keep the body for autopsy."

Findlay used a small stool to get down from his desk chair. Standing, he was no more than four feet tall. "I know none such thing," he said, thumping papers into a file. "The autopsy's already been done. The body's been cremated. Nothin' to see here."

Mark was beginning to flush with annoyance. "What do you mean, the body's been cremated? On whose authority?"

Mr. Findlay looked up and gave an owlish blink. "Don't you know? Two men came last night. From the government."

"MI-Five?" Mark asked.

Mr. Findlay gave a disgruntled sigh. "No, no, not MI-Five— although a' you Londoners look alike to me," he grumbled, going through another file until he found the paper he was looking for. "Here," he said, thrusting it at Mark. "Ministry of Agriculture and Fisheries."

"*What?*" Mark read over the paper. "The Ministry of Agriculture and Fisheries? They have no jurisdiction here." He handed it back.

"They had the right documents," Findlay insisted.

A vein in Mark's forehead began throbbing. "This is unacceptable! The Ministry of Agriculture and Fisheries? This is a *murder*! Not a bloody fish fry!" He looked to Maggie. "Sorry."

"I've heard worse." Dizzy from the stench, Maggie had an idea. "They came and gave the orders, but has the body really been destroyed?"

"Yes, o' course," Mr. Findlay snapped. Then he looked up at the clock on the wall. "Er . . . maybe not. Bus crashed today. Lots of bodies. More than usual."

"Well," said Maggie, breathing hard with the effort not to be sick. "Shouldn't we check?"

The smell turned Maggie's stomach, but she was not about to take out her handkerchief in front of the two men. The feeling of nausea only increased, however, as they reached a large waiting area, filled with sheet-draped bodies on gurneys.

"Let's get on with it," she said, with as much bravado as she could muster. She went to the first in a line of gurneys and began pulling back the sheets to see the faces of the dead. *Surely the deceased have nothing to fear from me.*

Or I from them.

"And here she is," Maggie said, reading a toe tag and pulling back a sheet.

Estelle Crawford was lying on her back. Her stage makeup hadn't been removed, and her face looked Kabuki-like under the lights. The corpse was naked, her breasts and hips slight, and the muscularity of her legs imposing. She was white as marble, except for the open, black oozing sores on one hand and up the slender arm to her chest, where the makeup had worn away.

Oh, poor Estelle, Maggie thought. *You poor, poor girl.*

"Well, shall we begin?" Findlay said, rubbing his hands together.

"Yes, let's," Mark Standish said.

"By all means," managed Maggie, with far more enthusiasm than she felt.

Later in the day, after Frain had left, Dr. Carroll tried again to induce a trance state in Clara Hess. This time, he was surprised to hear a different voice—an older, rougher voice—coming from her lips.

It's as if yet another woman has slipped into Hess's body. This is definitely not Agna Frei, the doctor wrote in his notebook. *Could it be one of Freud's dissociation disorders, triggered by some sort of trauma?*

"What are you writing? Are you writing about me?" the voice asked.

"What do you think?"

Clara turned and looked through the cage bars and out the window. "I think I want a cigarette. But I know you don't like it when I smoke in your office."

"Whose office is this?"

"Why, yours, of course," she replied in impatient tones.

"Who am I?"

Clara sneered. "Well, if you don't know, I don't know why I should tell you."

The doctor scratched his head. He didn't know what office she thought she was in, or who she was—or who she thought he was. All he knew was that this was someone who was neither Agna Frei nor Clara Hess.

"I'm testing your memory," he told her.

She rolled her eyes. "Oh, for God's sake, Dr. Teufel, let's get on with it, shall we?"

"Is this your first time in my office?"

"Of course not."

"And where is the office?"

Clara barked a laugh. "What a stupid question."

"Answer, please."

"It's in Mitte, of course." Mitte was in central Berlin.

"What is the date?"

"Please. There's a calendar on the wall behind you." The wall behind Dr. Carroll was blank, but apparently Dr. Teufel's office had a wall calendar.

He tapped his pen on the pad of paper. "Well, then this should be a very easy question for you."

She answered scornfully, "Fifteen March, 1913."

"And why are you here in my office?"

"To get my vitamin shot, of course."

"And what is your name?"

"For God's sake—you *know* my name."

"For my research, please—what is your name?"

The woman threw back her head and laughed. "Clara," she said.

"Clara what?"

"Clara Schwartz."

Dr. Carroll looked down at his file, scanning until he found what he was looking for. Clara Schwartz was Agna Frei's stage name when she was first starting out as an opera singer. "Do you know Agna Frei?"

"Of course," she answered, sounding bored. "Really, I'd kill for a cigarette, you know."

"Who is she?"

Clara stared at Dr. Carroll. "She's a weak, pathetic little girl—that's who she is."

"And you—are you strong?"

"Of course I am. I'm a survivor. *I'm* the one who survived."

"Survived what?"

"Survived *who*," Clara corrected. "My mother, of course. And Agna was weak. I had to step in."

"And she let you?"

"I told you—she's weak. And when bad things happen, I step in."

"How do you 'step in'?"

"She gets a stomachache—terrible stomach pains."

"Do you feel bad about her pain?"

"No, why should I?"

"Do you like Agna?"

"Not particularly. But she serves a purpose."

"And what's that?"

"I get to come out sometimes." She curled a strand of hair around a finger. "I'm stuck with her, I suppose."

"What do you do when she's here?"

"It's boring," Clara Schwartz said. "Dark. I don't like it."

"Do you think it's right for you to take over her body the way you do?"

An eye roll. "She needs me. When she's weak, she needs me to step in. She wouldn't have survived without me."

"Is Agna ever strong?"

"No, that's what I keep trying to tell you—that's why I'm here. With me, there's no tears, no whining, no hiding. No backing down."

"Do you ever cry?"

"Never."

"But Agna cried when you weren't around?"

Again, Clara looked out the window. The view was of the White Tower. "She was weak. She was lonely. She was pathetic.

She wanted"—Clara Schwartz's eyes drifted to Dr. Carroll's—
"*love*." She spat out the word with contempt.

"And what do *you* want?"

Clara stared at him as if he were dim-witted. "To *survive*, of
course.

"I must *survive*."

David Greene, sheaf of papers in hand, went to find the Prime
Minister. It was just before cocktail hour at Chequers, and the
P.M. had typists taking dictation and private secretaries drafting
speeches, as he paced the floors like a mighty lion, mind bursting
with ideas, impatient and prone to the occasional roar.

Tonight, however, Winston Churchill was uncharacteristically
subdued. There were violet shadows under his eyes. He was in the
wood-paneled Hawtree Room, sitting in a leather armchair pulled
up to the fireplace, the only warm place in the big, drafty room.
Nelson, the cat, was in his lap and he was stroking him, watching
the orange-blue flames dance behind the andirons.

"Prime Minister?" David murmured, not wishing to disturb
the older man's reverie, but knowing the papers must be delivered.
"Sir?"

Churchill started, then looked up in irritation. "What? What
do you have there, Mr. Greene?"

"A number of things, sir. Would you like me to leave them with
you—?"

"*Read them!*"

David cleared his throat. "A decrypt from Bletchley regarding
Rommel and the Afrika Corps."

"I'll look at it later. What else?"

"Our navy has spotted five Japanese troop transports with
naval escort off China's coast, near Formosa, heading south."

"Interesting. Send to President Roosevelt. What news of Popov, our playboy spy? The information he had on the Japs making a grid of Pearl Harbor?"

"Popov went to Washington and met with J. Edgar Hoover, sir. But he reports back that Hoover was unimpressed and nearly had him thrown out of the country."

Churchill nodded, then motioned for David to continue. "Burns at SOE reports Operation Anthropod is proceeding. Jozef Gabčík and his new partner, Jan Kubiš, are working well together." Operation Anthropod was the code name for the planned assassination of SS-Obergruppenführer and General der Polizei Reinhard Heydrich. "They're still working on getting Kubiš's identity papers in order."

"Well, tell them to get a move on with the papers! When do they think they'll be ready to go?"

"Plans are to get them to Prague between Christmas and the New Year, sir."

"Where are they training now?"

"In Arisaig, sir. The same place Maggie Hope is working. And speaking of Miss Hope, sir," David continued, "there's also an update from Frain at MI-Five about Hess."

"Our caged bird," the P.M. said, nodding. He cocked an eyebrow. "Is she singing yet? Or is she still trying to negotiate peace?"

"I'm afraid not, sir. Hess refuses to speak with anyone but Maggie, and Maggie refuses to meet with her."

"And so the bloodthirsty Frain wants to execute Hess. Blindfold and shoot her, just like Josef Jakobs."

"Yes, sir."

"He's mentioned some rather interesting prognoses of her current mental state. Regression and whatnot."

"Yes, sir."

"It might be real—it might be an act. Frain seems to think she's playacting—as she did in her operas. The doctor doesn't." The P.M. contemplated the orange flames. "But just because she won't talk doesn't mean we can't use her." He cleared his throat. "Hitler and his cronies don't know she's not talking. And as long as she's alive, they'll wonder what secrets our little nightingale is singing. Tell Frain to keep his bloody hands off her—at least for now."

"Yes, sir." David waited a moment. "Will that be all, sir?"

The P.M. held out one hand. "Gimme." As Churchill scanned through the documents, David braced himself, knowing that there was a transcript of a particularly harsh speech about the British Prime Minister that Joseph Goebbels had given to a huge crowd in Berlin.

Churchill squinted and reached for the gold-framed spectacles in his breast pocket. He put them on and read aloud, "*. . . ever since Gallipoli, Winston Churchill has spent a life wading through streams of English blood, defending a lifestyle that has long outlived its time—*"

"That's not true, sir."

"Ah, but the monster does have a point, young Mr. Greene," Churchill replied, his face tired and eyes sad. "I grew up during Queen Victoria's reign, then came of age under King Edward the Seventh. It was a magical time to be an Englishman—'the sun never set on the British Empire,' et cetera, et cetera. Soldiers in red coats, the Union Jack. That world is gone now."

"Sir?"

"Britain will live through this war, but we will be changed, utterly unrecognizable. We are now too damaged, too small, perhaps even too gentle to compete in this brave new world. We are Tolkien's hobbits—small and provincial, yet surprisingly resilient in stern times. No, we have Hitler and Fascism, Stalin and Communism, and America—young, foolish, capitalist America—who are all poised to lead now."

David scratched his head. "If the British are the hobbits, who are the Americans, sir?"

"The Americans are the *eagles*, Mr. Greene! The American eagles, of course! It's their country's symbol, for God's sake—that Tolkien's none too subtle!"

The Prime Minister contemplated the fire. "The eagles save Bilbo and the dwarves from the bloody orcs. What did Tolkien write about the eagles? *'Eagles are not kindly birds. Some are cowardly and cruel. But the ancient race of the northern mountains were the greatest of all birds; they were proud and strong and noble-hearted.'* If that doesn't describe the bloody Americans, I don't know what does."

"But, sir—the Lend-Lease Act—all those destroyers, all the aid—"

"All of their oldest destroyers, held together with tape and taffy. They're keeping their best at Pearl Harbor, in order to defend their territories in the Pacific. And for those few, ancient ships, we are expected to give up our military bases, our gold, maybe even our art and manuscripts."

"But surely America *will* join the war?" David's voice had the edge of desperation.

"Sit down, my boy," Churchill said, gesturing to the chair opposite.

David did. "I'm not so sure anymore," the Prime Minister continued, taking a sip of cognac. "I do everything I can with President Roosevelt, and I flatter and cajole him as I would any woman I'd want as my mistress. But Roosevelt is, as we used to say in the Navy, a tease. I would like to believe America will choose to fight on the side of right in this war, but I no longer feel I can guarantee it, the way I felt a year or so ago. We can't depend on them. Unless . . ."

"Unless?"

Churchill stared into the red embers of the dying fire. "Unless their hand is forced."

"And if it isn't?"

"We've had new posters made, in case of invasion—'Keep Calm and Carry On.'"

"Miss Tuttle!"

Trudy Tuttle started when she heard Admiral Kimmel's bellow over the noise of the rusted rotary fan that did nothing against Hawaii's heat and humidity. She was young, in her twenties, in a new white cotton dress covered with a pattern of yellow hibiscus blossoms.

She rose from her desk and walked to the door of his office. It was dominated by a framed photograph of President Roosevelt. Turquoise maps of the Pacific speckled with colored pushpins covered the walls, and the window afforded a sweeping view of the Pacific Fleet, docked in Pearl Harbor. Outside, an American flag snapped in the warm, jasmine-scented breeze.

"Yes, Admiral Kimmel?" she said. Dorothy's boss, Rear Admiral Husband Edward Kimmel, was a handsome man in his midfifties, a four-star Admiral in the United States Navy and Commander in Chief of the U.S. Pacific Fleet. When he bellowed, people ran to fall in line—the Admiral was infamous for throwing books at walls, or even taking off his hat and jumping on it in frustration, a situation that happened so frequently when he'd been at sea that the mess boys kept an old sea hat handy, just in case.

But today Kimmel was with Major General Frederick L. Martin, Commander of the Hawaiian Air Force, a man about Kimmel's age. Kimmel was in Navy whites and Martin in Army browns. Both men were highly decorated.

Kimmel took off his horn-rimmed glasses, folded them, and placed them on his desk. Above his head, the blades of a ceiling fan turned lazily. "Major Martin and I are going to have an early supper in my office today, Miss Tuttle. Would you order us two burgers, french fries, and Coca-Colas from the canteen, then pick it all up? That's a good girl." His face crinkled in a smile. "Oh, and a thick slice of one of those Maui onions, if they have them."

She couldn't help but smile back. "Yes, sir."

"And two of those pineapple tarts, you know—the ones with the caramelized coconut on top? And order something for yourself too, honey, while you're at it."

"Yes, sir. Thank you, sir."

"You can have mine, Admiral. I'm not eating much these days," Martin admitted, after she left.

"Nervous stomach? You can't let it get to you!" Kimmel thumped his palms on the desk. "Don't let the damn Japs get you down!"

Kimmel rose and widened the angle of the wooden blinds. Outside, the Honolulu sky was a dazzling blue. Two orange butterflies chased each other beyond Kimmel's windows. The windows were open as far as they could go, and, if they'd wanted to, Kimmel and Martin could have reached out to touch the spiky stalks of bird-of-paradise that grew outside.

Martin shook his head. "It's not the Japs. It's the Army. General Short's insisting that we move all of our planes together in the center of Hickam Field, all bunched up together. They're sitting ducks in case of an air attack."

"Why the hell is Short doing that?"

"We have over a hundred thirty thousand Japanese on Oahu, and Short thinks those planes are far more vulnerable to sabotage on the ground than air attack from above—'It would be far too easy for the enemy to sneak in at night and blow up all the planes.' He thinks that with the new radar installations in place, there's no way any enemy aircraft could sneak in undetected."

"It's a good thing you finally put in that radar station."

"No thanks to the National Park Service, which didn't even want to give us permission—damn wildlife preservationists! Now we just have to get those men out there some telephones."

Kimmel sat and tipped back in his chair. "What are those boys supposed to do without telephones? Walk a mile to the nearest store and use a pay phone?"

Martin gave a nervous smile. "We're doing the best we can, with what little we have."

Miss Tuttle rapped on the door and then entered, carrying a white paper bag full of food, grease stains beginning to form on the bottom. The bottles of Coca-Cola clinked against each other. "Thanks, honey," Kimmel said. She nodded to the two men and left.

Kimmel dug into the bag and handed a burger wrapped in paper to Martin.

Martin accepted it, unwrapping the paper on Kimmel's desk.

"That's one good thing about this move to Hawaii—fantastic golf. Tennis, too."

Kimmel swallowed a french fry and took a swig of Coke. "I still think the fleet should have stayed in San Diego—but don't mention it to Roosevelt, he won't listen to any of us. Doesn't even seem to see the need for a Pacific Fleet these days—wants to send more and more of our ships to the Atlantic, to help the damn British. And then what are we supposed to do? I even brought up the British success toppling the Italian fleet at Taranto—they just used some old biplanes and sank nearly all of the Italian battleships. And the harbor at Taranto's similar to Pearl's."

Martin pushed his food away. "Pearl's too shallow."

"That's just what Roosevelt said. Here"—Kimmel said, reaching into the bag and pulling out a spear wrapped in waxed paper and handing it over to Martin—"at least have a pickle." He dunked a french fry into a small paper cup of ketchup and shoveled it into his mouth. "And I'll have Miss Tuttle call the club to set up a golf match for us this afternoon."

Chapter Ten

Later, when Estelle Crawford's autopsy was over, Maggie and Mark put aside their mutual distrust and went out for a much-needed drink. Mark chose the place, a tiny bar with dark wood paneling and chandeliers with fringed lamp shades. They secured a table by the crackling fireplace.

At the next table over, businessmen in double-breasted suits talked in low tones with a definite Scottish burr about where to hide their money—trust funds for their children and grandchildren—watched over by the glassy eyes of mounted red and roe deer with enormous antlers.

"You could have done worse, Miss Hope," Mark said as he sat down across from Maggie, having secured their pink gins.

Maggie had no illusions about her professionalism. "Mr. Standish, I threw up three times."

"At least you had the good sense to vomit over the drain."

"I do my best."

"I have a confession," Mark said.

"Yes?"

"At my first autopsy I didn't even make it to the sink."

"Ah." Maggie smiled crookedly. "Thank you for telling me that." She raised her glass. "To Estelle Crawford."

"To Estelle," Mark echoed as their glasses clinked.

They drank in silence. Maggie was grateful for the fire's heat after the long, chill hours in the autopsy room. A chocolate-brown Labrador snoozed in front of the flames while his owner, an older man with a pipe, read the newspaper. A large white-faced grandfather clock ticked in the shadows.

One of the men at the bar stood, leaning heavily on crutches. "Excuse me," he said, making his way to the loo. Maggie could see that not only was he in uniform, he was missing a leg and hadn't yet been fitted for a prosthesis. Realizing all eyes were on him, the man grinned and good-naturedly called out, "Graceful—like a gazelle, I am. Like a ruddy mountain goat!" That caused a few chuckles and raised glasses in the soldier's direction.

"I brought the pathology report." Mark took some papers out of his pocket and handed them over to Maggie.

She scanned the documents. They confirmed what they had witnessed. "Heart failure due to chronic emphysema, along with nonrelated psoriasis, which surely clears both Sarah and Mildred Petrie of murder charges. So where does that leave us?"

"It still doesn't explain why the Ministry of Agriculture and Fisheries ordered the body to be cremated immediately, without an autopsy," Mark mused, chewing on the end of a pen. "How did they know? What could be their agenda?"

"You've been at MI-Five for—how long now?"

"Almost eight years."

"So you're well aware of how much red tape most British offices produce. Might be one of those situations where departments overlap?"

"Maybe . . ." He shook his head. "Sorry I was rough on you earlier."

Maggie was determined to take it like a man; she knew too well that hazing was part of the job. Only the toughest survived. "It's all right."

"No, it's not. I let it get personal. But you must understand that Hugh's one of my best friends, and—"

"I understand. And I'm sorry it ended the way it did, too. But I was . . . confused, and it didn't seem fair to Hugh to string him along while I tried to figure things out. I thought, given everything that happened, a clean break was best. Fairer to him."

Mark gave a grim smile. "And now you're reunited with your RAF pilot?"

"No," Maggie said, her face stone. "It didn't work out."

They sipped in silence.

"Rotten luck," Mark said finally. "Does Hugh know?"

"No. After my last mission . . . Well, let's just say I'm not exactly in a position to be stepping out with anyone, let alone someone as wonderful as Hugh. Quite frankly, he's better off without me."

Maggie changed the subject. "You're married, yes?" She knew the answer, having seen photographs of Mark's wife and child on his desk when she worked with Hugh at MI-5.

He smiled. "Sixth anniversary next month and second baby on the way."

"Congratulations!" *A baby. How brave, in the midst of all this chaos and destruction.* "If you don't mind my asking," she ventured, sensing a change in his mood. "What *did* happen with Hugh on his last job? Why was he fired?"

"You truly don't know, do you?"

Maggie shook her head.

"I can't give you specific details, of course—"

"Of course."

Mark lowered his voice. "Instead of sending visual confirmation that a certain mission succeeded, as he'd been ordered, he sent a photograph. A different sort of photograph." He took a swallow of gin. "Of his—" Mark had the grace to redden. "—er, naked buttocks."

"No!" *Oh, Hugh . . .*

"And I'm sure you can imagine who these photographs were addressed to?"

No. No. Surely Hugh couldn't have. "My . . . mother?"

Mark tapped his nose. "Exactly."

Oh, Hugh, Hugh . . . Maggie's eyes narrowed as she thought. "And so her boss found out their spy had been turned . . ."

". . . and that's most likely the reason she gave herself up to the British and offered to work as a double—or maybe a triple?—agent."

Her head was spinning, putting it all together. "And poor Hugh was fired for it."

"He was." Again they drank in silence. A log broke in two, and the dog twitched in his sleep.

"Mr. Standish, I have just one question."

Mark had finished his gin and gestured expansively. "Anything, Miss Hope."

"When Hugh pulled down his pants, who was taking the pictures?"

He looked like a guilty little boy.

"I thought so. More tea, Vicar?"

Mark grinned. "If you insist. My glass is a bit lonely."

Maggie caught the bartender's eye. "Another round, please, when you have a moment? And this one's on me."

"I *told* you I didn't do it," Sarah croaked from the bed, as Maggie opened the door. Then she coughed, a long, hacking jag.

"I know," Maggie said, taking off her coat, hat, and gloves and kicking off her pumps, noting the new holes in her stockings. "I never thought so for a moment." She walked to the bed. "Don't take this the wrong way, but you look terrible."

"I *feel* terrible. It's this horrible northern cold and damp."

Maggie touched her hand to Sarah's forehead; her friend was burning up. "You have a fever," she said. *Good God.* "Would you like me to call a doctor?"

"No, no—just my overnight in the chokey taking its toll. I'll be right as rain in the morning. I just need to get some rest. But first— tell me about Estelle."

Maggie thought back to the autopsy. There were details she could spare her friend. She padded in stocking feet over to an over-stuffed armchair, where she slumped, legs akimbo—decorum be damned. "The autopsy revealed nothing worse than emphysema and a case of psoriasis. Her body just gave out. But she's at rest now—and her family is coming here to pick up the body for the funeral and burial."

"Thank you," the dancer said, after a moment. "You always believed I was innocent."

"Of course," Maggie said. "And I really didn't do anything. The evidence acquitted you."

"Still. I suppose since this is over now, the Vic-Wells will finish our Edinburgh run."

"Where are you and the company off to next?"

"Glasgow, I think." Sarah gave a thin smile. "It's hard to tell the cities apart after a while—all you see are hotel rooms, studios, and stages."

"I'm sure." The bleat of the telephone in the hall made them both startle. Maggie rose and walked to the corridor, then picked up the receiver. "Hello? This is Maggie Hope speaking."

"Miss Hope, it's Mark Standish," she heard over the crackling line. "I'm afraid I have some bad news."

Maggie braced herself for what might come next. "I'm listening."

"Well, no beating around the bush—I'm calling from Chalmers Hospital. Officer Craig at the police station was kind enough to let me know that after Mildred Petrie was cleared of any sort of murder charge, she was taken directly to hospital."

Maggie's hands tightened on the telephone receiver. "Why? What's wrong with her?"

Sarah looked over. Maggie put up one finger, to say *wait*.

"I haven't spoken with any of her doctors yet, but Officer Craig says she was coughing horribly and running a high fever." Mark cleared his throat. "What's odd is that, like Estelle, Mildred also had black sores running from her right hand up to her shoulder."

Maggie looked to Sarah in the next bed, pale and haggard. "Sarah's under the weather, too, and has a nasty cough. Maybe it's flu?"

Sarah sank back against her pillow and closed her eyes.

"Given we have one dead dancer and another in critical condition, I don't want to leave anything to chance. Let's get Miss Sanderson to hospital immediately," Mark told Maggie. "Bring her to Chalmers—I'll meet you both there."

Maggie called for an ambulance and they managed to transport Sarah from the Caledonian to Chalmers Hospital, which had been requisitioned for civilian casualties. The trip to Lothian Road took only minutes, but to Maggie it felt an eternity before they reached the hospital's emergency entrance on Lauriston Place, with Sarah slipping in and out of consciousness. Maggie squeezed her hand, desperate to transfer whatever health she herself had to Sarah.

As the medics took Sarah from the ambulance and transferred her to a waiting gurney, Maggie spied Mark in the lengthening shadows. "Mildred Petrie is here," he reported, walking up to her, "in quarantine. Miss Sanderson will be quarantined, as well."

"Quarantine? Under whose orders?" Maggie asked.

"Cyrus Howard, head of the Ministry of Agriculture and Fisheries."

"Howard again? What does he think—that three ballerinas went fly fishing and picked up some sort of strange disease along with their trout? These are professional dancers—they don't have time to cavort in the great outdoors."

"You can come with me and ask him yourself—he's getting a cup of tea down in the cafeteria."

"Let's get Sarah settled first," Maggie decided, keeping pace with Mark and the gurney. Sarah's eyes were jerking back and forth beneath the lids and she was muttering in a fever dream. "Then we can question Mr. Howard."

To Sarah she said, "You're safe here—you're in the hospital. The doctors and nurses will take good care of you." She had a momentary pang thinking of another nurse she knew—her half-sister, Elise, who'd been a nurse at Charité Hospital in Berlin.

At the sound of Maggie's voice, Sarah's eyes fluttered open. Her breathing was ragged.

"You'll be in a bed soon. And I'll be right here beside you, I promise."

"Wha—what's wrong with me?" Sarah managed to gasp.

"Probably just flu, darling." Maggie forced a reassuring smile. She brushed damp tendrils of dark hair from Sarah's face. Her forehead was burning, perhaps even hotter than before. "Pneumonia at worst. You ballerinas—always so dramatic." She reached again for Sarah's hand, but then stopped. The dancer's graceful hand was covered in angry black blisters.

Maggie's and Mark's eyes met. They didn't know what Sarah had, but they both knew it wasn't flu.

Sarah's doctor was one of the many Polish doctors, most of them from Warsaw, at the University of Edinburgh's Polish School of Medicine. It was a unique institution that provided medical education and training to medical students and doctors exiled after the Nazi invasion and occupation.

Dr. Janus was a slight man, with a large pink bald spot. What hair remained was thick and silver, and wrapped around his head like a ladies' fur stole.

After his examination of Sarah, he went to the waiting room to speak with Maggie and Mark.

"How is she?" Maggie asked.

"Not well, I'm afraid." Dr. Janus spoke in heavily accented English. "She is extremely ill. We have another dancer here, from the same company, who is extremely sick as well."

"What is it? What do they have?" Maggie pressed.

The doctor rubbed his nose. "We will have to run tests . . ."

"There was a third dancer with the company, a woman named Estelle Crawford. She had the same symptoms." Mark reached into the breast pocket of his jacket and pulled out the pathology report. "You may find this helpful."

Dr. Janus accepted it, looking it over. "And this woman, this Miss Crawford—?"

"She's dead," Maggie told him. "Please, Doctor—please save Sarah!"

"We will do everything we can," the doctor said softly.

"We're with MI-Five." Mark showed his identification papers. "We're concerned there may be foul play involved with all three dancers. May we look in on Mildred Petrie?"

"That's not possible," the doctor told them. "Mr. Cyrus Howard of the Ministry of Agriculture and Fisheries has ordered that no one goes in or out without his express permission."

"But—" Mark began.

"Well then," Maggie said, pulling at Mark's sleeve, "we'll just have to have a little word with Mr. Howard."

Mark raised his wrist to look at his watch. "It's after midnight, Miss Hope."

"Well, Mr. Standish, this is where I suggest we 'wing it.' "

Down in the hospital's all but deserted cafeteria, the air was thick with the steamy smell of cabbage and potatoes. "Look, I'll bet you that's Cyrus Howard." Maggie pointed to an older man in tweed, sitting at one of the tables and reading Edinburgh's *Evening Dispatch*. The headline blared, U.S. DESTROYER SUNK—HUNT FOR NAZI U-BOATS CONTINUES.

"Why do you think so?" asked Mark.

"Because he's the only man not wearing a long white doctors' coat, Sherlock," Maggie whispered as they approached the older man, "but he also looks a bit like a trout." It was unfortunate, but his lips were thick and definitely trout-like. He was also astoundingly blond and pale. Maggie had the sudden absurd thought that if he were naked, one could see his entire circulatory system.

She addressed the man. "Mr. Howard?"

"How do you know who I am?" he said, peering up at them through a gold-rimmed monocle, which magnified one red eye and the surrounding wrinkles.

"This is Agent Standish from MI-Five and I am Margaret Hope, his . . . associate. We're here investigating the death of Estelle Crawford and the quarantine of Mildred Petrie and Sarah Sanderson."

Mr. Howard threw down his paper. "This is all top secret, by orders of the Prime Minister's office. I must ask you to leave. I have nothing to say to you two." He rose and clapped a tweed hat atop his thin gray locks. "Good evening," he said, turning on his heel.

They watched him leave, stunned.

Then, "Come on," urged Maggie. "Let's go back to Mildred's room."

"We're not allowed. I'll have to call Frain and he'll have to get on it. There's a lot of red tape involved—I don't expect you to understand—"

"I'll tell Dr. Janus that I had a word with Mr. Howard."

"Yes—and Mr. Howard just told us to go away."

"I'll say I had a word—I'm not going to say *which* word."

"Maggie—"

"Mark, if you don't want to be involved, I understand. But this is one of my closest friends, and she may be dying. If I can help, find out anything . . . Well, let's just say I'm not going to let anything like red tape get in my way." She walked away, heels clicking resolutely on the linoleum floor.

Mark looked to the ceiling as if to say a silent prayer, then followed her. "I can now see why Hugh managed to get into so much trouble with you. You're stubborn, you don't follow the rules—"

"Yes, and if we waited for every *i* to be dotted and *t* to be crossed, where would that leave Sarah and Mildred? Oh, that's right—*dead*."

"They may die anyway."

"But we need to try. I'd never forgive myself if we didn't."

Despite her growing concern for Sarah and the grim nature of the situation, Maggie realized that for the first time in a very long time, she was free of the Black Dog. He'd whimpered and turned away, settling down with his paws tucked underneath him—at least for the time being.

Mildred Petrie was tossing in her narrow white bed, moaning.

While Mark hung back, Maggie approached the bed. "Miss Petrie? Mildred?"

The dancer's eyes were closed, but her head flailed on the pillow. "I did it! It was I!" she muttered. She coughed, a long and racking cough, then gasped for air.

"Mildred?" Maggie repeated. "I'd just like to ask you a few questions—"

"We were right to do it! Estelle had to pay! But I didn't know . . . It wasn't my fault I touched them, too . . ."

"Who is 'we'?" Maggie pressed. "What did you touch, Mildred?"

Mildred opened her eyes and opened her mouth to respond. But when she tried to speak, she began to cough again, a cough that swiftly turned into a choke. She struggled for breath, her hands clawing her neck.

Mildred Petrie was dying.

Maggie whirled to Mark. "Get the doctor! Go!"

As the medical staff descended on Mildred Petrie's room, Maggie and Mark waited in the hall outside. Maggie was knitting furiously, muttering profanities under her breath. Mark stopped pacing and looked over.

"Socks," she said by way of explanation.

He looked blank.

"You know, 'Our Boys Need Socks—Knit For Your Brit.' Or however the propaganda offices are phrasing it these days. Look—" Maggie said, showing him the knitting, "I've even put in tiny *V*'s in Morse code—*V* for Victory. This is very patriotic work I'm doing. Very important, very patriotic work."

Mark nodded, distracted. "Right, right."

Dr. Janus finally emerged from the room. Both Maggie and Mark froze. "I'm sorry to have to tell you this." He shook his head. "We did everything we could."

If Estelle is dead and Mildred is dead, then what about Sarah?

"Dead?" Maggie managed. "What's the cause?"

"I understand that Miss Petrie is—was—a ballet dancer." The doctor took off his glasses and wiped them with his handkerchief. He looked bone-weary. "But the blisters on her skin look to me like Woolsorters' or Ragpickers' disease. And that would account for symptoms mirroring pneumonia or emphysema."

"Woolsorters' disease? What's that?" Mark asked. "Because Estelle Crawford had the black sores, too, as does Sarah Sanderson."

The doctor looked down at the chart. "Woolsorters' disease is caused by the spore-forming bacteria *Bacillus anthracis*. Or, as it's more commonly known, anthrax." He cleared his throat and looked up. "Humans generally contract anthrax through an injury to the skin or mucous membranes. But it's often found in agricultural or industrial workers who work with infected animals or animal products—such as wool, or buttons made from horn, for example."

Maggie's and Mark's eyes met. Now they knew what the Minister of Agriculture and Fisheries was doing there in the hospital—and why he'd wanted to dispose of Estelle's body before an autopsy could be performed. If a fatal disease was spreading, the authorities would want to quarantine those with it, and not cause panic. Keep the information from the public.

Still, something puzzled Maggie. "But Estelle Crawford, Mildred Petrie, and Sarah Sanderson were—are—ballet dancers, not wool sorters. How on earth would they have come in contact with anthrax?"

"Have they traveled to any farms recently?" Dr. Janus asked. "Within the past week or so?"

"I don't think so," Maggie said, "but we'll check, of course. How does one contract the disease, specifically?"

"Infection occurs through the skin. Or by inhalation or ingestion of bacterial spores."

"Does it mean anything that all three women have the blisters on their *right* hands?"

"They may have touched something with their hand that was covered in the bacteria."

"Is there any cure?" Maggie asked. Sarah was so desperately ill. Surely . . .

"Rest," answered the doctor grimly. "And a lot depends on the baseline health of the patient."

"You've examined Sarah Sanderson, yes?"

"I have."

"And what's your prognosis?"

"We'll do everything we can for her. But I'm afraid I must say that at this point—it's touch and go. Does she have any family?"

"Her mother lives in Liverpool."

"Well," the doctor said, "it's time to let her know. She might want to come and say her good-byes."

Good-byes? Maggie's heart stuttered. *Oh, no. Not yet . . .* "May I see her?" she managed.

Dr. Janus nodded. "But not for too long. She needs her rest."

———

"Mildred said, 'I did it,'" Mark said, pulling Maggie aside. "But then she said she 'didn't know'—and that she 'touched them, too.'"

"She was delirious," Maggie replied, thinking of Sarah. "I wouldn't take her words literally."

"It's a *confession*. That she played a part in the death of Estelle Crawford. Sarah was collateral damage. And she, herself, somehow touched something she wasn't supposed to—and was poisoned, too. Mildred Petrie killed Estelle Crawford. Somehow, she and Sarah were accidentally poisoned?"

Maggie shook her head. "It's not a confession. How could she have committed murder if she 'didn't know'?"

"The doctor said that infection occurs through the skin or by inhalation or ingestion of the bacterial spores. What if she touched something that was poisoned?"

"You mean, did she prick her finger on a spindle? I believe that's an entirely different ballet, Mr. Standish."

Mark ground his teeth in frustration.

"In the Windsor case I was too quick to let personal prejudices cloud my judgment, and too quick to jump to conclusions," Maggie reminded him. "You said so yourself."

"But—"

Maggie took his arm. "Come on. Let's see Sarah."

In Sarah's room, raindrops spattered against the high windows, and there was an overwhelming scent of rubbing alcohol. Sarah's eyes were closed. But when she heard the door open, they fluttered open. "Maggie . . ."

Maggie went immediately to her friend's side. "Shhhh . . . No need to talk, sweetheart. Just rest."

Sarah gave a choked laugh. "I don't think I'll be dancing *La Sylphide* anytime soon . . ."

Maggie looked at her friend's hand clutching the gray blanket. "Sarah, do you remember touching anything with your right hand? Raw wool for your toe shoes, perhaps? Horn buttons?" The black sores seemed to be worse on her right ring finger.

Sarah didn't reply.

"Did Mildred have any grudge against Estelle?" Mark asked. "Did she do anything to endanger her? Would she have any reason to . . . kill her?"

Sarah gave a low cough, then closed her eyes. ". . . No . . ."

She was in no shape for questioning. Maggie stroked her friend's pale cheek. "The doctors will take good care of you. And I'll do everything I can to figure this out—I promise."

Sarah didn't reply.

Chapter Eleven

After a restless night at the Caledonian, Maggie woke. It was just after seven.

The Black Dog bared his teeth and warned her against trying to go back to sleep, so she washed and dressed. When it was time for visiting hours at Chalmers, Maggie met Mark in Sarah's room.

Sarah was asleep. She was pale, and the bones of her face looked more pronounced. *Almost more like a skull than a . . .* Then, *Stop it! Just stop!*

Maggie didn't want Mark to see her cry, so she turned and walked quickly to the window. Outside, the sky once again threatened snow. It was gray and heavy, just as the Victorian soot-stained buildings were gray and heavy. She swiped at her eyes with her gloved hands. *Very Victorian train station,* David had once said about the Langham Hotel, mocking its pretensions. *Victorian . . .*

"Victorian," Maggie said suddenly. She turned to face Mark. *"Victorian!"*

"Er, yes?"

"Everything here's *Victorian.*"

"Well, many buildings are, although you can also see other architectural influences, depending on if you're in New Town or Old Town—"

"No, no," Maggie interrupted impatiently. "Not just the architecture. Tussy-mussies. Ballerina bouquets. Floriography. The language of flowers." She began to pace.

"Sorry, not following."

"There was a huge bouquet for Estelle in the dressing room, arranged in the Victorian tussy-mussy style—"

Mark scratched his head. "So?"

"Mark, we need to go to the library!"

"The library?"

"We need to find out the meaning of the flowers. When we do, we'll have an idea of the message the murderer was trying to send—and, maybe, who it was. Come on," Maggie said, pulling Mark by the arm, "hurry!"

The Edinburgh Central Library was an imposing building on George IV Bridge, between Old Town and the University quarter. They raced up the wide central staircase to the Reference Library, on the top floor. It was an enormous room, with Roman arches, high windows, and banks of wooden card indices.

Maggie wandered the high stacks until she found what she was looking for, pulling several books off the shelf. Henry Phillips's *Floral Emblems*, Frederic Shoberl's *The Language of Flowers; With Illustrative Poetry*, and *The Language of Flowers* by Kate Greenaway. She brought them to a table and started reading.

"Ah-ha!" exclaimed Maggie, paging through the Greenaway volume.

"Ah-ha?" said Mark, who was checking his watch. "Look, Miss Hope, I've been patient, but—"

Maggie put the book down. "Floriography is a sort of cryptological communication—code—using flowers. It's been used for thousands of years, all over the world, in works like the Bible and Shakespeare's plays.

"Floriography was popular in Victorian times. Bouquets called tussy-mussies were sent as a coded messages, allowing the sender to express feelings that couldn't be spoken aloud. You could say almost anything with flowers, in the right combination. There was a tussy-mussy in the dressing room at the ballet. Estelle, Mildred, and Sarah all touched it. I remember thinking the flowers were odd, especially for wartime Edinburgh."

"But odd doesn't mean murder . . ."

"In Oscar Wilde's *Picture of Dorian Gray,* Wilde used specific flowers to define character. Basil Hallward is associated with the rose—the symbol of love—while Lord Henry Wotton is paired with yellow laburnum, a poisonous plant symbolizing evil. Estelle's bouquet was made up of white roses, yellow laburnum, purple carnations."

Maggie flipped through the Greenaway until she found what she was looking for. "White roses signify death, while yellow laburnum symbolizes poison." She flipped through more pages. "Purple carnations mean infidelity."

"So the bouquet is really a coded message, saying—"

"I'm going to kill you with poison because you were unfaithful."

"And Estelle was unfaithful with whom?"

"It wasn't *Estelle's* infidelity—she was unmarried. But her lover was married. And what if Mildred found out about the affair? But how would she have had access to anthrax?"

"Wait one moment—first we need to find the bouquet, to see if there's actually anthrax on it."

"Then we need to find out if Mildred sent it," Maggie finished.

Frain had left messages for Edmund Hope at both Bletchley Park and MI-5, to no avail. But he did know one place he might find the man: his club in London.

Edmund was sitting, naked, in a dimly lit fog of eucalyptus-scented steam. The room was Romanesque, high-ceilinged, an oasis of marble and heat. A low fountain with a statue of Diana and Actaeon burbled in the room's center, splashing into a pool. The walls were lined with benches. The lights were low, with a single high-mullioned window boarded over in compliance with blackout regulations. Edmund sat and read *The Times* in one corner, lit by a bare lightbulb. The headline blared: RAF SINKS TANKER *IRIDIO MANTOVANI* 60 MILES OFF COAST OF LIBYA AND BRITISH CRUISERS HMS *AURORA* & HMS *PENELOPE* SINK STEAMER *ADRIATICO*.

He had a tumbler of scotch next to him.

"Thought I might find you here." Frain sat next to Edmund.

There was a protracted silence between the two men as the water continued to trickle in the fountain. Frain jutted out his chin, indicating the statue. "Odd choice for a bastion of male privilege, don't you think?"

Edmund folded his newspaper and set it down. He was sweating heavily. "I think it's rather perfect," he replied, finally. "In Shakespeare's *Twelfth Night,* Orsino compares his unrequited love for Olivia to the fate of Actaeon. *'Oh, when mine eyes did see Olivia first, Methought she purged the air of pestilence. That instant was I turned into a hart, And my desires, like fell and cruel hounds, E'er since pursue me.'"*

"Very pretty. Your former wife's still in custody, you know."

"I know. I went to see Clara. Warned her off Maggie. Clara's done enough damage for more than two lifetimes."

Frain stared into the clouds of steam. "The doctor at the Tower thinks that Clara's reverting. Into past personalities. She certainly has him wrapped around her little finger."

Edmund grimaced and took a gulp of scotch. "She certainly had us all wrapped and tied with pretty bows, didn't she? *All* of us."

"I think you should see her again," Frain said. "It might be your last chance. Her execution date has been set—December seventh."

At this, Edmund finally looked up. His blue eyes were rimmed with red and puffy, his face bloated from too much drink. "Why?"

"To settle things between you. To make your peace. To say good-bye."

"And you're really going to shoot her."

"Yes."

"Even though she's a woman."

"Afraid so, old thing. She's dangerous and not making herself very useful."

"The press would have a field day if they found out."

"They're not going to find out."

"No," Edmund said, rising and displaying a midsection bloated and turned to fat. "I'm done with her. I'm done with everyone, quite frankly."

Frain took in the ruin of the other man's body. "Don't be a coward, Edmund. And don't drink so much. You'll drink yourself to death, if you're not careful."

"Don't tell me what to do, Peter." Edmund picked up his newspaper and tucked it under his arm, then reached for his glass. He downed the whiskey in a single gulp. "Don't you think you've done enough harm?"

"So, how does this work?" Maggie asked. "How do we find the bouquet?" They were walking from the library down St. Patrick and Nicolson Street to St. Leonard's Police Station. The rain had turned into a light mist.

"Well, when the police take over a crime scene—in this case, the theater—they bag and tag everything. After everything's secured, the detective in charge would package the evidence and dust for fingerprints."

"Package, how?"

"They quite literally wrap it in brown paper and put a property and evidence tag on it."

"Including flowers?"

"We can hope."

"Tell me about Dr. Teufel," Dr. Carroll asked Clara. She was in the cage in his office, but no longer bound to the bed.

"*You're* Dr. Teufel." Clara was sitting up on the bed, gazing out the window.

"Well, I need to know what you think of me. For scientific purposes."

"What do you want to know?"

"Does Agna know . . . me?"

"Of course," she snapped. "She thinks you're her doctor. She thinks you're helping her with her stomachaches."

"And I'm not helping her?"

"Everyone wants something." Clara Schwartz leaned back and lit a cigarette. Dr. Carroll had given her cigarettes, to encourage her to talk, and she relished the one she had lit, sucking in the smoke, savoring it before blowing it out contemptuously. "He was helping to release me."

"And how did Dr. Teufel release you?"

"He told Agna they were vitamin shots. And she believed him." Clara Schwartz took another puff. "What a ninny." She laughed, a mean, tight laugh.

"What were the vitamin shots?"

"They weren't even shots. The medicine was given through an IV drip. What fool thinks vitamins are given through an IV drip?"

Dr. Carroll made a note. "What was in the drip?"

"Something else," Clara said. "Something bad."

"Do you know what it was specifically?"

She smiled, her eyes lit from within. "Hate."

"Who do you hate?"

"You know."

"Tell me."

"The Jews, of course. The kikes."

"Who else?"

"The niggers."

"Who else?"

"The Italians, the southern ones. The northern Italians are all right. The French—well, they can go either way. Gallic blood is unpredictable."

"Who else?"

"The Russians. The Commie Jews."

"And what does Dr. Teufel—what do I—want you to do to them?"

"Not do—avoid. Keep racial purity at all costs." Clara flicked ashes on the floor. "I want to go out. I'm tired of being in here. I want to look up at the sky."

"You can see the sky from the window."

"I want to feel the moonlight on my skin. Don't you ever want to feel the moonlight on your skin?"

"But Agna doesn't get out of here, either, does she?"

"I'm bored!" Clara spat. Then, "You know her mother is sick, don't you?"

The doctor leaned back in his chair. "No, I didn't."

"The dirty disease. The nasty disease. Syphilis." Clara's smile was cat-like. "She's a whore, you know."

"Does Agna know her mother is sick?"

"The whore's not sick, she's *dying*. No, Agna's not strong enough to know."

"Was her mother ever kind to her? Before she became sick?"

A grimace twisted Clara's face. "No. She never had time for Agna. And when she was around, she was constantly criticizing her. The girl couldn't do anything right, ever. Her mother broke her, broke her spirit, broke her heart. She broke Agna and the father pretended not to see. All he did was hide behind his books. He pretended not to know."

"And where were you?"

"I was watching. I was watching as her mother broke her."

"And why didn't you come out?"

"Because . . ." Clara Schwartz smiled, revealing pearly teeth. "Because if I'd been let out to play, I would have slit her mother's throat—and her weak, impotent father's as well."

Wearing gloves, Maggie and Mark found the boxes that had been in Estelle and Sarah's dressing room, crammed with tubes of lipstick, pans of pancake foundation and sponges, and cakes of mascara with black comb brushes. There was a vase, but no flowers.

"No!" Maggie said, refusing to accept the facts staring her in the face when they went upstairs to confront Officer Craig. "No—maybe they were put somewhere else. Maybe somewhere to dry?"

"I'm afraid if it's not here, then we don't have it, Miss," Officer Craig said, rubbing the back of his neck. "I'm sorry, but if there were fresh flowers, and it's been how long?" He whistled through his teeth. "They were probably moldy—stinking up the place."

"So, then what would happen?" Maggie persisted.

"What d'you mean, Miss?"

"Say the flowers were at the theater. If they'd been brought here, cataloged as evidence—but then thrown out. Where would they have been thrown?"

"Well . . ." More neck scratching. "The compost bin, Miss. We've a wee Victory garden out back—back o' the building, next t' the garden."

Maggie started running. Mark followed at her heels.

"But someone may have given it a turn—you might need to dig through the muck, Miss!"

"So when he said 'given it a turn,' he meant . . ." Maggie's nose crinkled.

They looked over the police department's small Victory garden. Sure enough, there was a wooden composting bin off to one side. Made of wooden slats with space between to allow the air to circulate, it gave off a distinctly unpleasant odor.

"Mixed it all up, with a shovel. Meaning if the bouquet's in there, it won't be anywhere near the top. We're going to have to dig for it."

Maggie stepped closer. "Fantastic. Simply marvelous."

"There might be worms in there, as well—to help with the composting."

"This just keeps getting better and better now, doesn't it?"

Mark shrugged. "Not so bad. I grew up on a farm."

"Well, thank you, Farmer Standish. Even if the bouquet's been 'turned,' it's probably still here, yes?" As Mark lifted off the lid, Maggie grabbed a rusty shovel leaning against a stone wall. She began to dig in the compost, taking shovelfuls of muck from the heap and flinging them behind her.

"Oi, mind where you're throwing that, if you please, Miss

Hope!" he cried, ducking and moving out of the way. "I can do that, if you'd rather—"

"No, I'm fine," Maggie responded, taking a moment to scratch her nose and leaving a streak of mud on her cheek as she did so. "Of course someone turned it," she muttered, as she continued to dig. "Of *course* . . ."

Her growing pile was mostly decomposing garden scraps, with the occasional wriggling fat worm. Finally, her shovel exposed the bouquets.

There were all sorts of ballet bouquets: lilies, narcissus, forced hyacinth blooms—now wilted and starting to rot. But not the bouquet Maggie remembered from the dressing room. Not the bouquet that was possibly the murder weapon.

"Here, give me a hand, please," Maggie told Mark, realizing she couldn't get enough leverage with the shovel from outside the composting bin.

Mark was gobsmacked. "You're—you're going in?"

"Well, do you see another way of digging through to the bottom?"

"Er, no."

"Hmmm . . ." Even though she was hobbled by her skirt, Maggie clambered into the bin and resolutely continued to dig. Her nose twitched. *I wish I had my SOE boots and jumpsuit . . .*

"Quite the aroma you've unearthed," Mark remarked, watching. " 'Unearthed'—you do see the joke, yes?"

Maggie stood upright, resting one hand on the shovel, the other on her waist. Her face was filthy. "Perhaps *you'd* like a turn, Farmer Standish?"

Mark looked down at his cashmere overcoat. "Er, as long as you're already in there . . ."

Maggie rolled her eyes. "That's what I thought."

"Here," he said, taking off his leather gloves. "Mine are thicker. More protection if we do find these poisoned posies."

Maggie quickly stripped off her own thin gloves, pocketed them, and put on the fur-lined ones. She continued to dig, then looked up. "Nothing," she reported.

"Nothing?"

She shook her head. Her voice was desolate. "Not a blasted thing."

"Well, we can at least track down the florist who made it. Maybe there's more information there."

There were four florists in Edinburgh.

They went to three of them, finding nothing, finally ending up on Queen Street. The rays from the setting sun turned the castle rose-gold, as children played in St. James's Park, the church's bell tower swathed in scaffolding. Twin girls in matching blue coats were playing jump rope, while a little boy in overalls and a Fair Isle sweater clung to his grandmother's hand and pointed up. *"Castle! Castle!"* he lisped, pointing a chubby finger.

The older woman bent down to adjust his hat. "I know! It's a great, big castle, innit, darlin'?"

"Of course it's the last one," Mark grumbled as they turned onto Northumberland Street to find Mary Mason's Florist. "It's *always* the last one."

"Actually, that's not statistically probable," Maggie replied. "You just find the times when it's the last one after a long search to be more memorable."

"I don't know what Hugh saw in you," Mark grumbled, "I really don't . . ."

"Tut, tut," she admonished. "We're here. Be professional."

When they pushed open the door, a tiny silver bell jingled. "I'll be right with you!" a woman's voice rang out from the back room. Inside, it was warm and humid, and smelled of cut stems and narcissus blooms. There weren't many flowers for sale, but there were several large and formal bouquets on the counter, ready to be wrapped in brown paper—velvety red amaryllis blossoms and heather, punctuated with thistles.

A tall woman with broad shoulders and a gray bun walked in from the back room. "Good afternoon," she said and smiled, wiping her hands on her apron as she did so. "May I help you?"

"I'm Mark Standish from MI-Five and this is my associate, Miss Hope." He showed his papers. "We're investigating a series of murders, and would appreciate your help."

The woman's face paled. "Of—of course."

"Do you remember making a bouquet of white roses, yellow laburnum, and purple carnations?" Maggie asked. "It would have been sometime during the last week of November," she added.

"O' course," the woman responded. "Such a strange bouquet. And in wartime, too! But she was insistent, she was. Some o' the flowers I had to bring in from Glasgow."

"She?" Mark said.

"Yes, it was a woman, older. Looked so sad, really, for buying such a pretty bouquet."

The florist opened the cash register and took out an accounting book. "I remember writing this one down, because of all the special flowers. Was a pretty penny, I remember." She put on tiny silver-rimmed spectacles.

"Ah, here it is." She put her ledger on the counter for them to see. "No, sorry to say I have no record of who made the purchase. That bouquet was paid for in cash."

"But do you remember anything about the woman—anything at all?" Maggie pressed.

The woman thought for a moment. "Well, there was one odd thing about her—"

Mark leaned in. "Yes?"

"She had some green paint—or makeup or something—left around the edges of her face."

Chapter Twelve

"I knew it!" Mark exclaimed, as they walked out of the shop. "Green makeup—left over from a performance as the evil witch! Mildred Petrie is the killer!"

"Mildred bought flowers," Maggie reminded him, stopping on the damp pavement. "That doesn't mean she killed Estelle."

"But you yourself said the flowers meant—"

"The flowers meant, 'I'll kill you with poison because you were unfaithful.' But Richard Athol wasn't stepping out on Mildred. He was unfaithful to his *wife*—Diana Athol has motive and fits the message of the bouquet. Not Mildred."

"Then why was Mildred buying the flowers?"

"That's a very good question," Maggie said, starting to walk. She called back to Mark, "Come on, let's go."

They stepped over puddles and avoided crumpled packets of cigarettes. Looking down on a cemetery, the stones and walls covered in lurid green moss and lichen, Maggie saw a French letter. "So much for the grave being 'a fine and private place,'" she muttered.

The offices of the Ministry of Agriculture and Fisheries were on Queen Street. "MI-Five," Mark said to the receptionist, a middle-aged woman, plump and prune-faced. Her glasses were so thick her eyes were magnified. "We have official and urgent business with Mr. Howard."

"I'm sorry, sir, but he's not here."

"I don't believe you."

The woman pushed up her glasses and glared. "Well, I don't care if you believe me or not, sir—I'm telling you Mr. Howard is not here."

"Look, not only are two civilians dead, but a third is dying! I don't have time for this nonsense. There may be a widespread health epidemic occurring!" Maggie shivered. Neither of them had put it into words before, and the truth was so very ugly spoken aloud.

"And, as I said, I'm very sorry, but—"

Ignoring her protest, Maggie pushed past to the door. She opened it.

There sat Cyrus Howard, at his desk, chewing on a slice of Dundee cake, cup of tea in hand.

"Why, look—it seems Mr. Howard is in after all," Maggie said pleasantly. "Come, Mr. Standish. I believe it's time for an impromptu meeting."

"I know who you two are," Howard said. "You've caused me nothing but trouble. The situation is under control." He set down his cup, holding on to his cake.

" 'Trouble'?" Maggie hissed. "Two people are already dead. If this is your idea of 'under control' . . . Well, then obviously MI-Five needs to investigate."

Howard's face purpled. "While it's unfortunate some of the civilian population was infected, I can assure you that this was an isolated incident. And this is all top, *top* secret, I'll have you know. There's absolutely no need for MI-Five to poke its nose into this."

"You can't keep MI-Five from investigating when the civilian population's in danger." Mark's voice was even.

"The civilian population is not in danger!"

"Ragpickers' and woolsorters' disease . . ." Maggie said, thinking it through. "If it were just an isolated incident on a farm, that would be one thing . . . but *three* ballet dancers infected?"

"Obviously it was some sort of mistake—"

"Wait—" Maggie interrupted. Suddenly she saw the larger picture, and knew why such deep secrecy was necessary. "Anthrax. Britain is developing biological weapons!"

"I can't say—"

"Biological weapons . . ." Maggie interrupted. Her friend might not just have been a casualty in a love affair gone wrong and revenge, but collateral damage in a top-secret military operation. "Good Lord," she murmured.

Maggie thought back to the sheep she had found on the shore. *The sores. The same black sores that Estelle and Mildred had. And now Sarah has them. And the men in the boats, herding the sheep to those islands. Arisaig,* she realized, piecing it all together with the satisfying click of a math problem solved. *They're carrying out experiments with anthrax disease on an uninhabited island off the coast of Arisaig.* "Mr. Churchill—the Prime Minister—he can't possibly know about this!"

"I can't say," Howard insisted.

"This isn't part of the experiment," she said, thinking aloud. "This is someone associated with the tests, who's using the bacteria to murder someone. So, to cover up Britain's biological poison experiments, you let someone get away with murder?"

"I can't say."

"My friend is *dying*—there is no big picture. And what's the cure? What sort of medicine can help? Oh wait, let me guess—you can't say!" Maggie blazed. "There are things I would very much like to say, Mr. Howard. But, as opposed to keeping secrets and protecting killers, I choose not to say them because I am too much of a lady. Good day!"

"Sarah's dying. I can't just sit on my hands!" Maggie protested, as they sat on a bench overlooking East Princes Street Gardens. Mark's long legs were crossed in front of him. She wished she could be with K. Things were better with a small purring friend. *How could Dr. McNeil ever have thought of . . .*

Then she remembered the sheep, covered in sores. Like her beloved calculus problems, the variables slid and shifted and then clicked into place. The sheep were poisoned. The British were developing biological weapons. The British were developing them on an island on the western coast of Scotland, near enough to Arisaig that one of their dead sheep could wash ashore.

Dr. McNeil had said that the sheep with the two triangular-shaped notches in his right ear and red paint on his rump belonged to a farmer named Fergus Macnab. Therefore, Macnab must know something about the experiments. Or at least have a link to the person buying his sheep for experimentation. Would Macnab know anything useful? And did they have enough time to save Sarah?

"Mr. Standish, how would you feel about a little field trip to Arisaig?"

Three long, drafty, and freezing train rides from Edinburgh later, they stumbled out on the Beasdale platform, the nearest stop to Arisaig House. Mark had slept most of the way, and had crease marks on his face from where it had been pressed up against the blackout-covered window. "This is your territory, Miss Hope," he said, yawning. "Where to?"

"To Macnab's farm, of course."

"Is it far?" Mark looked around at the muddy paths and then down at his shiny oxfords.

"I'm wearing heels and stockings recently in a compost heap, Mr. Standish," she retorted. "It would be quite churlish of you to complain. And no, just a few miles south."

"Also, Miss Hope?" Mark peered at his watch in the moonlight. "It's late. I suggest we get a few hours' sleep now. Even farmers aren't up this early."

Maggie had been so focused on getting to Macnab that she'd completely lost track of time. *Hmm, he has a point.* "Fine," she said, leading the way at a fast clip. "We'll go back to my flat. But you're taking the sofa." She was sorry K was with Mr. Fergus, but there was no time for a visit.

The next morning before anyone else was awake, they walked from Arisaig House to Macnab's farm, only a mile down the coast. This time, Maggie was prepared, dressed in her jumpsuit and boots. "So much better than heels," she sighed as they walked along the icy paths. The grass and fallen leaves were coated with frost, which crunched under their feet.

As they came upon the dirt road to the farm, they could hear the clucking of chickens and the mournful *baa*s of sheep. A black-and-white dog, dark spots circling his eyes like a mask, cornered them on the front walk to the small stone farmhouse, growling.

"What now, Miss Hope?" Mark asked. The dog bared his teeth.

It was impossible to approach the house without incurring the further wrath of the dog.

The door banged open. "Oh, *do* shut up, Jasper—that's quite enough!" the older man said to the dog, who whined and went to greet him, tail wagging, licking his fingers. The man was silver-haired, with a neck hidden by fallen flesh, and mud-caked boots. "And who are you two interlopers?" he demanded, one hand on his hip, the other carrying a rifle.

"Are you Fergus Macnab?" Maggie asked.

"Who's asking?"

Once again, Mark pulled out his identification cards. "I'm Mr. Standish with MI-Five, and this is my colleague, Miss Hope. Are you the owner of sheep—"

"—with two ear notches and a red dot on their rumps?" Maggie interrupted.

"Aye, those are mine," Macnab said. "What business is it of yours?"

"I was the one who found one of them, washed up on the shore near Arisaig House, covered in sores."

"What of it? Sheep get sick, they die."

"Who do you sell your sheep to, Mr. Macnab?"

His eyes narrowed. "The government, o' course," he retorted. "Wool for clothing, horns for buttons, meat for the ration queue."

It was quite possible that the man had no idea what was happening to his sheep. "Do you know the names of the government officials who buy your sheep, Mr. Macnab?" Maggie asked.

"Too many to keep track of," the farmer muttered. "But it's the installation just down the road, by the shore. Took over my land, they did, the blighters, just like they took over Arisaig House!" Macnab shook his fist. "You got problems with what happened to those sheep, you ask those buggers. You give them what for!" he barked. The sheepdog barked too, as if in agreement.

"Yes, sir," Maggie said. "We most certainly will."

"Not too much farther, Mr. Standish," Maggie said as they walked down to the shore. "Almost there."

"Almost where?" Mark panted, not used to country paths any-more. "If we took the road, we'd get there quicker."

Maggie couldn't believe that Mark was most likely several pay grades above her. "Yes, but then they'll see us coming. Do you really think they'll just give us the key to all their files and tell us to go on and have a look?"

"Well . . ."

"If we can observe them from the shore, we have a chance to see what they're really doing, without them being aware of our presence."

"Very well, Miss Hope." Mark sighed. "Carry on."

The scent of salt water and seaweed was stronger near the water, as Mark and Maggie walked the pebbly shore. "They've launched boats from here," Maggie decided, looking at the ropes and the wear of the beach.

"Boats for what?"

Maggie found a grassy spot, just out of sight of a long wooden dock with several boats roped to it on the beach, and sat down cross-legged on a flat rock. "I don't know," she said. "But we'll wait and then we'll find out."

They waited for hours and nothing happened. There was only the lapping of the waves and the occasional cry of a seabird. As the sun continued to rise, the day grew warmer and Mark's stomach rumbled. "Don't suppose you have anything to eat?" he whis-pered.

"No," Maggie whispered back. *This is one of MI-Five's finest? God save the King, indeed . . .*

"It would—" From the corner of her eye, she spotted movement. She raised one hand to silence him. Men in uniform, each carrying a sheep in his arms, were walking down the dock and loading the animals into a waiting boat. When the boat was full, they pushed off, using a small motor to head to an offshore island. When the boat was out of sight and the rest of the soldiers had dispersed, Maggie stood, brushing off the bottom of her trousers. "Sixteen sheep," she said.

"Now what?" Mark asked, bewildered.

"Now we go after them, of course." Maggie gave a crooked smile. "You may not know this, but stealth water landings are one of my specialties."

They borrowed one of the other boats and went to the same island, but landing on the opposite shore. "Come on!" Maggie said. Mark and his city ways were really getting on her nerves.

They pulled the boat onto the pebbled shore and hid it beneath some trees, camouflaging it with dead branches. Then they made their way to the top of the hill, crawling the last ten feet.

Below them lay a grassy valley, dotted with grazing sheep. The scene was pastoral, bucolic, except for the armed soldiers stalking the perimeters. "Keep your head down!" Maggie growled through her teeth.

Mark did as he was told.

Maggie watched as the soldiers pulled on white hoods, gas masks, gloves, and orange jumpsuits. They looked like something from H. G. Wells's *War of the Worlds*, just as strange, and just as terrifying. In their protective garb, they grabbed at sheep, each carrying his to a row of pens. They looked like stockades in a line.

Then the soldiers ran to take cover. Maggie realized what was happening. "They're setting off a bomb . . ." she said. "They're seeing how far the effects will go. However many of the sheep die in the line—"

"—shows the circumference of the damage," Mark concluded grimly.

"And we're—"

"—downwind!"

They both scrambled and rushed down the hill to the coast.

An hour later, they climbed back up to ascertain the damage. Sheep carcasses were being pulled from the stocks and removed on stretchers by the men in gas masks. The ones still alive were re-leased to graze, while one of the men made notes on a clipboard. "So, that's how far the bomb carries," Maggie whispered.

The soldiers dumped the dead sheep into what looked like an incinerator, and soon the air was filled with the putrid smell of burning wool and flesh. Maggie longed to bury her face in the grass to escape the stench, but she kept watching. Sarah's life de-pended on it, she was certain.

The men washed off their gas masks, hoods, and jumpsuits in the water, then put them in a small shed. They made their way back to their boat.

"Come on!" Maggie said.

"Can't we go back now?"

"They must keep their research notes here—they're much safer than their offices on the shore. Come on—we're going to have a look around."

The sun was beginning to turn red as it dropped closer and closer to the horizon. It was increasingly cold, and the winds were picking up. "Of course we are," Mark muttered.

On the other side of the field was a hut made from corrugated metal. "I don't suppose you have the key?" Mark muttered. His sour mood was intensifying.

"Don't need one," Maggie informed him; "I've been taught by Glaswegian safecrackers how to unlock almost anything. This—" She looked at the three padlocks. "—is a breeze."

It was dusk when Maggie finally got the door open.

"Finally," Mark said.

"I said I was good. I didn't say I was fast."

Inside were military-issue desks and chairs, bookcases and file cabinets. Maggie switched on a light.

"Really?" Mark said, his voice rising slightly. "Really?"

"Are you worried about blackout rules here and now? There are no ARP matrons to fine you, I assure you," Maggie said tartly. There was a safe in the corner. She went straight to it.

Mark found an apple on one of the desks and grabbed it. "Want some?" he mumbled, his mouth full.

"No thanks," said Maggie, taking stock of the safe. She was familiar with the model, but that still didn't mean it would be easy. She sat down in front of the metal box and patted it. "Now we're going to have a nice little chat . . ." she said.

"What?" Mark asked. He was going through the researchers' desks, finding a few sugar cubes, which he popped into his mouth. "Here!" he said, tossing one to Maggie.

She caught it with one hand, then turned back to the safe. She dropped the cube on her tongue. It was delicious. Then she shook her head. *Back to the safe, Hope.*

She twirled the knob back and forth, her ear pressed to the cool metal door, listening. Every tiny click and clack meant something. Finally, finally, the door swung open.

"Bingo," Maggie breathed, taking out the papers and paging

through them. There, in a manila folder, were all of the research notes on the experiments, all neatly typed, all stamped with TOP SECRET in red ink.

"Bingo?"

"It's American for 'We got you, you bastards.' And now, Mr. Standish, I think it's time to go."

Chapter Thirteen

They dragged their boat back into the water and sailed to shore, with Maggie navigating by the stars, as she'd been taught. Once ashore, Mark asked, "Back to the train?"

Maggie looked at him, then down at herself. Their feet and legs were caked with mud, their clothes were filthy, and they had grass snarled in their hair. Mark's cashmere coat was torn. "We'll only draw attention on a train," she said. "And we don't have time to clean up. Come on."

In the darkness, they made their way to the researchers' parking lot. Maggie ignored the cars and went straight to one of the couriers' motorbikes.

She jumped on the leather seat, glad she'd worn trousers, and put on the helmet and goggles. "Come on," she said, using a kick start to ignite the engine. Mark nicked a helmet and goggles from another motorbike and climbed on behind her, grabbing her around the waist. She revved up the motorbike, then—with the headlight's blackout slats on—made for the exit to the road.

The four guards didn't see the motorbike in the darkness, but they did hear the roar of its engine. It was boring work, being a guard, and the night shifts were long. Usually, they passed bottles of hard cider back and forth, and smoked cigarette after cigarette.

Which was why Maggie on her motorcycle had already broken through the wooden security gate before they could react. *"Bloody hell!*" said the first guard, drunk and rubbing his eyes in disbelief. But the other three were already running to their own cycles. "Hurry! After him!"

The guard left behind pressed the alarm button, and a wail of low sirens pierced the darkness.

Maggie didn't hear them—the rush of wind in her ears was too strong. She knew they were carrying information of great importance. Lives were at stake. Sarah's life was at stake.

She opened the throttle full and adjusted the rearview mirror. Sure enough, in the distance she saw bright yellow pinpricks of light. Headlights.

She revved the engine. A narrow dirt path headed off from the main road, and she swung right to follow it. She knew it, having made her trainees run it often.

The path was narrow and full of stones, but she'd run it on foot enough times to be able to navigate it even in the darkness. Maggie clenched her teeth as her bike bobbed and weaved around the larger of the stones. Behind her, Mark tightened his grip.

The pinpricks of lights followed them. *Damn,* she thought, wondering how much of a lead she had, and how long she could hold on to it. She decided to take a risk. She hit the accelerator, rocks be damned.

It was a good thing she did.

If she'd been going any slower, she wouldn't have made the jump over the ravine. The incline leading up to it served as a ramp, and the motorcycle was already airborne before she knew what was happening.

One exhilarating moment of flight and freedom as the motorbike soared.

When Maggie hit the ground on the opposite side, her front

wheel made contact first, out of alignment with the back wheel. The bike swerved and tipped over, hurling her into the dirt. Gasping for air, she spit dirt out of her mouth and tried to move. Although everything hurt, nothing was broken. Her nose was bleeding.

"You all right?" she managed to say to Mark. She rubbed blood from her nose.

"Oh just ducky," he panted, spitting out blades of grass. "Right as rain."

"As my instructor Mr. Burns used to say, 'Any landing you can walk away from is a good landing.'"

Then she saw the headlights in the woods behind them. Their pursuers were coming, fast.

She and Mark grabbed the bike and dragged it behind some bushes, then hid behind a tree to watch.

The guards were not so lucky.

The first biker didn't make it across the gully—he hit the dirt-and-stone wall opposite. Bike and rider fell, bursting into orange flames at the bottom.

The two other riders, seeing what happened, pulled up short on the opposite side. "Bloody hell!" one exclaimed, getting off the bike and running to the ravine, seeing the dancing flames and smelling the burning petrol.

"He's dead," said the other.

"Is the other driver dead, too, then?"

The first driver listened, then shrugged. "Probably. I don't hear a motor. But we'll have to see in the morning. If he's not dead, he won't get far."

That, Maggie thought, wiping more blood from her nose with filthy and scraped hands, *is what you think.*

Her mouth was parched. Her stomach was growling, too. She knew she could last without food, but she couldn't keep up this breakneck pace without drinking something soon. Still, she didn't want to stop. She had to get back to Edinburgh. Surely what they had found would help Sarah and find the murderer.

She was thirsty, bleeding, dirty, and tired. She stank of fear and desperation. Another man had just died—a Brit—one of their own. *One who was working on biochemical weapons,* she reminded herself. She would not cry, she would not—there would be plenty of time for a cry later.

To their right, through the evergreens, she knew there was a small pond. She led Mark to it, through cool pine-scented air. At the water's edge, they both dropped to their knees and drank as long as they dared.

The icy water tasted of dead leaves, but she didn't care.

She dropped back on the stones, panting, looking up at the dark sky encrusted with stars. "So, Miss Hope—this is winging it?" Mark dropped down beside her.

"Indeed," Maggie said.

Mark groaned. "And what now?"

"And now we ride as fast as we can, back to Edinburgh."

Many, many hours later, back in Edinburgh, they both went to their respective hotels to wash and change clothes, then met in Maggie's room at the Caledonian.

Mark knocked and she let him in, the room illuminated by a circle of golden light from the lamp on the nightstand.

Maggie had already read through the papers. "Well, it's official," she said, handing him the folder. "The British are developing what they're calling N—anthrax, the official name for *Bacillus anthracis.* The weapons-grade anthrax itself is made at Porton Down, but the experiments are being carried out on the island they've code-named Neverland."

Mark sat down on the chair and began to read. "Holy pish!" he said, flipping pages.

"My thoughts, exactly." Maggie started to pace restlessly. "We certainly have enough now to make Howard talk. But that still doesn't bring us any closer to our murderer."

"There's a payroll," Mark pointed out. "And a list of contacts at Porton Down."

Maggie stopped in her tracks. "We'd have to get a list of everyone associated with the ballet company and the Lyceum, and then cross-check with Neverland and Porton Down."

She flung herself on the bed. She was exhausted. Two dancers and a man were dead, Sarah was dying, the British, whom she always thought of as the White Hats, were developing anthrax . . . Dead sheep burning . . .

"I may not have been all that useful on our mission, Miss Hope," Mark said, taking out a folder of papers, as well as a fountain pen from his breast pocket, "but I can assure you, paperwork—and tracking people down—is where I excel." He went out to the hall to use the telephone.

While Maggie napped, Mark made call after call, using "MI-Five" often, as well as calling in some personal favors. Finally, he returned and slumped back in his chair. The folder and the papers fell to the floor.

"What?" Maggie gasped, startled. She sat up and rubbed her eyes. "Anything?"

"Damn it, no. We seem to have reached a dead end. At least until I can think of another angle."

"Let me see," Maggie said, stretching out her hand. Mark gave her the papers.

She read through them all again. Nothing. "And then—what do you have? A list of everyone at the Vic-Wells?"

"Yes, and the theater, too. No one's name checks out."

"Stage names," Maggie said.

"What?"

"A lot of the dancers use stage names. And women, of course, take their husbands' names. We need to find their legal names and see if any of them match. Maybe Mildred Petrie used a stage name? And be sure to check for Diana Atholl."

But Mark was already struggling to his feet. "I'm ordering us an enormous breakfast from room service, and then I'm on it. What are your thoughts on haggis for breakfast?"

"I think I'd rather have toast, thank you."

After dawn had broken and office hours had begun, Mark continued with his research. Maggie decided she had somewhere else to be. She was waiting outside on the steps of the Ministry of Agriculture and Fisheries when Cyrus Howard arrived.

"I have nothing to say, Miss Hope," he said, taking out his keys to open the door.

"Really, Mr. Howard?" she said, pulling out her trump card, the file. When he saw what she had, he paled.

"Come in, Miss Hope," he said.

"Thank you. Don't mind if I do."

In Howard's office, he sat and Maggie paced.

"My friend is dying," she told him. "My friend is *dying* from anthrax poison that you and your cronies are making at Porton Down and testing on an island off the coast of Arisaig. 'Neverland,'" she spat.

"Miss Hope—"

"Somehow, this poison has infected at least three civilians—two are dead and one is dying. And yet you cover it up . . ."

"We have everything under control. There's no need for MI-Five or police involvement."

"I don't think you understand that my friend is *dying*," Maggie snapped. "I can go to any number of people at this point. I can go to the Prime Minister. I can go to the King. I can go to the BBC . . ."

"Don't you know?" Howard shot back. "The Prime Minister is behind these experiments. If you go to him, you'll be arrested for treason."

Mr. Churchill? Developing anthrax? Maggie felt her legs buckle. "That doesn't stop me from going to the press," she retorted.

"You'll be *hanged*."

"At this point, Mr. Howard, I don't really give a *flying fig*!"

Howard snorted, then made a steeple of his fingers. "Miss Hope, I think I can help you. We can help each other."

"I highly doubt it."

"There's an epidemiologist here in the city. He's worked with some of our boys who've accidentally been infected with the anthrax spores. He has a seventy-five percent success rate. You give me all of the evidence you have and promise you'll never speak of it again—and I'll call the doctor and have him save your friend."

Dr. Janus met Maggie outside Sarah's hospital room. "I just spoke with the epidemiologist," he said in low tones. "Now that we know she's come in contact with cutaneous anthrax, we're going to wash her thoroughly. He also recommended that we put her on a new medication we're calling an 'anti-biotic.' That should give her a fighting chance."

"What *are* her chances, Doctor?" Maggie managed. She opened the door gently and saw Sarah, gaunt and gray, eyes closed, looking almost like a corpse already. She felt dizzy with fear. "Of survival?"

"We're doing the best we can, Miss."

Maggie went back to the Caledonian. Mark was on the telephone. When he hung up he asked, "How did it go?"

"In exchange for our silence, he gave me the name of a epidemiologist who's helping Sarah," she answered, her voice flat.

"How is she?"

"It's touch and go."

Mark shook his head. "I'm glad. But I haven't found the murderer. As far as I can tell, Mildred Petrie never used a stage name and she has no connection to Porton Down."

"And what about Diana Atholl?"

Mark rubbed his eyes with his fists. "No connection to Diana Atholl, either."

"Mark," Maggie said, thinking, "what about Diana Angius. Can you look up the name Angius?"

Mark returned to his papers. "Angius, Angius . . ." He stopped, eyes wide. "There's a Simon Angius here, who's a scientist. Works on the spore research for 'N.'" He read further. "From his date of birth, he might be Diana's father. Let me check."

Mark went to the telephone in the hall and made a few calls. "Yes, Diana Atholl is Simon Angius's daughter," he panted when he returned. "And Diana visited him last month for two weeks. And she signed into the lab—under her maiden name."

Maggie brushed loose hair out of her face. "Diana Atholl had motive and access to the poison and to the theater—that's enough to arrest her."

"And Mildred Petrie?"

"She was no doubt involved, but I don't think she's Estelle's killer. It's something we could ask Mrs. Atholl when we question her."

"When we arrest her, you mean." Mark raised an eyebrow. "Would you like to do the honors?"

Maggie shook her head. "You're the actual MI-Five agent on the case. Frain just let me in as a courtesy."

"You've earned the right to make the arrest, Miss Hope. I'm just glad I'll be there to see her face when you do."

At the other end of Edinburgh, at the Balmoral Hotel, the Atholls were having tea at the Palm Court. A harpist played Debussy's "First Arabesque" as waiters in black and white circulated under the tall Victorian glass dome with silver trays.

There was a tiered tray of sandwiches in front of the Atholls, though neither was eating. Richard Atholl looked as handsome as ever. Diana, his wife, looked even shorter and stockier in a floral dress with gaping spaces between its buttons. And although waves of genteel conversation passed over them, they did not speak.

Maggie and Mark walked in, shrugging off an offer to be seated. They went directly to the Atholls' linen-covered table.

"I'm Agent Standish and this is Miss Hope of MI-Five." Mark showed his identification. He looked to Maggie.

She continued, "Mrs. Diana Atholl, you are under arrest for the murders of Estelle Crawford and Mildred Petrie."

Around them, conversation stopped as curious eyes looked over.

Mrs. Atholl pressed her lips together, then stood. "Do you need to use handcuffs?" she asked. "I promise not to make a scene."

Maggie had expected more protest, but Mrs. Atholl seemed

almost relieved. "Just come with us, Mrs. Atholl, and there's no need for handcuffs."

"Are you coming?" Mrs. Atholl turned toward her husband.

"You? *You* killed Estelle?" the conductor said softly.

"Yes, I killed Estelle," Mrs. Atholl replied tonelessly. "And it still didn't make any difference. Even with her gone, you still don't love me."

"What did you do to her, Diana?" the conductor asked, voice breaking. "What did you do to *my* Estelle?"

"We'll talk about that at the station," Maggie interposed, motioning for Mark to hurry. "Will you be coming, Mr. Atholl?"

He was staring at his wife as if he'd never seen her before. "No. No, I won't be coming."

"Richard!" Diana half screamed, half moaned. "Please! *I'm your wife!*" The harp music stopped. Everyone in the tearoom waited, on edge, to see what would happen.

"Not anymore," he told her. "Our sham of a marriage is over."

Diana Atholl's eyes were wild. She was still for just a moment, like a startled bird, and then she broke from Mark's hold, lunged to her feet, and began to run.

"I've got this," Maggie called, setting out.

The women's heels clattered on the floor. Mrs. Atholl slammed into a startled waiter, then staggered into a potted palm. But she kept running.

Maggie dodged a woman swathed in furs and reeking of perfume and leapt forward at Diana. Both women slammed to the marble floor. She straddled Diana's facedown body, forcing her hands behind her back.

"You nearly killed one of my best friends," Maggie growled in her prisoner's ear. "Two women are dead because of you. Why is Mildred Petrie dead and Sarah Sanderson in the hospital, Mrs. Atholl?"

"Mildred," she gasped, "Mildred bought the flowers for me. I didn't want to be spotted. I never thought she'd touch them after I'd left them for Estelle . . ."

"So Mildred touched the bouquet after you poisoned it. And Sarah accidentally touched it, too," Maggie finished. "Revenge didn't bring back your husband, but it did kill two, maybe three, women."

Diana began to cry. "I'm sorry," she sobbed. "I'm so, so sorry . . ."

Mark handcuffed her and brought her to her feet, then looked to Maggie, who stood and brushed herself off, ignoring the shocked looks of the hotel guests and staff. "Are you all right?"

"Yes," Maggie answered. "But if you wouldn't mind taking her to St. Leonard's, I'd like to get back to Sarah."

Chapter Fourteen

Dr. Carroll continued to update Frain with telephone calls. Elbows propped on his desk, he watched the Union Jack snap in the stiff breeze outside his window.

"I consider this a visit to the mad tea party, Dr. Carroll," Frain said. "Frau Hess is playing you."

The doctor shook his head. "I'm no Sigmund Freud, but I don't think she is."

"You don't know Clara Hess."

"I know her better than you do."

"You know what she *chooses* to show you."

"I've done my research. The woman we know as Clara Hess was born Agna Frei—Agna Clara Frei. She changed her name to Clara Schwartz when she began her opera career, and became Clara Hope when she married Edmund Hope, and then became Clara Hess when she returned to Germany and married the conductor Miles Hess."

"So she knows her name," Frain deadpanned. "Remember, she's an actress—she knows how to create a role and how to perform it brilliantly."

"I don't believe this is a performance, Mr. Frain."

"You have a few more days. If she doesn't start talking and giving us information, she'll be executed."

The doctor looked at his desk calendar. It was December 3.

Four days left until her execution. "I think that would be a terrible mistake."

"Get some intel out of her that I can use—or just flip her to our side. Unless you can do that, she's going to end up like Josef Jakobs—dead."

"I want books, Dr. Carroll." This time, Dr. Carroll was visiting her in her room at the Tower. He had ordered the cage and the restraints removed.

"I'm sorry, Frau Hess, but prisoners do not have the privilege of receiving books."

"What do you think I'm going to do with them? Make paper airplanes? Pinprick code? It's not as if everyone wouldn't be on the lookout for that." Clara rose from her chair and stretched.

Then, she doubled over in pain, clutching her stomach. It was the telltale sign of another personality coming to the fore.

"Frau Hess?"

"I'm—I'm—" She struggled to speak. When she did, a different voice came from her mouth.

It was Agna. "My favorite book is Hoffmann's *Der Struwwelpeter*. Do you know it?"

"I do." Dr. Carroll's voice gentled as it always did when he spoke with the child Agna.

"Am I banished?" she asked, looking around, eyes wild. "I must be. I'm in my room and I can't get out. Mother must have locked me in!"

She flung herself on the narrow bed and began to weep. "I don't know what I do to her! She's always locking me places—the closet, the pantry. She locks me away! Sometimes she forgets about me!"

"Is that what you think is happening?" the doctor asked.

"Isn't it? And I don't even have my dolly. Or my books."

"Well, surely a book wouldn't hurt," Dr. Carroll said. "I'll see if I can hunt up a copy of *Der Struwwelpeter* for you. I'll bring it tomorrow."

Agna smiled.

Churchill was in bed, surrounded by a half-eaten breakfast and various papers and files, as well as his precious Box of top-secret documents, wearing nothing but his dragon-embroidered silk dressing gown. "Cars and refrigerators!"

"Sir?" Churchill's long-suffering manservant, Mr. Inces, was unruffled by his boss's sudden exclamations.

"The Americans!" The Prime Minister crumpled a memo and threw it into the fireplace, where it burst into flame. "While we fight for our last breath, American factories are producing cars and refrigerators, not planes and tanks!"

"Yes, sir," Inces agreed, tidying up the overflowing ashtrays and drained brandy snifters.

"Their ships are being sunk by Nazi U-boats in the Atlantic, and still they make cars and refrigerators! Meanwhile, Kurusu goes from Hitler's snake pit in Berlin to Washington, DC. 'Special envoy' my arse."

"I thought Admiral Nomura was the Japanese Ambassador to the United States, sir?" Inces remarked.

"Looks like Tōjō's sending in reinforcements," the Prime Minister growled. "The Japs are up to something . . . And where the hell's the Japanese fleet? Well, don't just stand there—get me Mr. Sterling and Mr. Greene!"

"Yes, sir," Inces said.

The two private secretaries reached the P.M.'s bedchamber less than three minutes later. "Yes, sir?" David managed, out of breath.

"The bloody Japanese are up to something. Get me all of the intelligence reports from Bletchley. Call my Chiefs of Staff. We need to consider all options—Japan may attack our holdings in Thailand, Singapore, the Philippines—maybe even they'll attack Russia, now that they've signed that blasted pact with the Nazzies."

"And what if they do attack us in the Pacific, sir?" John knew as well as anyone that all of Britain's power, not that it was much, was tied up with defending her home island.

"Just get me the goddamn papers!" the P.M. roared. "And find out where the damn Japanese fleet is!" he thundered, flinging a pillow at the two young men, who departed hastily.

Minutes crawled by until the two private secretaries reappeared in his doorway. "No one seems to know where the Japanese fleet is, sir," David reported.

"Not good enough!" the Prime Minister shouted. "Gimme decrypts!" Bletchley Park had broken the Japanese naval and diplomatic codes. Still, the codes only gave part of the picture.

Churchill pulled out one particular piece of paper from the rest. "What's this one mean?" he asked, putting on his gold-framed spectacles to take a closer took. " *'Climb Mount Niitaka 1208'*?"

"It's a JN-25 transmission from Tokyo, sir," David replied. "It went out on the second of December."

The P.M.'s face hardened. "Where the hell is Mount Niitaka?"

"I—I don't know, sir," David stammered.

"Well, bloody well find out! That's why I have you young pups here! Why the devil—"

"Mount Niitaka is the highest mountain in Formosa, even higher than Mount Fuji. It's often referred to here in Britain as Mount Morrison," John interposed.

"Highest mountain . . . A naval message to climb a mountain?" the Prime Minister growled. Nelson, who'd been curled up at the end of the P.M.'s bed, had endured enough and jumped off. "That's an attack code! That's a *bloody attack code!*"

John and David looked at each other, realizing he was right. "Yes, sir," they both managed.

"And 1208—the eighth of December?" John ventured. He'd run his hands through his hair, causing it to stand on end as if he'd been electrocuted.

The P.M. was lost in his thoughts again. "But why so much time?" he murmured. "And where's the damn Jap fleet?" Then, "Gimme map!"

John hurried to the perimeter of the room, where there was an antique globe in a Queen Anne stand. He took out the orb.

"Just throw it, young man!"

John tossed the world, and the P.M. caught it with ease. David almost whistled in appreciation.

"Mount Niitaka . . ." the Prime Minister mumbled, searching for it on the globe. " 'Climb Mount Niitaka' must have been the order to begin a mission—the climb—*not* the order to attack . . . The Japanese fleet was last spotted off Formosa almost a week ago . . . So they're at sea . . . But where? God blast it to hell and back!"

"They'd probably be sailing about three hundred miles a day, sir," David ventured, trying to make up for not knowing Mount Niitaka.

The P.M. thrust up a finger. "Remember, I was First Lord of the Admiralty, young pup! I know bloody well how fast a ship can sail! But they won't go in a straight line . . . Let's give them three thousand miles . . . They were last spotted off the coast of China, near Formosa . . ."

"Yes," John said. "We sent all of that information to the Americans in Washington, both the Army and Navy. And our double agent, Dušan Popov, went to J. Edgar himself, with the intel we received, about the Japanese making a grid map of Pearl. Popov said Hoover threw him out of his office, then tried to throw him out of the country . . ."

"Popov. Pearl Harbor. The Americans . . . Good God." The globe slipped from Churchill's hands, falling to the floor with a crash, then rolling across the carpet. "They're not going to attack us or our holdings in the Far East—the Japanese are going to attack the American fleet at Pearl Harbor on December eighth!"

Chapter Fifteen

When Maggie burst into Sarah's room at Chalmers, her friend's eyes were open.

"How are you feeling?" Maggie exclaimed, sitting gently on the edge of the bed.

Sarah gave a weak smile. "The doctor says I'm going to live."

"I'm so glad! You can't even imagine . . ." Maggie bent down to hug Sarah.

"We arrested her," she went on. "It was Diana Atholl. She . . ." Maggie couldn't mention anthrax. "Well, she put poison on the roses for Estelle. So Estelle was poisoned, and you and Mildred Petrie were, as well."

The dancer shook her head. "You mean I almost died because of an *accident?*"

"I believe the technical term is *negligent homicide*. But you're going to be fine . . ."

"Estelle and Mildred won't be fine . . ."

"Shhhh," Maggie soothed. "Just get some rest—"

But Sarah's eyes were already closed.

The next morning, Dr. Carroll brought the book of German children's tales for Agna, but it was Clara Hess who received him. "What's that?" she demanded, eyes narrowing.

"Something for Agna."

"Morality tales? Of course that's what *she'd* pick. Here, let me see it."

She held the book up to her nose and sniffed. "Ah, I love the smell of books. Even if they are sentimental drivel." She turned the pages. "Look at this one!" she said, pointing to *Die Geschichte von den schwarzen Buben*. "Do you know it?"

" 'The Story of the Black Boys.' I may have read it as a child, but I don't remember."

"In the story, St. Nicholas catches three boys teasing a Negro. To teach them a lesson, he dips the three boys in black ink, to make them even darker than the boy they'd teased." She looked at the doctor. "But they were right to tease the black boy. They are racially superior."

"I'll take it away, if you don't want it—"

"No, no, no," Clara said. "Beggars can't be choosers. The only thing is . . ." She smiled at Dr. Carroll, her lips curving in what looked to be an embarrassed grimace. "I'm over fifty now. My eyes aren't as good as they once were. Do you—do you think," she asked, her voice gentling, "that you could bring me a pair of reading glasses?"

Dr. Carroll smiled, relieved he'd seen the first crack in Clara Hess's façade. "Yes, Frau Hess. I'm sure that could be arranged."

"And my daughter. You have contacted her? She knows about the—" She avoided saying the word *execution*. "—Sunday?"

"No, Frau Hess. I'm terribly sorry to tell you that your daughter is in the midst of important government work. She cannot receive any messages."

Clara gave a bitter laugh. "Is that what she thinks she's doing? *Important government work?* Yes, yes, of course. And Edmund?"

"Mr. Hess, I'm sorry to say, is also busy with government work."

"Edmund? Doing something important? My, how the worm has turned!" She hesitated. "And Peter?"

The doctor blinked. "He is also——"

"Busy with government work," she finished sourly. "How fortunate the government has such busy little bees."

"Frau Hess, we can have a clergy member visit you the night before and be with you the day of . . . Would you like me to make a call? Are you Lutheran or Catholic?"

"I have no God!" Clara spat. "He turned his back on me, and so I turned my back on Him. And never looked back. Not once."

"With your permission, Frau Hess, *I* would like to be there for you . . ."

But Clara's attention had already turned away. "Fine, fine," she said, waving a careless hand. "How droll—my last audience."

"Frau Hess . . ."

Her neck snapped around and she looked him straight in the eye. "Get out," she whispered.

When he didn't move, she repeated, "Get. Out. Now."

Then, *"Get! Out!"*

The next day, Maggie woke early. It was too soon to visit the hospital. It was too early for breakfast. It was still too dark to do much walking in the blackout. And so Maggie decided to go to St. John's. As she picked her way through the darkness, the unexpected reflection of the crescent moon in a puddle startled her.

The stained-glass windows at St. John's were boarded, but the arches were still beautiful. Inside the thick wooden doors, the church smelled of incense and age. And flowers, from the forced hyacinths on the window ledges and the amaryllises on the altar, next to a wreath of pine boughs with purple and pink Advent candles.

Maggie, alone in the vast space, lit only by a few bare bulbs, listened to her footsteps echo on the marble floors. She lit a candle at a side altar, then went to the nearest pew to pray, knees on the worn needlepoint cushions. Or, at least, as well as an atheist and scientist could pray.

She thought of Estelle, and Mildred, and Sarah. Of Diana Atholl.

She thought of her half-sister, Elise, back in Germany. What was happening to her? Had she been arrested? Taken to a concentration camp? Elise had seen her shoot a man. Surely she wouldn't want to have anything more to do with her. The thought pierced Maggie's heart with guilt and shame.

She thought of Gottlieb Lehrer. She thought of the Jews of Germany. She thought of the women Diana Atholl had murdered and of Sarah, who had nearly lost her fight for life. Maggie didn't know how to pray, but she tried to hold each in her heart, with as much love as she could. She thought, too, of Chuck and Nigel, and their little baby Griffin, only a few months old.

What would Griffin's future be? She recalled his sweet face and little bald head. He was so tiny, so fragile. Surely they had to make sure the world was a better place by the time he grew up. Surely they had to do better. *Surely I can do better.*

Suddenly it came to her, clear as the dawn that was breaking outside in the purples and pinks of Advent candles. This wasn't about her. This wasn't even about all of them—Elise, Gottlieb, Hugh, John . . . This was about the next generation—the little Griffins and all the babies yet to be born.

Once she'd been so sure of black and white, of right and wrong. She wasn't anymore. But she was certain of one thing— while there was no such thing as a good war, this particular one was a *necessary* war. The stakes were as high as they could be. And it had to be the *last* war.

On the one side was anger, arrogance, bigotry, victimhood, lust for power, unbridled sadism, and apathy. A brutal enslavement mentality. An utter lack of empathy in a world obsessed with power and racial purity.

And on the other side were courage, perseverance, selflessness. The dignity of the individual. Empathy, faith, and freedom. These were what was important. It wasn't about her—it was about Griffin. It was about the children. It was about the children's children. If the world could be a better place for them, her own Black Dog, her own life—well, things were complicated, but a glimmer of possibility shone through.

The possibility of peace.

"Are you awake?" Maggie whispered at the doorway to Sarah's room.

Sarah moaned, but sat up and smiled at her. "Dr. Janus says I'll be ready to be discharged soon, but I probably won't be able to dance for months. So, touring with the Vic-Wells is out. Maybe I could go stay with my mother, back in Liverpool—"

"Absolutely not," Maggie said firmly, pouring a glass of water from the carafe on the table. "You shall stay with me," she decreed, holding the water to Sarah's lips to let her sip. "You'll need some help until you're back on your feet, and until then I can give you a helping hand."

"I wouldn't want to intrude—"

"On me and my nun-like life? On my new cat, who will simply adore you?" Maggie kept her tone light. "Nonsense—the fresh air of western Scotland will be just the tonic for you. It's beautiful there—the mountains, the woods, the shore . . . I'll just have a little chat with Mr. Burns. Sort it all out."

Then she shook her head, as if to clear it. "Sarah, dear, I do have one very serious thing to tell you. When you were very sick and it looked—well, it looked as if we might lose you—I called your mother."

"My mum? Is she all right?"

"Your mother's fine, darling, but I'm afraid there's bad news about your grandmother. Your mother asked that I relay the news. I'm sorry to have to tell you that . . ." Maggie took a breath. "Your grandmother is dead."

Sarah sat in silence, struggling to take in the enormity of the news. "No!" She shook her head. "No, it can't possibly be—you must have heard wrong—my mum must have heard wrong—"

"I'm sorry, Sarah. Your mother has official confirmation."

"How—?"

"The Nazis. She was shot just outside her apartment on the Île Saint-Louis. No reason given. But she didn't suffer—your mother wanted you to know that."

"I can't believe it. Those Nazi bastards. I'll kill those Nazi bastards! *Salauds de Nazis! Je les déchirerai en petits morceaux quand je sors d'ici!*"

Churchill walked about the frost-encrusted gardens of Chequers with John and David.

"Not that I think Chequers has been bugged, but we'll have complete privacy out here. Look at it!" He swept his walking stick at the sprawling vista—tree-covered rolling hills, several horses grazing in a field, and sky. "England!"

John and David nodded. They were used to the P.M.'s theatrics.

They walked farther along the path. "I've been thinking about

Mount Niitaka," the Prime Minister began. He plopped down on one of the wooden benches, with a view of the rolling hills. He was humming "There Will Always Be an England."

"How can we help, sir?" asked David.

Churchill looked at both the young men, who'd stood by him through so many years. "I'm asking you not to say anything."

"Sir—?"

"If we tell Roosevelt, he'll publicly denounce the Japanese. Then they'll call the attack off, swearing it was a training exercise or some such falsehood. Pearl Harbor will be put on alert, and so the Japs will never have the element of surprise again. They'll turn their attentions to *our* territories in the Far East . . . And then we'll be at war with Japan, as well as Germany and Italy."

"But sir," John began, "there are over two thousand American servicemen stationed at Pearl Harbor. To not warn them of a potential attack—"

"—is wicked," Churchill finished glumly. "Evil, even. Despicable. Don't you think I've wrestled with this? If I don't tell them, I'm the Devil himself.

"But if I do warn them, they still won't join the war. And the Japanese will destroy us in the Pacific. While Roosevelt smokes his cigarettes with his ivory holder and talks out of both sides of his mouth, we will be destroyed. We'll become Nazi slaves. And, personally, I have a cyanide pill handy, should things come to that."

"You—you do have some time, sir. We have until the eighth," John reminded him.

Churchill got to his feet, walking stick tapping. "Yes, Mr. Sterling, that's true—we have until December eighth."

The very same message that Consul Kita had sent to Admiral Yamamoto was also picked up by "Magic" in Washington.

That afternoon in Washington, one of the young men from the Intelligence service gave it to Kramer's secretary, Mrs. Dorothy Edgars, to file until a translator came on duty the following Monday.

But Dorothy was bored, restless. She didn't like to be idle. She'd already typed everything that needed to be typed, filed everything that needed to be filed, washed the coffee cups, and sharpened all the office pencils. She looked up at the ticking clock—still another three hours until her shift ended. And so when the next "Magic" landed in her in-box, she decided to take a crack at it herself, using her hard-won knowledge of Japanese learned while her husband had been stationed in Tokyo.

She took one of the freshly sharpened pencils and began. The more she read, the more engrossed she became. It was Kita's message to Admiral Yamamoto explaining Otto Kuhn's signals for last-minute information to be communicated to ships offshore—by lights lit at certain times in certain windows, code hidden in newspaper advertisements and radio spots, and even burning garbage for smoke signals.

Dorothy was new to Washington, and she was brand-new in the Intelligence department. Still, she knew that something was wrong, and she sensed that this particular decrypt was of paramount importance. The Japanese had plans for the military base at Pearl Harbor—and the U.S. fleet was in jeopardy.

She showed her translation of the decrypt to Chief Bryant, her supervisor. "It's interesting, to be sure, Mrs. Edgars," he murmured, glancing at his watch. It was Friday, and he was eager to start his weekend. "But surely it will keep until Monday."

Dorothy bit the inside of her lip in frustration. "I'll keep working on the translation, sir," she said. "If you don't mind."

"Yes, yes, of course." He waved her off. "Would you mind getting me a cup of coffee first? Milk, no sugar."

But back at her desk in the deserted office, Dorothy continued the translation, hoping that when Lieutenant Kramer arrived, he, at least, would see its importance.

She finished the final lines: *If the above signals and wireless messages cannot be made from Oahu, then on Maui Island, six miles to the northward of Kula Sanatorium . . . at a point halfway between Lower Kula Road and Halakala Road (latitude 20°40′ N, longitude 156°19′ W, visible from seaward to the southeast and southwest of Maui Island), the following signal bonfires will be made daily until your EXEX signal is received: from 7 to 8, Signal 3 or 6, from 8 until 9, Signal 4 or 7, from 9 to 10, Signal 5 or 8.*

"Oh my stars," she whispered, reading the translation again. "Oh! Oh my stars!"

She waited, heart thumping, pencil tapping, until Kramer arrived. "Look, sir!" she exclaimed, jumping up even before he entered the room.

"Mrs. Edgars, please allow me to take off my coat and hat before you start badgering me," Kramer snapped, not happy to be working the weekend shift, especially after Bratton's false attack alarm of the previous weekend.

When he'd settled in at his desk, she walked to his open office door and knocked. "Please, sir," she said, holding out her translation of the decrypt. "Read this. I think it might be important."

Kramer looked cross as he took the papers. "I don't know why you're staying after hours to work on something that isn't even in your jurisdiction."

He picked up a pen and began to edit her copy. "You need to make your translations sound more professional, Mrs. Edgars."

After working at it a few minutes, he said, "Why don't you run along now, Mrs. Edgars. Although you've made a brave attempt at a translation, it still needs a lot of work. I'll have to finish the editing properly myself next week."

"But, sir—"

"Go home, Mrs. Edgars," Kramer insisted. "Your shift is over, and your husband is probably already there, waiting for his dinner. We'll get back to it on Monday."

Dr. Carroll knew he didn't have long if he wanted to solve the mystery of Clara Hess. "Tell me about the first time you revealed yourself to Dr. Teufel."

Clara smirked. "I thought he was going to piss his pants. He was trying to get her to change her name—he wanted her to have a spy name. So she told him about me—and how I was her doll when she was little, how I was her friend, how she thought I was alive. She was convinced I would talk to her. And of course I did!"

"Then what happened?"

"He gave her an IV drip—and she began to get a horrible stomachache."

"Do you know what was in the drip?"

Clara shook her head.

"Can you see the writing on the bag?"

She squinted. "S-sodium amatol," she said, as if reading.

Sodium amatol was a barbiturate that induced trance-like states. "And then?"

"And then she was I—I was she. I was in control of the body. I had the power."

"And what did you do?"

"I grabbed Dr. Teufel's arm. I said, 'It is I!' The idiot—he actually had to say, 'Who?' And I replied, 'Clara Schwartz!'"

"What did he do?"

"You should have seen his face!"

"What was it like?"

"Afraid. Very afraid."

"And after that, what did he do to get you to come out?"

"He would call my name—'Clara Schwartz! Clara Schwartz!' "

"And then what would happen?"

"Agna would get a horrible stomachache—and I would appear."

"And this required the medication?"

"At first. Then I didn't need it anymore. Oh God, she's coming back!" She doubled over as if in pain, clutching her abdomen. She moaned in agony, then slumped back to her bed.

After a few moments, her eyelids fluttered open. "Where am I?" she asked in a sweet voice.

"Where do you think you are?"

"England? Is it London?" She turned to him, her voice Agna's but older, a young woman's voice. "Where is my husband? My daughter?"

"What are their names?"

"Why, Edmund and Margaret. Edmund and Margaret Hope, of course. May I see them? I *must* see them!" Tears began to spill from her eyes. Suddenly she started, as if pierced by memory, and put a hand to her heart. "And Peter."

"Peter?" Dr. Carroll looked down at his file. "Peter who?"

"You can't tell them," she whispered. "No one must know."

"No, no, of course not—but who else must you see?"

"Peter. Peter Frain."

The woman clutched her abdomen. "It hurts, it hurts so much . . ."

Then came Clara Schwartz's rough voice again, as if nothing had happened. "The Aryan woman is not the concubine of the Jew! It's revolting and wrong! It's against the natural order of racial purity! Does a lion mate with a tiger? No! It's all about *breeding*. If a Jew mates with an Aryan, they should be sterilized. Any offspring should be *sterilized*."

"This is what you are taught?"

"Yes."

"Why were you taught to hate?"

"To get me ready for the mission."

" 'The mission'?"

"To London. To Edmund Hope."

"Who were you when you were with Edmund Hope?" Dr. Carroll decided to press further. "Did Agna know Edmund Hope?"

"I went to London, and Edmund knew only Agna. Grown-up Agna."

"Why?"

"Why?" Clara shrugged. "Agna is . . . lovable." She grimaced with disgust. "Like a fluffy cottontail bunny. And Edmund was an idiot. Plus, Agna didn't know anything. Not about the training, not about the mission. She could never confess anything, even under torture. Agna was the perfect dupe."

She smirked. "Of *course* they fell in love."

Dr. Carroll was on the telephone in his office. "Frain, I know what you think. But you must come, you must see her for yourself."

"I'm not up for a dog-and-pony show, Carroll. We're at war, if you haven't forgotten, and while we're bracing for the Kraut invasion, that doesn't mean we don't have any number of domestic threats, as well."

"Half an hour. Give me just thirty minutes. There's a new personality I want you to observe—an adult Agna. She's the one who was present in London—she's the one who married Edmund Hope, who gave birth to Maggie Hope . . . It was the personality of Clara who was the spy, but Agna was also in London."

"No."

"If she indeed has multiple personae, some of them are innocent. Then I must insist on getting another medical opinion before letting you proceed with this execution."

"Get as many opinions as you want, Doctor. But they won't sway mine. Unless Clara Hess is willing to cooperate, she'll be shot on December seventh. Let's see—that gives you until Sunday."

The phone rang, the bell shrill in the empty office. Kramer waited for Mrs. Edgars to answer it for him, then realized he'd already sent her home. He picked up the black receiver and barked, "Kramer."

"I've found something." It was Bratton. "You need to come over, quick."

"After your crying wolf last week?" Kramer snapped. "I don't think so."

"Just because the wolf wasn't there last Sunday doesn't mean there's not a wolf," Bratton retorted.

"Fine, fine." Kramer sighed. "I'll be right there." He dropped Mrs. Edgars's translation into his overflowing in-box, to be dealt with the following Monday.

When Kramer arrived at Bratton's office, he was cold, damp, and even more annoyed. "You scared everyone to death last week," he admonished, brushing melting snowflakes off the shoulders of his overcoat. "What is it *this* time?"

Bratton seemed oblivious to Kramer's sharp tone. "Tokyo's alerted its embassy here to stand by for a long message in fourteen parts."

"So?" Kramer took off his hat and coat and sat down. It was the weekend. Only a skeleton crew was working, all of them exhausted from last week's false alarm.

"After the transmission, the Japanese Embassy has been instructed to burn their code books and destroy their decryption machines." Bratton's eyes shone with determination, and his jaw was clenched. "This is it! This means war! I don't care—I'll stake my reputation on it! I'll stake my very *life* on it! The Japs are going to attack us!"

"Calm down," Kramer snapped. "You nearly gave me a heart attack last week. No one's in the mood for another false alarm, especially not on the weekend. Let me tell you, my wife sure was sore at me. I'm not going through that again."

"I'm sorry about your wife," Bratton said. "And I'm sorry I was wrong about the date. But I know I'm not wrong about the plan to attack. I *know* it."

Kramer began to think. "What about their aircraft carriers? Where are they?"

"We don't know," Bratton replied, his expression dour.

"We don't *know*?"

"We've lost them."

"You've *lost* the Japanese aircraft carriers?"

"Yes."

"Well, this just gets better and better, now, doesn't it," Kramer grumbled, shaking his head. "Have any scotch?"

Bratton pulled a bottle out from a desk drawer, handed it to Kramer, then pulled out two glasses. Kramer poured and both men sipped, lost in their own thoughts.

"I know it looks as if I'm crying wolf again, but I'm convinced they're going to attack us on Sunday. *This* Sunday. Sunday, December seventh."

"So, what can we do?" Kramer sounded resigned.

"Tokyo's holding the final part until morning, but if you would make the rounds with what we have, I'd appreciate it, Al."

Kramer started at the first use of his Christian name. "All right, Ruf," he replied at last, returning the compliment. "Let's wait for a few more parts to come in—and if they do, *then* I'll go to the President."

Maggie took Sarah by taxi back to her room at the Caledonian, where she fussed over her, fluffing her pillows, tucking a rose silk quilt over her, and making her tea. The blackout curtains were drawn, and the radiator clinked and hissed.

The telephone in the hall rang. It was one of the men from the front desk, saying there was a Mr. Mark Standish in the lobby for Miss Hope. "Do you mind if I meet with him?" Maggie asked Sarah, who was drifting in and out of sleep.

"Go . . . I'll be fine, kitten . . ."

"All right, but I won't be long, I promise."

Downstairs, Maggie crossed the lobby quickly. Mark started when he saw her. "How's our patient?" he asked, taking off his hat.

"Better," she said with a smile. "It's going to take a while, but I have no doubt she'll pull through."

Mark nodded. "Come, let me get you some tea to celebrate. Or something stronger?"

"Stronger, definitely."

The bar at the Caledonian had dark wood paneling hung with Sir David Wilkie paintings, full of shadow and menace. Picture lights glinted off the oils, and a fire crackled on the far side of the room.

They sat at a table in a corner near the fireplace. Mark ordered them both scotch. " 'The best thing for a case of nerves is a case of scotch,' as W. C. Fields likes to say," Mark remarked as the waiter set down two heavy glass tumblers.

"I'm not sure I'll need that much, but this is lovely, thank you."

"Least I could do." He lifted his glass. "To you, Miss Hope. I spent a lot of time thinking you were a waspish shrew and a willful, dangerous girl. But now I can see where 'winging it' can be a valid course of action."

Maggie lifted her glass and they clinked. "Thank you, Mr. Standish. Whatever my mistakes may be—and I know I've made plenty—at least I don't make them twice." She took a sip of the scotch. "And I am only occasionally a waspish shrew."

"Cheers. And please call me Mark. I think, after this case, Christian names are permitted?"

"Please call me Maggie." She smiled. Then, "What's happening with Diana Atholl?"

"She's been formally charged with the murders of Estelle Crawford and Mildred Petrie. She'll be in prison until the trial, which is scheduled for January of the new year."

Maggie watched the flames dance behind the grate. "Meanwhile, Richard Atholl, the man who had the affair, goes free."

"His lover's dead, his wife's in prison . . ." Mark pointed out. "Surely that's retribution?"

"You know," Maggie said, "they really are Atholls."

Mark stared at her, and then began to laugh. He laughed so loudly that the other patrons began to look over in curiosity and annoyance.

"Please, I've been waiting all week for someone to finally say it. And look, whether things work out between you and Hugh someday—well, regardless, it was a pleasure to work with you, Maggie."

"Likewise, Mark." Her eyes dimmed. "But alas, I believe that ship has sailed. Hugh and I . . . Well, even if we'd stayed together, can you imagine the dinner conversations? 'So, about that time your mother killed my father . . .' No." She shook her head. "It just wouldn't have worked out."

"And your RAF pilot?"

"Also not an option, for many reasons." For a moment, seeing Mark's wedding band glint in the firelight, Maggie felt just the slightest bit sorry for herself. And lonely. *But that's ridiculous.* "I do have a cat now." Maggie had a sudden longing to hold K and feel his fur against her cheek and the warmth of his compact body. "And, you know, I'm happy with that. Freud would have a field day with my so-called daddy issues—and so maybe it's best that I'm on my own."

"But not forever, certainly?"

"Mark, I don't know. In this line of work . . ." Maggie started, then realized she was thinking more of being an agent than an instructor. *Am I ready to go back into the field? But what about my old friend, the Black Dog?* ". . . Well, let's just say that at this point in time—given what I do—a cat is probably a better option than a beau. And certainly a better option than a husband."

Sarah will live. There is no public health scare. "You realize a man died that night, when his bike didn't make the jump over the ravine?" she asked.

"Yes," Mark said. "I do."

"And I'd do it all again, if I had to," Maggie said bleakly. Surprised, she realized it was true—to protect those she loved, she would kill. There was no hand-wringing now, as over the dead German boy she'd shot. And the Black Dog was silent.

I've become a professional, Maggie realized. *No more plucky ingenue.*

And whether that's a good thing or a bad, I have no idea.

———

Nomura was sitting on a leather sofa in front of a crackling fire in his embassy office. "When the transmission is finished, they want us to destroy our code books and our machines!"

Kurusu was sitting in a winged armchair opposite, his face impassive.

"*Only specially screened members of your communications staff are permitted to process the fourteen-part message and prepare the typed translation,*'" Nomura read. He looked to Kurusu. "It will be hard without the help of a skilled typist."

Kurusu pursed his lips. "Even though your employees here are Japanese, they have picked up the lazy American habit of the 'weekend.'"

"True," Nomura said, not wanting to argue. He, too, was fond of the "weekend." He was in the office on a Saturday night only to wait for the message. "But this is too sensitive to have one of the girls type it up. Who can we get, at this late hour?"

"I'll alert the code room," Kurusu said. "The situation right now between Japan and the U.S. is extremely delicate. We must be prepared to have each part of the message decoded as soon as it comes in—don't want things piling up."

Nomura studied his compatriot, his usually jolly face apprehensive. "Do you know what this is all about?"

"No," Kurusu said, his face poker-serious. "But I suspect all will be revealed tomorrow."

Dr. Carroll was not going to give up without a fight. He was determined to question Clara Hess once more, convinced that if he could just find the link between the adult Agna and Clara, perhaps the split could be repaired. "Do you consider Dr. Teufel to be your father?"

Clara played with her hair. "I suppose. I always thought I was hatched."

"Like Athena, from the head of Zeus?"

Clara snorted and lit a cigarette. "Nothing so grand. Like a chicken egg. Dr. Teufel was my mother hen."

"But Agna created you."

"I was with Agna when she was small, yes."

"But Dr. Teufel made it possible for you to come out fully, to take over Agna's body. What does she do when you're here?"

Clara blew out blue smoke. "She rests," she deadpanned.

"Rests? She's asleep?"

"Life is hard for her. My being here gives her a chance to rest."

"How do I control you?"

"The IV drips help me come out, but no—at a certain point I learned I could appear whenever Agna needed me. When life was too hard. When she wanted to rest."

"And why did he hatch you? What was his purpose?"

"To be the perfect spy, of course. Which I became. Which is what I was in England during the Great War."

"Were you ever afraid of him?"

Clara threw back her head and laughed, a rough, harsh laugh. "He—" She raised a finger and stuck it in Dr. Carroll's face. "—*he* was afraid of *me*."

"And what did he have you do?"

"Assignments—simple at first. Receiving an envelope, then holding it for pickup. Delivering packages around Berlin. Continuing Dr. Teufel's lessons.

"Agna doesn't care that the kikes are pigs," she said suddenly. "But they all stick together and try to cheat the Aryan. If you turn your back, they'll stick a knife in it."

"What if I were Jewish—would you hate me?"

"I only hate things that are worth hating."

"Do you hate yourself?"

"There's hate in everyone—and sooner or later it will always come out."

"But do you hate *yourself*?"

"No." Clara laughed, her disdainful laugh. "But I do hate Agna. And they don't just teach you how to hate—they teach you how to destroy."

"Destroy what?"

"You mean, destroy whom."

"Murder?"

"How to hit, how to kick, how to use your opponent's own strength and weight against him. Detect, destroy, demolish. We climbed ropes, took furniture apart with razor blades, loaded and unloaded guns . . ." She smiled proudly. "I became the perfect weapon. Dr. Teufel was proud of me."

"How do you know?"

"He liked to show me off. To his colleagues. Other doctors."

"What did he do?"

Her face darkened. "I don't want to talk about it."

"What did he do?"

Perspiration began to break out on her forehead. "No, no," she said, looking flustered for the first time since she had emerged. "No. I passed the test, I don't want to think about it anymore. They made it so I wouldn't remember!"

"What test?"

Clara put her head in her hands, unable to meet the doctor's gaze. "Dr. Teufel gave me the drip. Well, he gave Agna the drip, and then I appeared. It was a special performance for the other doctors." Clara began to tremble.

"What's wrong?" Dr. Carroll asked.

"I'm scared," she answered, looking up with large green eyes, sounding more vulnerable than she ever had before. For a moment, Dr. Carroll thought he might be speaking with Agna, but from her facial expression, it was still clearly Clara.

"Why are you scared?"

"They kept me over the weekend," she whispered.

Dr. Carroll made a note—Clara was reliving an experience. "The doctors?"

"Yes."

"Do you know the date?"

"It's 1914, right before I'm supposed to go to London. Dr. Teufel needs to prove to them that I'm perfect—the perfect agent. That I will do anything." She shuddered. "Absolutely anything."

"Where are you now?"

"In a sort of operating room," Clara said, her voice small. "Dr. Teufel is with me. There are some other doctors up in the gallery. It's a performance." She took a deep breath. "No food. No water. I felt sick."

Her eyes darted back and forth. "The nurses are pushing me down!" She appeared to struggle. "No! Stop it!" she shrieked.

"Are they administering the IV?" Dr. Carroll asked.

"No," Clara answered in a low voice. "I was already there." She squeezed her eyes shut. "He has a candle."

"A candle?"

"It's part of the performance. He lit it." She began to breathe faster. "No, no!" she cried. "No!"

"What's he doing?"

"He's asking me questions! He's trying to get me to denounce my blood, my race!" Clara gasped. "No! No!" She began to struggle. "He says it won't hurt, that he has total control, but . . ."

"What won't hurt?"

"He's trying to put the candle . . . he's trying to put the candle . . ." Clara's eyes were wild. "No! You said I wouldn't remember! That I'd *never* remember!"

"Was this part of the experiment?"

"Yes! To prove that I would let them do anything to me!" Then, "I hate you!" She growled, low in her throat, like a wounded animal. "I want to kill you!"

She made an ungodly sound, more of a howl than a scream. Then she went limp. Tears rolled down her cheeks. "He pushed it between my legs," she said in a little-girl voice. "And they all laughed and clapped. They *laughed* at me!"

She turned her face to the wall. "That was when I started to hate him. And that's when they realized I was ready."

"Ready for what?"

"Ready to go to England," she said flatly, without emotion. "Because they had created the perfect spy."

Chapter Sixteen

Dr. Carroll was in his office. It was late at night. He had Clara Hess's file in front of him.

As he read through, he tried to put the pieces together. A German woman named Clara Hess had surrendered herself to the British. She claimed she wanted to disclose Nazi secrets, but would only speak with her British-born daughter, Margaret Hope. When Miss Hope refused to see her, Clara refused to speak with anyone else, and fell into what he considered a depressive state.

Then, without any warning that he could see from her medical records, she not only revealed another personality, but regressed, into a girl of about five, named Agna Frei, who was sweet and innocent. Agna Frei had, in fact, been Clara Hess's maiden name, Agna Clara Frei. Clara had started out as a doll, but eventually became a facet of Agna's personality. She was created by the trauma of witnessing her parents' fighting, her mother's narcissism, and her father's neglect. Clara was brash and tough, with a sneer on her face and a chip on her shoulder. Her voice was different—lower and harder, harsh. She fiercely protected Agna, although she also longed for her own existence.

From what Dr. Carroll could put together from their fractured conversations, Agna Clara Frei had been recruited by Sektion, a precursor of the Abwehr, the German intelligence agency, who exploited her childhood trauma in order to create a completely separate alternate identity. Thus Agna Clara Frei became the woman known as Clara Schwartz. Clara Schwartz was an aspiring opera singer, but was also being secretly trained by Sektion to become a spy. When her training was complete, as evidenced by the trial with the candle—here Dr. Carroll shuddered—she was sent as Clara Schwartz to London. There she met Edmund Hope. But Edmund met and fell in love with Agna, not Clara. They married, and she had a daughter, Margaret Hope.

At some point her mission was concluded and she changed back into Clara, then went back to Berlin, leaving her husband and daughter to believe that she had died in a car accident. Secretly, though, she had staged the accident and escaped from the hospital, substituting the body of a prostitute in the morgue for her own, and making her way back to Berlin.

He sagged back in his chair and sighed wearily. It was ingenious, really. As part of the split personality, Agna could be kept in the dark, perfect for a cover. And Clara could step in when needed, obtaining the information Sektion wanted and then planning her escape. It all made perfect sense. Except for one thing.

Dr. Carroll made a note on Clara's chart. *What is Agna/Clara's relationship to Peter Frain?*

He looked at his desk calendar. Only twenty-eight hours until Clara's execution.

Across town from the Japanese Embassy, Kramer was pacing as Bratton went through the latest of the decrypts. "You're sure this is all thirteen parts?"

"Yes," Bratton said bleakly. The strain of the last month was showing. "Tokyo's holding the final part until tomorrow morning."

Kramer sniffed. "Well, I'm going to make the rounds with what we have so far. Thank God the President's back on the Magic distribution list. And let me know the moment the missing part arrives."

"Of course."

With his wife as his driver in their trusty blue Chevrolet, Kramer planned to deliver the message in locked briefcases to every single one of the addressees on his distribution list—General Marshall, Secretary Knox, Admirals Stark and Turner, Captains Ingersoll and Wilkinson.

At the White House, the President was in bed with a sinus infection. Kramer gave it to Harry Hopkins—who didn't have a Magic key. Hopkins accepted the thirteen-part decrypt, saying he would deliver it to the President. "But don't worry, the Old Man just sent a personal message to the Emperor. He's sure it will get negotiations back on track again."

At Admiral Stark's residence, his aide answered the door. "Admiral Stark can't be reached tonight, sir."

"Well, where the hell is he? I need to get this to him!" It was late, and Kramer was cold and tired.

"I'll do my best, sir."

At General Marshall's, the butler checked his watch. "It's after ten, sir, and General Marshall always retires early."

By now, Kramer was apoplectic. "Get me his private secretary!" he bellowed.

The butler was unruffled. "Yes, sir."

An assistant came and looked over the document. "I don't want to disturb the General for something that's incomplete, sir," the young man said, handing it back. "Let me know when the final part is in, and I'll give it to him then."

At Secretary Knox's residence, the windows were dark and no

one answered the door. Kramer had his wife drive him to the nearest phone booth, where he fumbled for change and cursed at his cold, stiff fingers as he struggled with the dial. At the Secretary of the Navy's residence, the telephone rang and rang.

Cursing, Kramer hung up.

Chapter Seventeen

The next day, Maggie and Sarah took the train from Edinburgh to Glasgow, changing trains at Queen Street Station under the great glass ceiling, pigeons pecking on the platform. Maggie had arranged for their things to be sent. Sarah leaned on a walking stick.

On the train from Glasgow to Fort William and then Arisaig, both young women were silent, watching the scenery as it passed. Fields neatly arranged and dotted with white farmhouses. Swiftly running streams and low fences. Telephone lines black against sky as blue as the Scottish flag.

Scotland's history flashed before them, the snowy mountains, created by ancient volcanoes and cut by primeval glaciers, the ruins of pagan stone circles, towns and lonely church spires, ancient graveyards set back on the curve of hills.

As they wended higher into the mountains, Maggie looked over at Sarah. "How are you doing?"

"My feet are freezing."

"It's not too much longer."

"I look at this and think of it being invaded."

"I know."

"Can you imagine this as Nazi territory?" Sarah asked, gesturing to the landscape out the window. "Since France was invaded, I haven't been able to banish the image from my mind. And now, my grandmother . . ." Her face clouded, but she didn't cry. Maggie took her hand.

She thought about the deadly anthrax Britain was developing. Would it keep the Nazis from invading? If anthrax was right to use as defense, what about offense? Was it being developed to be dusted over cities, cities with civilians?

At the highest elevation, the train pierced through clouds, the ground covered in snow, the evergreens becoming more sparse. Finally, after a stop at Fort William, the train pulled into the Beasdale station, where Mr. Burns was waiting to meet them and drive them back to Arisaig House. There was the sharp blow of a whistle, the scents of wood smoke and pine, and the tang of the sea. The tall pine trees were dusted with snow.

"Welcome, Miss Sanderson," Mr. Burns said, pipe clenched between his teeth. "I hear you'll be staying with us for a time."

"Yes, thank you, I do appreciate it."

"You must sign the Official Secrets Act."

"I have already."

His bushy eyebrows raised. "You have?"

"Yes, in July 1940. It should be on record." Sarah shot Maggie a look. "So, what exactly *do* you do for the war effort, Maggie?"

Maggie gave a sly grin. "Oh, a little bit of this and a little bit of that."

"Your cat missed you," Mr. Burns remarked as they climbed into his jeep. "And he was quite vocal about it. Mr. Fraser was not pleased. Neither was Riska."

It was cold and damp, the omnipresent damp that seeped into bones. The kind of cold only a hot bath and hours by the fire would dispel.

And so once they were back in her little apartment, Maggie lit a fire and ran Sarah a bath. While Sarah was in the W.C., she went through the icebox. Arisaig House's cook, Mrs. MacLean, had left a pot of stew that Maggie put on the stove to reheat. The aroma of the rich stew filled the room as the flickering fire warmed it.

However, K was nowhere to be found.

"K? K?" Maggie called. "Mr. K?"

She found him on her bed. He gazed at her, rose, stretched, and began to speak. If it had been English, it would have been profanity of the worst sort. *"Meeeeeeeeeeh!"* he chided. *"Meh! Meh! Meeeeeeeeh!"* And then turned his back on her, wrapping his tail around his body.

"I think you're in a bit of hot water there, Maggie," Sarah said, fresh from the bath, wearing one of Maggie's flannel dressing gowns, her hair in a towel. "He seems a bit put out."

Maggie was disappointed and tried not to show it. "Well, let's get you settled. Would you like a cup of tea? Dinner?"

"Something to eat would be lovely, thank you. It smells marvelous."

"That's good—if you're hungry, that means you're feeling better."

Sarah curled up in the worn armchair by the fire as Maggie banged and clattered in the tiny kitchen, ladling out bowls of venison stew. "Just glad it's not mutton," Maggie muttered, thinking of the sheep being poisoned with anthrax and repressing a shudder.

"Sorry?" Sarah called.

"Oh, nothing— No wine, I'm afraid, but I do have some of Mr. Fraser's cider put away, would you like a glass of that?"

"Yes, please."

When Maggie came out with Sarah's half-pint of cider, she found K on her friend's lap, purring and rubbing his cheek against her.

"Well, I see someone's making friends," Maggie said, setting the glass down. She tried not to be jealous.

K ignored Maggie, instead getting up on his hind legs and using his front paws to knead at Sarah's bosom.

"You know, K," Sarah said, smiling down at him, "I'm usually treated to cocktails and dinner before I let any taxi tigers make moves like this."

"Shall I remove him?" Maggie asked.

"Oh, no," Sarah said, petting his silky head. "Yes, you are a fine and handsome old thing," she said to the cat, rubbing under his chin. "But it's amazing what you can get away with. If any human tried this without so much as a by-your-leave, I'd have cut his hand off, just so you know."

The women began to eat their stew. Sarah finally had a chance to look around her and take in Maggie's living quarters. "Oh, Maggie, this is charming."

"And wait until you see the views tomorrow morning— mountains, the shore, and even a bit of the loch. When you're a bit stronger we'll take a walk down to the shore—it's absolutely beautiful. And until then, you will be a princess in a tower, with plenty of tea, healthy food, books to read . . ."

"So, is this handsome fellow the only man in your life?" Sarah teased, stroking K.

"Yes, he is," Maggie said, setting down a small bowl of stew on the floor. K eyed it, then begrudgingly wandered over to Maggie. After a brief standoff, he rubbed his furry face against her legs. "That's my K," Maggie said, scratching behind his ears. He butted his head into her leg, hard. All was forgiven.

She scooped K up and went back to sit near Sarah. "Cats and knitting," Maggie said. "That seems to be my lot in life right now."

"Socks come in pairs," Sarah said.

"Well, people don't. Or at least they don't have to. My life was just too complicated in London. But now it's simple—I work, I have a cat, I knit. I am Diana, the Virgin Huntress."

"But Diana's celibate!" Sarah cried, in mock horror.

"Believe me, I know."

"That's awful." Sarah dabbed at her mouth with her napkin and took a sip of cider. "Honestly, with two men in love with you, I don't see why you had to choose at all, Mags. Haven't you ever heard the phrase *ménage à trois*?"

Maggie choked. "Sarah!" Then, "Do *you* have someone special?"

"Not really. There was for a while, but . . ." Sarah rose and went to her bag, returning with a silver case of clove cigarettes and a lighter.

Maggie raised an eyebrow. "With your cough?"

"Oh bother, you're probably right. This being an invalid is a rather trying role."

"You must miss performing. Will you rejoin the ballet when you're well?"

Sarah shrugged. "Maybe. I was feeling frustrated already. Now I think . . ."

"What?"

"I'd like to do something to help the war effort. I'm not sure. Remember how back in London, I was torn about doing something so frivolous while there's a war on?"

Maggie remembered that day in Regent's Park well. "I do. And I also remember what I said then—that we need beauty and art—a reminder of all that's worth fighting for."

"Well, I'm not sure it's enough for me now," Sarah said. "Paris has been invaded . . . My grandmother was shot. *Shot.* I'm not sure I can just dance anymore. I want to *do* something."

Maggie chose her words carefully. "Whatever you decide to do, you know you'll always have my wholehearted support . . . Your French is very good, you know."

"How do you know?"

"When you were angry, at the hospital, you spoke perfect Parisian French."

"Merci beaucoup. Je parle Français depuis toujours."

"I have an idea," Maggie said.

"What?"

"Tomorrow I'll go and have a little chat with Mr. Burns."

"Yes?"

"I can't say. But if you're serious about helping the war effort, and you speak perfect French, I think that perhaps they can find you a little something."

In the darkness of night in the Pacific Ocean, 230 miles north of the Hawaiian Islands, all 183 Japanese planes were in their final positions on the aircraft carriers. The midget submarines had already been launched. And now the pilots were waiting, nerves strained, for their next order.

Admiral Yamamoto spoke to them by broadcast, played over the ships' loudspeakers. "You have just heard the Imperial Proclamation from the Emperor. The success of this mission depends on the element of surprise. If and when we achieve it, the code words *Tora! Tora! Tora!* will be sent out.

"Now that the time of battle draws near, I will not burden you with the usual pep talk. Instead, I shall hoist the famous Z flag, beneath which Commander in Chief Togo led his fleet to victory in the historic battle against the Russians."

Throughout the Japanese fleet, men cheered, all their training and courage leading up to this moment. Privately, Yamamoto still had questions. Once the microphone had been turned off, he said to his aide, "There's still one issue to be resolved—when to declare war officially. Our Emperor demands that war be declared before commencement of hostilities, as mandated by Article One of the Third Hague Convention, which we promised to uphold."

"Sir," the young man said, handing over a sheaf of papers, "Section Chief Toshikazu Kasc has written a diplomatic note for Ambassador Nomura to hand to Secretary Hull, prior to the launching of military operations. It is a declaration of war—but without immediately alerting the United States and losing the surprise element of the attack."

Yamamoto accepted the document, the *saigo no tsukoku* or "Final Notification," and read it through. There was no mention of Pearl Harbor or any immediate outbreak of hostilities. Still, the meaning seemed clear.

"Please take a message," Yamamoto said, "and send it to the Emperor and General Tōjō—that the Final Notification is adequate. And hostilities *must* not start until after it is delivered. It must be presented in Washington at precisely one P.M., exactly thirty minutes before the attack is to begin. This is crucial."

"Yes, sir."

The aide departed, and Yamamoto was left alone. His eyes went to the small kamidana altar on his credenza. "It's a gamble," he muttered. "I only hope it isn't a terrible mistake."

As Yamamoto prayed, the first wave of Zero planes launched from the Japanese task force's aircraft carriers in the darkness, flying off through the fog and clouds, en route to Pearl Harbor.

Chapter Eighteen

The next morning, Sarah still felt weak. But after tea and porridge, she began to do barre exercises holding on to the windowsill—a few demi-pliés and tendus, slowly building back her strength.

Maggie watched from the armchair, shoes off, feet tucked under her, hot cup of tea in hand. The blackout curtains were open and it was a glorious day in Arisaig, the sky a warm blue velvet. The windows were cracked open, and the air smelled clean and fresh after the previous night's rain. "Spring is coming," she said, sniffing. "I know it's winter, but you can smell it, can't you? Or at least the promise of spring."

Maggie sprang to her feet. "I must go to work now, but I'll check in with you later. Be good." She waggled a finger. "Naps. Lots of tea. And *no* clove cigarettes!"

The band at the Manoa Hotel was playing a cover of the Andrews Sisters' "Boogie Woogie Bugle Boy." Admiral Kimmel, with his wife on his arm, walked into the "Ball for Britain." The Manoa was known as the "First Lady of Waikiki"—a turn-of-the-century four-story Beaux-Arts building, right on the beach. The evening air smelled of jasmine.

They made their way through the hotel lobby, with high

Corinthian columns painted cream, and with huge vases of red anthurium and lazily turning overhead fans. They cut through to the back beachfront garden, where the party had already started. The courtyard was filled with chattering couples, clustered around ancient parasitic banyan trees with trunks the size of small cars, strung with fairy lights that glittered against the darkness. Torches burned around the perimeter, while candles shone in hurricane glasses. The ball was being held to raise money to send to support the British war effort.

Most of the men were in uniform and all the ladies were in bright-colored silk and satin gowns that glinted in the lights. Many of them had a flower, a plumeria or an orchid, in their hair. They wore the blooms Hawaiian-style—left for those taken and right for those looking. Kimmel and his wife, Dotty, found their table, and he pulled out her chair as she sat down. He took his seat.

"Those B-17s are coming in from California tomorrow, Admiral," one of the young men in a naval uniform already seated at the table said.

Dotty smiled. "Now, Captain—can't we have at least one night off from military talk?"

"My apologies, Mrs. Kimmel," the young man said, offering his hand as the band segued into "Stardust." "Would you care to dance?"

"Why, thank you, I would *love* to dance," she replied, with a significant look in her husband's direction. Kimmel grimaced and motioned to one of the waiters with a silver tray of drinks.

As they left for the dance floor, another sailor, a private, leaned in to speak with Kimmel. "They've arranged for Honolulu air to stay on all night, so that the signal can guide them in, sir." He had carrot-colored hair and a galaxy of freckles across his nose.

Kimmel laughed, accepting a Mai Tai garnished with a slice of pineapple and a maraschino cherry from a waiter's silver tray. "I hope they like the ukulele—only music the damn station ever plays!"

"Yes, sir. I'll be manning the Opana radar site tomorrow, sir."

"What time does your shift start?"

"Oh-four-hundred, sir."

Kimmel quirked a bushy white eyebrow. "Then shouldn't you be in bed?"

"Yes, sir!" he said, jumping to his feet and saluting. "Thank you, sir!"

Kimmel smiled. "What's your name, son?"

"Private Daniel Mathis, sir!" he said, saluting again from sheer nerves.

"Well, Private Mathis—I wouldn't say anything to your commanding officer if you had another drink before you left. Or a dance with a pretty girl."

"Yes, sir! Thank you, sir!"

Kimmel winked and downed his Mai Tai, motioning over the waiter for another. "It's not as if it's the end of the world."

Maggie went to the main house first, for any messages and her schedule. "Here you go, Miss Hope," Gwen Glyn-Jones said, handing her yet more messages from David.

"Thank you—" Maggie almost called her Twelve. "—Miss Glyn-Jones."

"You know my name!" the girl cried. She smiled, a warm, wide smile.

"Of course I know your name," Maggie said, feeling slightly ashamed of how she'd treated the trainees. "And I know I was a bit tough on you. But you're going to face . . ." Maggie had no idea what Gwen would face, where she would be sent, what she'd be up against—but she knew it wouldn't be easy.

"I just want you to survive," Maggie finished. "When this is all over, I'd like to know you've come back to Blighty in one piece. That's all."

"Thank you, Miss Hope," the girl said shyly.

Mr. Burns entered. "How's your friend feeling? It's Miss Sanderson, isn't it?"

"She's feeling a bit stronger this morning, thank you, Mr. Burns. By the way, I recently learned that not only does Sarah Sanderson have a beautiful French accent, but she's well acquainted with Paris—spent several summers there. She's recovering from an illness, but she's a trained dancer. She's strong and flexible."

"Really?" Mr. Burns said. "Do you think she'd like to interview for The Firm?"

"I think she would. Can we set it up?"

"Of course. If she's a dancer, she'll do well with the physical requirements. Not like—" He looked askance at Maggie. "—some people. And how was Edinburgh? You look better."

"I feel better, thank you."

"You were gone a bit longer than expected."

"An old friend at MI-Five needed some help."

"Glad we could lend you to them, then. But also glad you're back."

Satoshi Nagoka entered the room and went to his mail slot, picking up files, memos, and a few airmail letters with American stamps. "Thank you, Miss Hope, for teaching my class."

"Sorry?"

Then she remembered. The jujitsu class she'd taught before she'd left. How long ago it all seemed . . . "You're American," she realized, putting together the accent and the stamps. "I didn't know that. I'm from Boston," she said, holding out her hand.

"Nice to meet you, Miss Hope from Boston," he replied. "Satoshi Nagoka, from California, at your service. Thank you again for teaching the class."

Maggie nodded. "How did you get here?"

"The train from London, most likely the same way as you."

She laughed. "No, no—I meant from the U.S. to Britain. To Scotland. To SOE."

"Oh, that's a long, long story." Satoshi smiled. "You keep to yourself, don't you?"

Maggie blushed. "I suppose." Then she offered: "I have a cat."

"In Japan, cats are considered wise spirits. There are many *maneki-neko* statues, said to bring good luck."

"How do you know that?" Maggie asked. "Are you Japanese? Or American?"

"My parents are Japanese, and I've spent time there. But for the most part, I've lived in Northern California."

Maggie had never been to California. "In San Francisco? Japan Town?" she asked.

"No, Berkeley," he said, trying not to laugh. "My father is a professor at UC Berkeley."

"Oh," Maggie said. She had assumed . . . *I'm an idiot.* "I'm sorry for my mistake."

Satoshi smiled. "It's a common one—don't fret."

They walked to the large windows overlooking what used to be the formal gardens and badminton lawn. "What does your father teach?" she asked.

"Physics. For over twenty years."

"And what did you major in?"

"Trouble."

Outside, Maggie could see Riska frolicking in the grass, chasing a squirrel. "Oh, come now." As a professor's adopted daughter, Maggie knew opportunities were few and far between. "I'm a faculty brat, too—and so I question how much mischief you really made."

"It's true!"

"You made trouble at Berkeley? What did you do—break into a lab and release the mice?"

"I had a little trouble in J Town—or Japan Town, as you called it, in San Francisco." He winked.

"And is that where you learned jujitsu?"

"Well, it's not exactly a course offering at the university." Then, "So, you're a faculty brat, too?"

"My Aunt Edith, who raised me, is a professor of chemistry at Wellesley College, in Massachusetts."

"You didn't get into any trouble back then?"

"Long ago and far away, I was devoted to my studies—mathematics. Now—" Maggie held up her hands. "Well, let's just say that since I came to Blighty, about four years ago, I've been in my share of hot water." *If he only knew* . . . Maggie reached for the hard outline of the bullet in her side. She realized she hadn't thought about it while she was in Edinburgh.

"Anything you can share?"

"Not really. I'm sure you understand."

"I do. There are all sorts of rumors about you, you know. And since you don't actually talk to anyone, they keep growing. Soon you'll become the stuff of legend."

"I talk to Mr. Burns," Maggie said, feeling defensive. "And Mr. Fraser, the gardener. And, as I mentioned, I now have a cat."

"You're angry."

Maggie was surprised. "No. I'm not angry." But she thought about it. "Yes, I'm angry. But not with anyone here."

"I was able to see you teach the last part of my class last week. I watched from the dining room windows. You're hiding anger. That's not good."

"When you were trouble, were you hiding your anger?"

"Back then, I was fighting everyone—and everything. Yes, I was very angry. But I've learned a lot since." Satoshi grinned. "Good luck, Miss Hope."

"And good luck to you, too, Mr. Nagoka." They both bowed.

Maggie had some time before teaching her class, so she went down to the shore, with its view of the isles of Skye, Mudd, and Rhum, past the stones and broken shells, and rhododendron trees with buds promising pink blooms. On the beach, she was alone, with just the cries of the seabirds and the sound of the surf.

She sat down on a rock and looked over the water. Watching sparked a jumble of thoughts and images: *fluid dynamics, Sir Isaac Newton, kinetic energy, stationary action, the Euler-Lagrange equation* . . .

Maggie watched the waves crashing on the shore, then receding to gather strength, then crash once more. A warm breeze tugged at her hair, loosening tendrils from her tight bun. *The wave has to fall back in order to gather strength, before it can crash back onto the shore. Maybe that's what I'm doing here at Arisaig House, in Edinburgh. Receding and gathering up my strength. Maybe it's time to go back—to the SOE, to London, to where I can be useful again* . . .

She took off her jacket, laid it on the rock, jumped down, and took a few steps toward the water. Maggie took a deep breath and shook out her limbs.

She closed her eyes, breathing in and out, taking in as much oxygen as possible. With great deliberation, she began a series of movements, done slowly, gracefully—more like modern dance than martial arts.

She remembered what her first teacher had said: *"First, it will teach you how to breathe. When you breathe, you relax. When you relax, you clear the mind. Clearing the mind allows you to focus, and being focused allows you to live in the present moment.*

"As you begin, you step out, then turn in, with your weight in your bent knees—double weighted," she remembered. *"Let all the weight sink into the balls of your feet, keeping the bend in the knee."*

Maggie continued her sinuous movements. *"Now relax into the knees and let the energy fill you up, from your toes, up into the arms, and out into the fingertips. Now you want to relax and bring the arms back into the body, relaxing the hips, letting the weight sink back down into the balls of the feet. Let the energy draw back up into the fingers, then relax the arms back down to your sides."*

She wasn't the best at it, but remembered her instructor's words: *"Breathe. There is no great and no terrible here. Just doing and not doing. And you're doing."*

She took another deep breath of cold salty sea air and did the sequence again. And again.

"You could spend your whole life trying to get this move right, and it would not be a wasted life." She'd never before known what that meant, but now she did, her movements slow and graceful, her mind at rest, focused only on the present. She was both in it and of it, connecting with the sand, the water, the sun, and the sky.

In that moment, she felt strong again.

In that moment, she felt truly alive.

She felt a lightness, a change. Her cheeks were now rosy—flesh and blood instead of wax. *The force that through the green fuse drives the flower,* Maggie thought. She'd read it at school, but now she finally understood.

Finally, Maggie floated her hands down to rest at her sides. There were tears in her eyes. She looked out over the water, at the large black rocks rising above the waves, and saw that she'd attracted an audience. Eight gray seals had stopped to sun themselves there, and perhaps wonder at the sight of the curiously moving human. There was a brief moment when seal eyes met human eyes and the light changed just slightly to a more rosy hue, and the wind gentled, just a little.

Maggie suddenly remembered all the times she'd come to the shore and thought of death, of filling her coat pockets with stones, like Virginia Woolf, or swimming out too far, like Edna Pontellier.

Maggie took off her wristwatch. She removed her shoes and sweater, then dropped the rest of her clothes. She walked naked over the sand to the water.

She stepped in and gasped. The water was icy on her toes, then feet, then legs, until she was up to her neck. She dove under the water, and came up giggling. It was cold, but agreeably so, the Gulf currents making it less frigid than it looked.

Something bubbled up inside her, warm and delicious, and for a moment she didn't know what it was.

Then she remembered.

It was happiness—and it flowed through her veins until it reached her mouth, turning it upward into a smile. For a moment she was afraid to move. But then she realized, it was like the waves—even if it disappeared, even if it disappeared for a long, dark time, it would eventually come again.

"I think," Maggie called to the seals, who were still regarding her curiously, "that after I teach my class today, I'll have that bullet removed."

It was a beautiful Sunday morning in Washington, chill and blue. The streets were still quiet, with birdsong louder than the usual traffic. Dead leaves swirled and eddied in the breeze.

Bratton and Kramer were in the "Magic" room, going over the fourteenth part of the message from Japan to the United States as it came in, the clicking of the typewriters loud in the silence. Both men had stayed up all night and were pale and hollow-eyed. Their jackets were off and ties askew.

Bratton read the latest decrypt, translating it as it came in: *"Will the Ambassadors please submit our reply to the United States government at precisely one p.m., December seventh, your time."* He looked up at the row of clocks. "What the hell's the significance of one P.M.?"

Bratton kept reading and translating. *"After deciphering part fourteen, destroy at once your cipher machine, all codes, and secret documents."*

The two men looked at each other. "They're going to attack at one, Eastern Standard Time," Kramer said.

Bratton started to pull on his jacket. "I'll find General Marshall, you find Admiral Stark." He looked up at the clock with wild eyes. "We still have time."

"Dr. McNeil?" Maggie said, pushing open the door to the veterinarian's office.

The doctor was at his desk, his bushy white hair as wild as ever, typing up invoices with his two pointer fingers. "Who are you?"

"Maggie Hope. I adopted the cat from your office last week."

"Well, I wouldn't have recognized you, Doreen. You're not half as pale and pinched as you were. But you can't give the cat back. No matter how obnoxious he is."

"No, no—the cat's fine," she said. "Dr. McNeil, I know you only work with animals—"

"Farm animals, lassie. Large brutes of the field. No dogs and no cats."

She looked at his typing. It was riddled with errors. "What about humans? A human's an animal. Sometimes not even as noble as animals."

"What are you getting at, lassie?"

Maggie took off her coat and untucked her blouse, revealing the flesh just above her waist. The scar from the bullet was red and angry.

"Looks like you have an infection, there."

"I have a bullet there," Maggie retorted. "And it needs to come out. I'd like you to do it."

"I don't do cats and dogs—and I don't do humans. Go find a people doctor—Fort William has a few. I can make a call—"

"Dr. McNeil," Maggie interrupted, "I want it removed *now*. It's been in there far too long, and now it's time to come out. And," she added, with a sly smile, "I'm an expert typist—even typed for Prime Minister Winston Churchill once upon a time. I'm sure I can help you with this batch of invoices. What do you say?"

The vet glared. "You drive a hard bargain, lass."

Maggie grinned. "I do."

"Should I even ask why you're carryin' around a bullet in yer middle?"

"Probably not. But let's get it out now, shall we?"

Bratton burst into the offices of the Deputy Chief of Staff of Intelligence. "Where's the General?" he barked.

The assistant covering the desk was freckled, slight, and fair-haired. "It's—it's Sunday morning, sir."

Bratton exhaled with impatience. "I'll need to use your phone," he said, reaching for the receiver.

"Yes, this is Colonel Bratton," he said. "Connect me with the Chief of Staff, General Marshall." He began drumming on the desktop with his fingertips. "Yes, at his quarters in Fort Myer."

There was an interminable wait while Bratton listened to the piercing ring of the telephone. He kept checking his watch. Finally, someone at Fort Myer picked up. "This is Colonel Bratton," he repeated. "I need to speak with the General, ASAP."

He rubbed at the back of his neck with his free hand. "What do you mean he's not there?"

Then, "He's out *riding*? Well, somebody better mount up and gallop after him!"

In the Japanese Embassy, the clicks and clacks of hunt-and-peck typing ceased. The typist, sweaty and disheveled from his efforts, burst into Ambassador Nomura's office, where he and Special Envoy Kurusu were waiting. They, too, had been up all night, and while their posture was impeccable, there were violet circles under their eyes.

The typist bowed deeply, then said, "Here's another part of the document, sir." He cleared his throat. "We are instructed to deliver the fourteen-part message at exactly one P.M., sir."

They all looked to the grandfather clock in the corner of Nomura's office. It was already after eleven.

"One P.M.?" Nomura shouted, standing. It was the first time the usually placid man had ever raised his voice in the office, and the other men stared at him, mouths agape. "Hurry! Or else we'll never have it ready for Secretary Hull in time!"

Kramer had reached the office of Admiral Harold Rainsford Stark, Chief of Naval Operations, out of breath, his white silk scarf undone, threatening to slip from around his neck. He handed the document to the Admiral, who looked askance at Kramer's demeanor, his own thick white hair perfectly combed and square jaw set.

Stark left Kramer standing as he read through the document,

taking his time, while sunlight through the government-issue blinds cast lines across both men's faces. A clock ticked on the mantel. Finally, Stark looked to Kramer. "This message indicates the Japanese are going to attack."

Relief flooded Kramer's face. "Yes, sir."

"Thank you." Stark waved a hand. "You may go now."

Kramer shifted his weight. "Sir, as hostilities seem imminent, shouldn't we telephone Admiral Kimmel in Hawaii?"

Stark's eyes widened. The Admiral was not used to being told what to do. "No. I'm going to call the President first." He looked Kramer up and down, taking his measure. "I need to speak to the President in private."

Kramer saluted and left. When Stark called the number, it was busy.

Chapter Nineteen

At the large desk in his office, General George C. Marshall, Chief of Staff U.S. Army, looked over Bratton's documents, as Colonel Bratton chewed the inside of his lip.

"*The Japanese government,*" Marshall read, "*regrets to have to notify the American government hereby, that in view of the attitude of the American government, it cannot but consider that it is impossible to reach an agreement with further negotiations . . .*"

He skimmed the rest of the papers, then looked up. "Colonel Bratton, I do believe you're right. This document convinces me that the Japanese will attack at or shortly after one P.M. today."

Bratton, who'd been dressed down by Marshall after the previous week's false alarm, swelled with pride and relief. Marshall scrawled a message down on a piece of his personal stationery for distribution to the commanding generals in the Philippines, the Canal Zone, and the Presidio. It read: *The Japanese are presenting at thirteen hundred EST today what amounts to an ultimatum. Also, they are under orders to destroy their code machines immediately. Just what importance the hour set may signify, we don't know, but be on alert accordingly.*

"Don't you think we should let Admiral Kimmel in Hawaii know, too, sir?"

"Let me call Stark first," Marshall said. He spoke a few minutes with Stark, and listened, and then hung up. "Admiral Stark doesn't think any additional warning is necessary."

The telephone rang, and it was Stark again; the Admiral had changed his mind. "Yes, sir—we'll take care of it." To the list of people getting the memo Marshall added in a scribble: *Inform the Navy.*

"Colonel Bratton, please take this to the communications center. They'll get it out to Admiral Kimmel and the rest of them in the Pacific."

"Yes, sir!" Bratton said, saluting.

"And if there's *any* question of priority," Marshall called after him, "get it to the Philippines first!"

Bratton ran down the hall to the Communications Center. "This is urgent!" he panted, thrusting the thick, engraved sheet out to Colonel Edward F. French, chief of Traffic Operations. "General Marshall wants it sent to all Pacific commanders by the fastest possible method!"

At his desk chair, French stared at the page for a long moment. He looked back to Bratton. "The General's handwriting . . ." he said, shaking his head. "What a mess. I can't read it. You're going to have to help put it into some kind of legible copy."

Bratton, at the limits of both patience and sanity, opened his mouth to spew profanities at the man—then closed it. He sat down to transcribe the note using the typewriter at the empty secretary's desk, hunting and pecking one key at a time.

When he handed the typed message back to French, it was precisely two minutes before noon.

———

At the Japanese Embassy, Nomura's typist was also still hunting and pecking. He took off his jacket and rolled up his sleeves. He went back to the document, hit a wrong key. *"Chikusho!"* he swore, sweat breaking out on his upper lip. Then he crumpled up the piece of paper and threw it in the trash. He took out a fresh sheet and rolled it into the typewriter to try again.

In the office adjoining, Nomura paced while Kurusu sat absolutely still. "The typist still isn't finished!"

Kurusu nodded, unruffled. "We will have to postpone our one o'clock meeting with Secretary Hull."

Nomura ground his teeth in frustration.

Bratton hovered as Colonel French sent the message from General Marshall. Finally, French sent him away, saying everything was in the works, and it would take thirty to forty minutes to get through.

But French struggled with the messages, especially the one to Admiral Kimmel in Hawaii. He took the message himself to the signal center, but the channel to Fort Shafter had been out since ten thirty because of bad weather.

"Direct channel to Hawaii's out, sir." The aide was young and untried, and annoyed to be at the office on a Sunday morning.

"Shit!" French began pacing. "The weather's that bad? No sign of it clearing?"

"No, sir. We—we could always give it to the Navy, sir."

French shot him a deadly look. "Do you think the weather will be more cooperative for the Navy than it is for the Army?"

The young man shrank in his seat. "No, sir."

French thought. "Well—then we'll have to send the damn thing as a telegram! Call Western Union!"

"Yes, sir. Right away, sir."

In his bed at his home in Honolulu, Kimmel was woken up by a shrill telephone. "Kimmel," he grumbled into the receiver, feeling the effects of both the late night and the cocktails.

He listened. And sat up, eyes widening. Then he spoke. "Do you mean to say a submarine was reported, and shots were fired, and it's taken you this long to report it to me? No—I don't *care* if it still hasn't been confirmed. I should have been informed *immediately*! Get the report and confirmation over to my office! *On the double!*" He threw both the telephone and receiver at the wall. It fell with a crash and the tinkle of bells.

"Honey—" his wife murmured from the bed, pushing away the quilt and rubbing her eyes.

"Not. Now. Dear," Kimmel growled as he went to put on his uniform.

It was barely dawn in Honolulu when the telegrams finally came in to the Western Union office. "Messages for Admiral Kimmel and General Short, sir," said a clerk, painfully thin with wide-set eyes.

"Are they marked urgent?" the manager asked. He was older, grayer, and had a cup of hot coffee and a Portuguese sweet roll on his desk he wanted to get back to.

The clerk looked over the document. "No, sir."

"Then just type them up and put them in their respective boxes. Their secretaries'll pick 'em up Monday morning."

"I don't have all the fancy anesthetic you might expect, being from London and all," Dr. McNeil said, scrubbing his hands with soap and hot water. "But we Scots do claim Joseph Lister as our own—so no need to worry about infection."

"That's all right," Maggie said, gritting her teeth.

"I think I have some brandy somewhere, if you want it . . ."

"No. No thanks." Her hands gripped the table, her knuckles turning white.

Dr. McNeil examined the wound. "It's close to the surface—that's good," he said, cleansing the area with raising antiseptic fluid on a cotton pad.

Just do it! Cut it out! was all Maggie could think.

And then he lowered the scalpel.

Clara felt in the darkness for the reading glasses she had next to her book. Dr. Carroll had even been kind enough to give her a leather case. Clara smiled as she opened it, then took out the glasses. She opened her blackout curtains and let the moonlight stream in.

She took the glasses and broke off both earpieces. She put one of the lenses under the leg of her chair, placing the glass carefully so that only one half of the lens would be crushed under the chair leg. She pushed down on the seat of the chair. Nothing happened. *"Scheiß, "* she muttered.

She sat down on the chair, and heard a satisfying crunch as the glass shattered. She knelt down to inspect the damage. There were splinters and shards of glass, which glinted in the moonlight. But there was one large piece.

She picked it up, holding it in her palm, almost as if weighing it. "Yes," she said. "This will do. This will do nicely." In the light of the moon, she smiled. "Through a glass darkly," she muttered.

And then she slit her wrists.

———

Yamamoto waited in silence in his office, at his desk, eyes closed, a globe next to him.

There was a knock at the door, and "Sir!"

"Enter."

The officer could barely contain his excitement. *"Tora! Tora! Tora!"* he exclaimed. "The strike force has achieved complete surprise!"

Yamamoto opened his eyes, his shoulders dropping slightly. He looked at the officer. "What about the U.S. aircraft carriers?"

The man's face dropped. "At sea, sir."

"And when did the U.S. government in Washington receive our final notification? Before hostilities commenced?"

"We're still waiting to hear, sir. There have been some issues in getting a signal through to Washington."

Yamamoto closed his eyes again and folded his white-gloved hands, as if in prayer. "The game hasn't even begun."

After hearing about the USS *Ward*'s bombing of an unidentified submarine in Hawaiian waters, Kimmel had canceled his golf date with General Martin and called for his driver. Even though it was Sunday morning, he was going in to the office.

There was a roll of thunderous noise from outside, but it went on too long to be thunder. Kimmel, uniform still unbuttoned, ran down the stairs to the front garden, along with his wife and the rest of the staff. From his front lawn he had a perfect view of Pearl Harbor.

They looked up at the sky and saw the outlines of Japanese Zero planes flying overhead, so close that the blowback nearly knocked them down. The morning sun had risen red, and its crepuscular rays looked like the flag of Japan.

Over Pearl Harbor, torpedoes began to fall and Admiral Kimmel, watching the destruction of the U.S. fleet, fell to his knees.

Chapter Twenty

When Clara regained consciousness, she was in a hospital.

Her wrists were bandaged in white gauze. An IV was stuck into a vein of her inner elbow.

There was a figure on the chair, a man in a rumpled suit, his usually perfectly Brylcreemed hair mussed, a file of papers, still unread, on his lap. He gazed, unseeing, out the window, at flakes of swirling snow.

But when he sensed Clara's eyes open, he trained his eyes back to her.

"Peter," she said, smiling weakly. "You came."

"If you'd really wanted to kill yourself, you would have slit your carotid artery—you wouldn't have wasted time with your wrists," said Frain, unable to tear his eyes away from Clara's.

She smiled, a satisfied cat-like smile. "I bought myself some more time," she said. "I know British law. Even though I was scheduled to be shot the next morning, you wouldn't have let me bleed out on the floor. The moral inconsistencies of your people amuse me to no end."

Frain put his thumb and forefinger to the bridge of his nose.

"No," Clara said. "I know your ways. I knew that you would hospitalize me, and wait until I've recovered, and *then* shoot me." She smiled. "You British are so civilized."

"Now that you're awake, I'll leave you in peace," Frain said, gathering up his belongings.

"No, no," Clara said, never taking her eyes from his. "It's been, let's see—how long? Twenty-five years now?" Her gaze flicked up and down his body. "You've aged well, Peter, I must admit. Except for the gray in your hair and a few more wrinkles, you look the same."

"I'm not the same, Clara," he said, putting his files in his briefcase and rising to his feet. "And neither are you."

"How do you know that?" she mocked. "You don't know me. You don't know what I've been through over there. In Germany . . . They're insane—do you understand? Hitler is insane and he's surrounded himself with yes-men who cater to his every whim. I did what I needed to do to stay alive. To keep my family in Berlin alive." She looked at him, eyes wide. "I did what I had to, to *survive*."

Frain put on his overcoat. "Yes, I'm sure," he answered drily. "And what of your family here? Did you ever think about them? And now that you're here, what of your family back in Germany?"

"Margaret, yes, of course. You know how I loved her. But Edmund—no. He was a means to an end. Miles—well, that marriage was dead long ago. And Elise . . ."

"Yes?"

Clara shook her head. "Too pious for her own good, but Elise is a survivor, too. I'll bet on it."

"And me?" he asked, putting on his hat and shrugging into his overcoat.

"Peter," she said, her eyes green and wide. "I loved you. I always loved you. And we both know you loved me, too."

———

The clock in Secretary Hull's antechamber ticked as Ambassador Nomura and Special Envoy Kurusu waited. It was five minutes past two in Washington.

Hull was just finishing up a telephone conversation with President Roosevelt. "Yes, Mr. President," he said, standing, his eyes like flint. "And it's been confirmed by multiple sources?" Then he sat, his knees buckling under him, hitting the leather seat with a bang he didn't even notice. "All right then. Yes, they're about to arrive. Of course I won't let on that we know when I receive them. Yes, Mr. President. Thank you, Mr. President."

Hull hung up the telephone and took a ragged breath. He called out to his secretary, "Send them in."

Nomura and Kurusu entered. Both bowed, then Nomura handed Hull the fourteen-part document, the so-called Final Notification.

Hull picked up his pince-nez and pretended to read it for the first time.

When he was done, he rose to his full height and began what his grandmother would have called a Tennessee tongue-lashing. "In all my fifty years of public service, I have never seen a document so crowded with infamous falsehoods and distortions. On a scale so huge, that I never imagined until today that any government on this planet was capable of uttering it." Hull would not meet Nomura's eyes.

While Nomura looked wounded, Kurusu's face remained unreadable.

"Mr. Hull . . ." Nomura began.

"Go," Hull said softly. "Go now and never come back."

Gil Winnant, the American Ambassador to London, was Churchill's special guest at Chequers. Still, the P.M. didn't go easy on him. "Where are the Americans?" Churchill asked as they drank in his study before dinner, his voice breaking. He was exhausted. There was no time left for flatteries and subtleties. It was do or die.

"Mr. Churchill," replied Winnant, "I wish I could say. You know if it were my decision, the U.S. would be in this war already, but the President—"

"*Your* president . . ."

"—by most people's standards FDR's doing enough with Lend-Lease. But even he can't declare war—"

"Yes, yes, only bloody Congress can declare war!" the P.M. roared. "I am half-American! My mother was Jennie Jerome, from Brooklyn Heights, New York! I know how these things work!"

"Of course, Prime Minister. But with public opinion the way it is . . ."

"The President told me he would find a way of going to war, even on a pretext. Nazi submarines have sunk American ships, and still he bides his time. After Hitler's done in Russia it will be our turn. And if we are gone, who's next in line? I had such high hopes after the Atlantic Charter . . ."

Winnant looked apologetic. "The President must walk—so to speak—a very fine line. He must support Britain, but not alienate the antiwar faction . . ."

The Prime Minister regarded Winnant from above his golden spectacles, then chose his words carefully, as if he had come to a decision. "I will tell you one thing—you're not going to be neutral forever. The U.S. is like Prospero in Poe's 'Masque of the Red Death'—war, like Death, will prove impossible to avoid forever. And now, please excuse me, Mr. Ambassador. I have a war to fight."

Admiral Yamamoto was still sitting statue-still, white-gloved hands folded in front of him. A military march played over the ship's loudspeakers, and officers chatted, some smoking cigarettes, and some drinking sake from small ceramic cups. With the exception of Yamamoto, the atmosphere felt like a party.

The Japanese radio announcer broke into the music. *"Just in—we have an announcement from the Navy Department, released today, December eighth. Before daybreak, the Imperial Navy successfully launched a large-scale air attack against the United States Pacific Fleet in Pearl Harbor, Hawaii, destroying the U.S. Fleet. We salute the Commander in Chief of our Fleet, Admiral Yamamoto."*

The men applauded. "The attack went as planned!" one called. "It was a success!" shouted another.

Yamamoto remained motionless. "Yes, but did the U.S. government receive the communiqué before one P.M.?"

One of the men sobered, facing Admiral Yamamoto. "Ambassador Nomura was late in Washington, sir. And Air Commander Fuchida was early in Hawaii."

Yamamoto shook his head. His face was tired and sad. "We didn't follow Geneva Conventions—and now we look every bit like the sneaky slit-eyed dwarfs their propaganda paints us."

Conversation in the room ceased. Yamamoto kept speaking, as though to himself. "I had intended to strike a fatal blow to the American fleet by attacking Pearl Harbor immediately after Japan's official declaration of war. But according to all our reports, we attacked *fifty-five minutes before* the message was delivered. I can't imagine anything that would infuriate the Americans more than what they're going to see as a 'sneak attack' by the Japanese. The Emperor, too, will be most displeased.

"The fact that we have had a small success at Pearl Harbor is nothing. The fact that we have succeeded so easily pleases people. But they should think things over—and realize how serious the situation will become."

———

News of the attack was spreading. *"Here is the news, and this is Alvar Lidell reading it,"* sounded the burnished tones of the BBC announcer over the hiss of the airwaves.

"Turn the damn thing up!" Winston Churchill bellowed from across the Hawtree Room at Chequers. "What's Lidell saying?"

"Winnie," his wife, Clementine, chided. "Language, dear—really."

"Not now, Clemmie!" the old man snapped, stomping over to the wireless. He fiddled with the buttons and dials of the Emerson. "How the hell do you fly this damn thing? Inces! Where are you, you damn fool?"

David stepped in and adjusted the knobs.

"This just in," Lidell was saying.

"Shhhhh," the Prime Minister growled to the assembled crowd, who were chatting over Martinis and silver bowls of smoked almonds: American Ambassador John Winnant; Averill Harriman, Roosevelt's special representative in the UK; Harriman's daughter Kathleen; and the P.M.'s daughter-in-law, Pamela Churchill.

Then Lidell's usual professional veneer broke. *"Japan has launched a surprise attack on the American naval base at Pearl Harbor in Hawaii, and has declared war on Britain and the United States,"* he squeaked, voice pitched slightly higher because of adrenaline.

"Turn it up!" the P.M. roared.

"The U.S. President, Franklin D. Roosevelt, has mobilized all his forces and is poised to declare war on Japan.

"Details of the attack in Hawaii are scarce but initial reports say Japanese bombers and torpedo-carrying planes targeted warships, aircraft, and military installations in Pearl Harbor, on Oahu, the third largest and chief island of Hawaii."

The Prime Minister looked up, shocked. He and John locked eyes, and John's eyebrows rose. *The date line,* John mouthed. Churchill nodded. It was December eighth in Tokyo. But it was still December seventh in Pearl Harbor. They had forgotten to factor in the date line.

"News of the daring raid has shocked members of Congress at a time when Japanese officials in Washington were still negotiating with U.S. Secretary of State Cordell Hull on lifting U.S. sanctions imposed after continuing Japanese aggression against China . . ."

Across the table, Winnant's face was stone. "No . . ." he muttered, as if to himself. "I can't believe it. Sure, if there was an attack, it was the Philippines . . ."

"America—like it or not—has finally joined this world war," the P.M. intoned, his voice rising in volume, as though he stood before the House of Commons. "Germany will honor the pact and back Japan. We, of course, will support the United States. And the U.S. will have no option but to declare war on Germany!"

With effort, he climbed up onto his chair and raised a fist. "We shall fight Japan!" he said, his usually booming voice breathy. "We shall declare war on Japan and support the United States of America!"

"Let me just have the details confirmed, Prime Minister, before you have the U.S. declaring war due to a radio announcement." Winnant's voice was shaking.

The Prime Minister waved him off with one hand. John and David ran to stand behind Churchill, should he topple over in excitement.

"This is a day of great joy!" the Prime Minister exclaimed, as though addressing his countrymen from the balcony of Buckingham Palace. "With the United States at our side, we will win, of that I have no doubt. England will live! Britain will live! The Commonwealth of Nations and the British Empire will live, I say! *Live!*"

He opened his arms wide, as if to embrace the whole of his people. "Once again in our long island history, we shall emerge—however mauled and mutilated—safe and victorious! Victorious, I tell you! There *will* always be an England!"

Winnant, still seated, took the Prime Minister's measure. He spoke slowly, still in shock. "We lost untold men at Pearl today," he said. "And now it looks as if we've been pulled into a war I'm not convinced Japan really wanted. With all due respect, I believe it is in poor taste to gloat over the bodies of the dead, Mr. Prime Minister."

Churchill's face darkened. "Men, Winnant. *Military* men," he said, enunciating each syllable. "Soldiers. Sailors. On duty. Do you know how many military men *we* have lost? Do you know how many civilians—women and children, babes in arms, the old and infirm—we lose nightly? Why, we lost as many men just yesterday on the *Repulse* and the *Prince of Wales*! And no one even blinks an eye! Do you think American blood is more precious than ours?"

Winnant shook his head and drained his Martini.

Churchill looked at Winnant, a long, hard look. "Welcome to the war, Mr. Ambassador," he said, as John and David helped him down, then pulling out a cigar from his jacket pocket and sticking it between his teeth. "Better late than never."

Then, to David: "And gimme President Roosevelt on the telephone. Immediately!"

Hugh Thompson had made it through the SOE training camps in Scotland, and was doing what was called finishing school at Beaulieu, a large estate in the New Forest. The last of the spy training camps was set in a manor house and cathedral on glorious grounds, with gardens, lawns, and walkways overlooking the Beaulieu River. It was where secret agents finished their training: in bur-

glary, forgery, sabotage, disguises, living off the land, and assassination.

Hugh had started out as an MI-5 agent, like his father before
him, until a situation with Abwehr spymaster Clara Hess had become so personal that he'd been fired for unprofessional behavior.
And so, when agent Kim Philby had shown up at a pub in London,
with his red tie and double-folded handkerchief, to recruit him, it
had seemed like divine Providence.

Suddenly Hugh's life had purpose again. He would be a spy. He
would use his knowledge of the French language to help a French
resistance group. *La Résistance!*

As Hugh finished up his training in F Section, he became restless. His fellow trainees were being sent off, parachuted God only
knew where. When would it be his turn? At the pub in town, Hugh
finished yet another beer as he listened to Lidell on the wireless.
When the news was announced, there was stunned silence, then
cheering, as people put together that the United States would finally be entering the war.

"Mr. Thompson!"

Hugh looked up from his glass. It was Philby. "Have you
heard?" Hugh asked. "About Pearl Harbor?"

"Yes," the older man said. "Walk with me."

Hugh put a few coins on the bar and the two men made their way
outside. "I wanted to speak with you. You see, I'm being re-
assigned. I'm leaving SOE and transferring to MI-Six," Philby said.

"Oh."

"But I do have a special mission in mind for you, and I wanted
to speak with you about it before I go."

"Yes, sir."

"In France, we've discovered that making connections with
and working with Communists is our only hope of fighting Fascism. I'm not sure where you stand ideologically . . ."

"I hate Fascism with all my heart and soul," Hugh vowed.

"Well, Great Britain and Russia are allies now. The bulldog stands with the bear."

"I had a brief flirtation with Communism at university," Hugh admitted.

"Where were you?"

"Selwyn College, for a degree in theology. But on scholarship." He shook his head. "The class divisions were hell."

"Ah," Philby said, nodding. "I was at Trinity. I know exactly what you mean."

Hugh cocked his head. "I was influenced by E. M. Forster: *'All men are brothers. All men are equal.'*"

"And so you'd have no issues working with French Communists?"

"No, sir, not at all."

Philby smiled. "Excellent. Your cover is that you are the newest member of the orchestra of the Paris Opèra Ballet. You are military excused from service because of a weak heart, and will take over as one of the cellists. I was told you play the cello quite well—is that true?"

"I play, I'm not sure I'm up to that level . . ." Hugh was flustered.

"Well," Philby said, "start practicing. We have several resistance contacts among the orchestra, the ballet, and the intelligentsia. They are an armed branch of French Communists, called Francs-Tireurs et Partisans—the Free Fighters and Partisans, or FTP."

"Who will be my radio operator?"

"We're still looking. There's someone we have in mind, but she has more training to do before she can be considered."

———

Churchill was finishing his transatlantic telephone call with President Roosevelt when David and John came in. "Yes, Mr. President—we're all in the same boat now. Good night." As he hung up the telephone receiver, the Prime Minister's face broke into a beauteous smile. "Gentlemen," he said, "pack your bags, we are going to America!"

"To Washington?" David asked, astonished. "For how long? How many staff?"

"Tell Cook to make some sandwiches and bring them up—it will be a long night. We have much to plan, much to arrange. We shall go to Downing Street first, and then I want to leave as soon as possible." He blinked, then looked at the two men. "Have either of you ever been to America?"

David and John looked at each other. "No—no, sir," they both said in unison.

"I need an American, or at least someone who speaks American . . . Look at the debacle between Popov and that Hoover chap . . . I'm sure it was a language mishap."

"They *do* speak English, sir," David ventured.

"Two nations divided by a single language—I shall need a translator! For language and customs! We don't want to misstep. *And* I'll need a typist." Churchill looked thoughtful. "Where is Miss Hope these days?"

David's eyebrows knit in confusion. "Maggie Hope, sir? She's still in Scotland, as far as I know."

"Well, bring the girl back! I need a typist, I need a translator, and it won't hurt to have yet another person on my staff for protection. I must have Hope. Hope shall go with us to America!"

"I shall telephone her immediately," David said.

"Excellent," Churchill said. "Tonight I shall sleep the sleep of the saved and thankful. Thanks to God. Good night, gentlemen."

Chapter Twenty-one

In the gardener's cottage, Maggie and Sarah had the wireless on. *"Meeeeeeh,"* yowled K, desperate for attention.

"Not now, you scoundrel," Maggie said, scooping him up and holding him close.

"And now a rebroadcast of President Roosevelt's address to Congress. It was made at twelve thirty today Eastern Standard Time—and we've just received word that the United States Congress has passed a formal declaration of war against Japan. The United States is at war with Japan."

"My God," Maggie said, rubbing her face against K's warm flank, listening to President Roosevelt, his aristocratic and nasal voice serious but strong: *"Yesterday, December seventh, 1941—a date which will live in infamy—the United States of America was suddenly and deliberately attacked by naval and air forces of the Empire of Japan."*

Unconsciously, Maggie inhaled sharply. "No . . ." she said.

"The United States was at peace with that nation, and, at the solicitation of Japan, was still in conversation with its government and its emperor looking toward the maintenance of peace in the Pacific. Indeed, one hour after Japanese air squadrons had commenced bombing in the American island of Oahu, the Japanese ambassador to the United States and his colleague delivered to our secretary of state a formal reply to a recent American message. While this reply stated that

it seemed useless to continue the existing diplomatic negotiations, it contained no threat or hint of war or armed attack."

"No!" Maggie cried. "It can't be!"

"It will be recorded that the distance of Hawaii from Japan makes it obvious that the attack was deliberately planned many days or even weeks ago. During the intervening time the Japanese government has deliberately sought to deceive the United States by false statements and expressions of hope for continued peace.

"The attack yesterday on the Hawaiian Islands has caused severe damage to American naval and military forces. I regret to tell you that very many American lives have been lost. In addition, American ships have been reported torpedoed on the high seas between San Francisco and Honolulu."

"This is it," Sarah said, looking at Maggie when it was over. Both women were pale. "This is what Britain's been waiting for. Maggie, are you all right?"

Tears glinted in Maggie's eyes. *America. Attacked. Bombed. And yet . . . And yet that means Britain will be saved.* She shivered, blinking back tears. "I suppose I never truly realized how much I love my country."

"Which one?"

Maggie wiped at her eyes. "Both of them."

The next morning, the Prime Minister and his staff moved from Chequers back to Number 10 Downing Street, where the P.M. was finalizing plans for his trip to Washington, DC, to meet with President Roosevelt.

The Prime Minister was in his claw-foot bath in his and Mrs. Churchill's apartment at the Annexe. His body was large and pink. "It's settled, then," he announced, sprinkling in a large handful of pine-scented Blenheim Bouquet bath salts. "We're going to Washington. We set sail on the *Duke of York* on December twelfth for the so-called Arcadia Conference." The P.M. peered at his two private secretaries over his gold-rimmed glasses. "And I must have Hope with me."

"Mr. Churchill . . ." David began. "I've tried to reach Miss Hope, but she's not responding . . ."

"Well, try her again! Tell her it is *I*, asking for her!"

"Also, no women allowed on ships crossing the Atlantic," John reminded him. "As per the Geneva Convention."

"Miss Hope isn't a woman," Churchill rejoined. "Well, she is, of course—but she's an *agent*, by Jove! And she types! And she speaks American. I need her! I must have her! The Prime Minister's secret agent!" He splashed his hands in the soapy bathwater to punctuate his enthusiasm.

"But sir, why?" David asked. "We can hire a girl to type when we reach the United States."

"No, no new staff!" Mr. Churchill kicked his feet under the water. "I must have Hope." The Prime Minister was child-like in his steadfast resolve.

"Miss Hope is still in Scotland now, sir—"

"Well, bring her back!" Churchill bellowed. "I'm not getting on the ship without her!"

"Sir?"

"Do you know what the symbol of Hope is, Mr. Greene—Mr. Sterling?"

"Er, no, sir," said John.

David resettled his glasses. "Afraid not, sir."

"And you claim to have a classical education! Hope is an anchor—because of its importance in navigation, it was regarded in ancient times as a symbol of safety. The Christians adopted the anchor as a symbol of hope—and Christ is the unfailing hope of all who believe in him. Hebrews six-nineteen says that when we have Hope as an anchor of the soul, we are firm and sure.

"As we sail to the United States, our new ally, we both literally and metaphorically are raising our Anchor and venturing forth into a new chapter of the war.

"And so I must have Miss Hope, my metaphorical anchor. Plus, I trust her to type decently. And tell me of the quaint American customs and verbiage of which I may not be aware. Hope shall be part typist, part diplomatic adviser, and all secret agent."

David and John exchanged looks. "I'll see what I can do," David said.

The Prime Minister blinked and dropped below the surface of the water, blowing bubbles.

"So, how do we get Maggie back?" John said.

"You, my friend," David replied, inspired, "shall go to Scotland, in person. You shall procure Miss Hope for the P.M.!"

John recoiled. "I? She hates me."

"Oh, jumping Jove, I sincerely doubt that. And even if she does, you must change her mind. It's about time you two kissed and made up."

"Maggie won't come with me."

"Well, throw her over your shoulder caveman-style if you must. 'I must have Hope with me in the New World!' says our fearless leader. Do you really want to be the one to tell the P.M. no?"

"Then *you* should go to Scotland. She still likes you. She'll listen to you," John insisted.

"Oh, but I'm not going. As I said, *you're* the one who's going to journey off to the Highlands of Scotland and return with our own bonnie wee secretary."

John cocked an eyebrow. "Caveman-style?"

"Well, it's about time you two were reunited. I never understood why you two didn't just have at it."

"I . . . She . . . We . . ." Then, "No, no, I'm not going."

David took a moment to examine his fingernails. "So dreadfully sorry to bring this up, John, but I outrank you now. And if the Boss wants you to go fetch Miss Hope, you're going. It's your duty to God and King. And Prime Minister."

John muttered something.

"What was that? Didn't quite hear."

"Nothing," John grumbled. "I'll return with our Girl Friday."

"Good, because I've already made your train reservations. Merciful Minerva! You'll need to hurry if you want to make it to Euston on time!"

Chapter Twenty-two

Maggie was with the others in the main conference room at Arisaig House when Germany formally declared war against the United States, with Reich Foreign Minister Joachim von Ribbentrop delivering a diplomatic note to the American Chargé d'Affaires in Berlin.

Now Hitler was addressing the Reichstag. "*. . . After years of negotiating with the deceiver Roosevelt, the Japanese government finally had its fill of being treated in such a humiliating way. All of us, the German people and, I believe, all other decent people around the world as well, regard this with deep appreciation . . .*"

"Turn the blighter off!" Charlie called from across the table.

But they listened to the full version of the Führer's rant before breaking for cups of tea. Maggie saw Satoshi and went to him. "Are you all right?" she asked. "You look a bit peaked."

"Do you remember my telling you that my parents live in Berkeley? Well, I'm worried about them."

"But your father's a physics professor . . . And you're here, helping train British agents. Obviously . . ."

"But it's not obvious to the U.S. government. All the Japanese in America have been ordered to pack a single bag and be ready for transport at any time in the next few months. My family, and everyone that I love back home, is being sent to internment camps."

"Internment camps?" Maggie blinked. *Internment camps—in the United States?*

Satoshi sighed. "That's what we hear."

"Where?"

"Rumor has it they're building in the southwest."

"Is there any evidence of any Fifth Column activity?"

He started. "Well, certainly not in my family."

"No, of course not," Maggie said. "I'm truly, truly sorry."

When Maggie returned to her cottage, she saw a dark figure on the steps to her flat. Above, the stars burned blue.

"Sarah?" she called. "Did you forget your key?"

But the figure was a man. It was John Sterling.

Maggie had imagined him so many times it took her a few blinks to realize it was actually him, not a daydream.

He held out his hand, revealing something that glinted in the moonlight. "You left these at my flat."

"You came all the way to Scotland to return my earrings?" she said, trying to ignore the shock of longing she felt at the sight of him. That he was wearing his RAF coat and hat certainly wasn't helping matters.

How had she described him to Charlie? *Tall, dark, and damaged,* she remembered. His eyes were still a dark and unreadable brown, his hair curly, his tie slightly askew, and his shoulders hunched from tension. But he was still John.

"Also, to give you a message from Mr. Churchill."

Maggie pulled out the extracted bullet from her coat pocket and held it out for him to see in the moonlight. "Those earrings will go nicely with my 'Berlin souvenir.' I'm thinking of having it made into a necklace."

"Glad you finally had it taken out," John said as he gave her the earrings. Their fingers touched, then Maggie pocketed the earrings.

"So, this is business?" she asked briskly.

"Special delivery from Number Ten." He took an envelope from his breast pocket. "By courier."

Maggie opened the envelope, slipping out the thick card. She caught a whiff of cigar smoke.

> *I need Hope.*
> *Come back to London.*
> *This is an order.*
> *Please.*
>
> *WSC*

Maggie put it in her coat pocket, with the bullet and the earrings, without comment.

"What he didn't put into writing," John continued, "is that he's going to be traveling to Washington, to meet with President Roosevelt."

Maggie shrugged, trying not to show how touched she was. "Good for the P.M. He has what he's wanted for so long."

"And he wants you to go with him. With us."

"So—you're going to America, too." A flicker of a smile played on Maggie's lips. *John in Washington, out of his element. Oh, I would love to see that.*

"Yes, and David, as well."

"And why does Mr. Churchill want me?"

"Well, ostensibly, he needs a secretary—"

Maggie threw up her hands. "Oh, for heaven's sake . . ."

"He has a number of reasons, including your being an agent, and your being an American 'diplomatic adviser,' too, but really . . . He wants you back. All of us do."

"*You* want me back?"

"Yes. Yes, I do. I'm sorry for my behavior in London over the last summer, Maggie. I'm very sorry. Because I was in love with you—and I'm still in love with you. And I will spend every day of my life making it up to you. I love you. Please come back to London with me."

"I'm going to say this once, very slowly, and make it quite clear," Maggie began. She looked him straight in the eye. "I'm not pouting, and I'm not being coy. I thought you died. And I mourned your death. And because I eventually moved on, with another man, you decided to punish me. You, John Sterling, are a narrow-minded self-centered fool."

Maggie was on a roll now, angry words tumbling over each other in her haste to get them out. "What's the biggest predictor of future behavior? Past behavior. If I let you back into my life I am sure you would hurt me again. So, please—go away."

"Maggie—"

Maggie held up a hand. "You may have come back today with all kinds of good intentions and pledges and promises, but I'm not interested."

John swallowed hard and was silent for a moment. "I thought if we could talk—well, I'm here and I'm ready to listen."

Maggie took one step up and got out her key. "Go to hell."

"Already been there, thanks." John shook his head. "Well, re-gardless, I have explicit orders to bring you back to London with me."

Maggie traversed the remaining stairs, and used her key to open her door. "I'm not going *anywhere* with you—and you can quote me to Mr. Churchill." She stepped over the threshold and turned. "And you—you can just . . . stick it up your jumper!"

And then she slammed the door.

"Well, you're quite the mucky pup." The woman's voice was deep and throaty. She was bundled in an overcoat and scarf from head to toe, walking slowly but resolutely up the path to the gardener's cottage with the aid of a cane.

"Sarah!" John smiled. "David said you were here. So glad to see you up and around."

They embraced. "I'm alive," Sarah said. "But you—*you* had us all terrified, what with that we-thought-you-were-dead prank," she said as she pulled away. "Naughty, naughty boy," she added, wagging her finger at him.

John gave a wry smile. "Well, it wasn't exactly a barrel of monkeys from my perspective, either."

"I know. You poor thing." She glanced up at the closed door. "Maggie not ready to make nice?"

"No would be an understatement."

"Well, I know just the thing—we'll get you a room in town, you can wash up, and then we can have dinner together and catch up on old times."

John's eyes went to the windows of Maggie's flat.

Sarah saw his look. "She'll come around," she promised. "She just needs a little time." She linked her arm through John's. "Come on, I know someone who can give us a ride."

Mr. Burns drove them to town, where John checked into a room at Arisaig Inn. After he'd gone up to the room, washed, shaved, and changed his shirt, he met Sarah downstairs at the inn's dining room.

It was small and modest, and a delicious smell of fried fish emanated from the kitchen. A number of older local men lined the bar, nursing beers. They eyed Sarah, still a beauty despite her recent illness, with unabashed curiosity. She placed their order at the bar, two bowls of cullen skink—a creamy smoked-fish stew—a plate of chips, and one pint and one half-pint of beer.

Sarah was used to men—and women—staring at her. When she was done, she sat down at one of the tables and listened to the news broadcast on the wireless over the bar, as a group played darts, showing off for her. "Turn it off!" growled a man in the corner, pulling out an accordion. The man sitting next to him had a fiddle, and another a small drum. Without introduction, they began to play, and the man with the accordion began to sing:

> *Duncan Gray cam' here to woo,*
> *Ha, ha, the wooing o't,*
> *On blythe Yule-night when we were fou,*
> *Ha, ha, the wooing o't,*
> *Maggie coost her head fu' heigh,*
> *Look'd asklent and unco skeigh,*
> *Gart poor Duncan stand abeigh;*
> *Ha, ha, the wooing o't.*

As John entered, Sarah looked up at him and smiled. "This song could be written about you two."

John sat down next to her. "I'll have you know I'm on an official mission from the Prime Minister, not here to pitch woo."

The dim light glinted off the rag marks left on the wooden table as the barkeep brought their cullen skink and beer.

"Winnie said there will always be fish." John pushed at it with his spoon. "Although he never specified what sort of fish."

Sarah took a spoonful, and then delicately removed a bone from her mouth, placing it on the plate. "It's not Sunday roast at The Pompadour, but it'll do."

At the table next to them, an older man was taking out his false teeth. "Lost 'em at Yprees," he explained to Sarah. "I'm your Prince Charming—invite me to tea!"

He was obviously a regular. "Come on, Prince Charming, Cook has some hot soup for you," said the barkeep, and the man trotted off to the kitchen, teeth in hand.

"Well, I do feel a bit better," John said.

"You look a great deal better, kitten. Cheers," Sarah said as they clinked glasses. "Like Lazarus, you have risen from the dead."

His eyes darkened. "I'd rather not talk about it."

"Of course. I won't mention it again. But if you ever do want to talk—"

"I won't."

"Well, why don't you tell me what brings you to Arisaig. And please don't say the lovely beaches, because it's a wee bit nippy for swimming." She raised one eyebrow. "I'm guessing it has to do with a certain red-haired secretary?"

"It's official business, actually."

"Is that what you're calling it these days?" Sarah said, sprinkling vinegar on her chips.

"It's true. David sent me."

"*David* sent you? I thought he worked for you?"

"Not anymore. He was promoted while I was convalescing in Berlin. You'd think *I* would have been promoted—the fallen RAF hero. But no . . . Apparently, being dead does nothing for one's career."

Sarah snorted.

"And I must say, David took great satisfaction in sending me— *ordering* me—on this little mission. As they say, power corrupts— and absolute power corrupts absolutely."

"I can see David enjoying his new influence." Sarah touched a napkin to her lips. "But even if it's official, you must have a fair amount of—how shall I phrase it—*unfinished business* to discuss with our mutual friend."

"I'm afraid that's top secret as well."

"She's only told me bits and pieces, but, really, John—I think you behaved like an arse."

John choked on a swallow of beer. "I—"

"Let's cut to the chase, shall we, Johnny? Since, in another lifetime, we used to step out, I know certain things about you, and what you're like as a beau. And you, my dear, have flaws."

"Really," he said, mopping up vinegar with a chip.

"Really," she said. "For example, you and the fireplace poker."

"Oh. So she told you about that." Then, "Well, I'd just returned from Berlin—"

"*She* had just returned from Berlin!"

"She was seeing another man!"

"Because she thought you were *dead*!"

Suddenly, they realized all eyes were on them. They dropped their voices.

"Well, I may have mentioned before," John said in a harsh whisper, "'reports of my death have been greatly exaggerated.'"

"Yes, but we didn't know that. *Maggie* didn't know that."

"Well, it certainly didn't take her long to move on."

"She was gutted, absolutely gutted."

"I'm sure," John said, finishing his beer.

"Look," Sarah continued in a low voice. "Her mother was a spy. Maggie was probably only conceived as part of some cover story. And when her mother went back to Germany, her father wasn't enough of a man to stay and fight for her. She was raised by her spinster aunt, who seems perfectly nice, but not much of a maternal type, if you get my meaning.

"And then when she finally finds her father—he's still . . . *off*. And she finds her mother—and she's a top-ranking Nazi.

"She finds out that Churchill, a father figure to her, has been using her for her family connections. And you, the love of her life, she thinks you're dead—another abandonment."

"Yes, but—"

Sarah held up a chip. "Wait—I'm not done. And *then* you come back. And when you find out she did something human, you abandon her again."

John was silent.

"She's damaged," Sarah said. "All she sees now is that love is mathematically improbable."

John sighed. "I wasn't really angry with her. It wasn't her at all. It was just . . . everything. The war, losing friends, being shot, being behind enemy lines for so long . . ."

Sarah nodded. "And maybe, if you're honest with yourself, it's because the world moved on without you. We thought you'd died. Maggie moved on with another man. Mr. Churchill's office moved on. David was promoted." She wiped her hands on her napkin. "Perhaps, just perhaps, you're angry because the earth didn't stop rotating for you."

"Good God," John exclaimed. "I think you're right. That makes me rather awful, doesn't it? When you put it like that."

"Yes, but you were angry. And hurt. And while the way you reacted wasn't the most sensitive thing you might have done, it was—just like Maggie's behavior—human."

"So now what do I do?"

"You apologize."

"I did apologize."

"Well, you continue to apologize. And you say you'll never do it again—and then you never do. And you'll tell her you adore her and cherish her and you ask—you get down on your knees and beg if you need to—for another chance."

John nodded, taking it in. His lips curled in a smile. "And how's *your* love life these days?"

Sarah rolled her eyes. "As you well know, near-death experiences aren't exactly conducive to romance."

"You're returning to the Vic-Wells when you're patched up?"

"I'm not sure. I might be done with that life."

"You're smart, you know. I'm sure you could do whatever you put your mind to."

She smiled. "You don't have to go to Magdalene or Wellesley to know things. In fact, you overeducated lot often seem awfully stupid on many occasions."

"I am aware." Then, "Do you think she'll take me back?"

"She took in a stray cat recently, Johnny—so really, darling, you never know."

Chapter Twenty-three

When Maggie opened her front door the next morning, she was astonished to see John sitting on her steps, reading a book. "You slept here?" she asked, one hand on a hip. She was dressed for work, in coveralls and boots.

He stood. "No—I ran into Sarah, had dinner with her, found a room at the Arisaig Inn, slept, shaved, and came back."

"What are you reading?"

"T. H. White's *The Sword in the Stone*."

"I'm reading that too," she said, coming down the stairs. "And grateful not to have been born a fish. Or a squire. Or a king, for that matter. Although in White's world, just being human is bad enough."

"Would you please take a walk with me?" John asked.

"No."

She attempted to pass by, but he reached out and took her arm gently. "What I have to say to you, on behalf of the Prime Minister, is top secret. I am under oath that I will verbally deliver this message to you."

"Fine. We'll walk." They made their way past the gardens, where Mr. Fraser had turned over the rich black soil dotted with earthworms. Birds chirped in the trees, and in the apple orchard the sap was running.

They took muddy paths past grazing sheep down to the beach.

There, they leaned against a large boulder, protected from the wind. The morning sky was tinged with pink.

"The Boss and the President have been in constant contact, via scrambled telephone," John began. "But Mr. C. thinks that Roosevelt's a slippery fish—wants to keep him focused on fighting Germany, not just Japan."

"Well, Hitler made that fairly clear with his declaration of war against the U.S.—President Roosevelt didn't have to lift a finger."

"Still, the Boss has it in his head to go, and you know when his mind's made up—"

"—there's no stopping him." Maggie picked up a small, flat rock from the shore and threw it. It skipped over the waves, until it finally vanished into the loch. "I still don't see what this has to do with me."

"Well, first of all, the P.M. needs a secretary."

"Again?" She laughed, in spite of herself. "But what about Mrs. Tinsley? Miss Stewart?"

"Geneva Conventions forbid women's ocean travel in wartime." John picked up a rock and skipped it, as well. "I don't suppose you've heard, but Mrs. Tinsley's also on compassionate leave. Her son died."

"Oh," Maggie said, remembering the picture of a handsome, serious young man in a naval uniform on Mrs. Tinsley's desk at Number 10. "Oh, I'm so sorry."

"So, not only does the Boss need a typist, but you've been cleared, because of your SOE training. You have, shall we say, special skills that may come in handy being in the Prime Minister's entourage. And he also says he needs you to translate for him."

"Translate? But we all speak English."

" 'Two nations divided by a common language,' says he. I think he just doesn't want to make any gaffes. Or miss any Yankee cultural nuances."

Maggie skipped another stone. "Tell him not to call anyone a 'bloody Colonial' and he'll be fine."

"There's a train back to London this afternoon. I have two tickets."

"Well, you'll have to convince someone else to take the seat, I'm not going." Then, "Besides, I have a cat now."

"Mr. Churchill would no doubt approve."

Maggie was silent. It had just been Thanksgiving. She missed the United States. She missed her Aunt Edith. After hearing about Pearl Harbor, she was filled with love for both her countries. And she had come to the decision that she would do whatever was in her power to fight Nazism.

She also had a sister behind enemy lines in Germany. And Mr. Churchill was probably the one person in the world who could get that sister out. If he wanted her help so badly, he would have to help Elise, too.

"Fine," Maggie said. "I'll come to London to speak to Mr. Churchill in person. But I'm not leaving my cat behind. We're a team."

"I understand."

"And I have to make sure Sarah's all right before I leave."

"Of course." John's lips twitched with a hidden smile.

"This isn't about you, you know," Maggie snapped, throwing another rock. "And I have a few things I'd like to say to our Mr. Churchill."

"I'm going back to London," Maggie announced to Sarah. The latter was already dressed and doing her barre exercises.

"Good on you," Sarah replied. "And I have a meeting today. With Captain Gordon."

Maggie sank down into the armchair. K bumped against her

legs and started to purr. "Of course, that's your decision. It's all voluntary. And, even at the last minute, you can decide not to do it—"

"If you could go back in time, would you do it again?" Sarah interrupted. "Volunteer, I mean?"

"I honestly don't know." Maggie stared at the fire. "I wish none of this had happened. I wish we could just turn back the clock and go back to better days—peaceful days." Her hand went to the bandage. "And I'm sure everyone involved with this horrible war feels the same way—but we can't. There's no going back, there's no putting our heads in the sand. Not unless we want to be slaves, and see the rest of the world enslaved as well. I think this war is terrible—the things I've learned, the things I've seen, the things I've done . . . But despite that, I do believe it's a necessary war. I even believe that it's a just war.

"But you have to know, while I will, with all my strength, defend our right to exist against a monster who would destroy everything honorable and good, I don't love what I do. In fact, I hate it.

"There's no glamour in it, Sarah. No glory. But I realized during my time here that I'll do anything to make sure the next generation knows peace." She turned to K. "Come on, pussycat, pussycat—we're going to London to visit the Queen!"

"*Meh,*" was his only response, but he seemed content to ride on her shoulder as she packed her things. And later, as she, K, and Sarah walked up the stairs to the main house, John followed behind with her trunk. Maggie was pleased to see the fuchsia rhododendrons were just starting to burst into bloom.

"I just wanted to say good-bye, Miss Glyn-Jones," she said to Twelve in the main room as they shook hands.

Then she went down the line, shaking hands. "Good-bye, Yvonne. Good-bye, Charlie. Good-bye, Mr. Fraser and Mrs. MacLean." Impulsively, she threw her arms around Mr. Burns and kissed his leathery cheek. He smelled of pipe tobacco. "And good-bye, dearest Burns. Thank you for everything."

Sarah walked to Maggie, now without the help of the cane. The two women embraced. "Thank you for everything, Maggie," Sarah said.

"You may not know it, but you helped me as much as I may have helped you—maybe even more." *Good-bye, Black Dog.*

"Well, I don't know how that could possibly be, but I'm glad." Sarah reached to rub K under the chin. "And good-bye to you, Mr. K." He began to purr, then rumbled even louder as Maggie settled him once again over her shoulders.

"Are you really going to take that animal on the train?" John asked, hoisting up the trunk once again.

"If anyone asks," Maggie answered, pulling on her gloves, "he's a fur stole with personality."

On the train, there was the usual assortment of pilots and soldiers, with their support crews as well—the fitters, the riggers, the mechanics, the crew chiefs. A sign read: PLEASE HAVE IDENTITY CARDS READY FOR INSPECTION. Ads extolled women's train conductor uniforms and warned TRAVEL AT YOUR OWN RISK.

Maggie and John traversed the swaying corridors until they found an empty compartment. John slid open the door, then hoisted her trunk up to the luggage rack. First class had two lights; there was only one in second and third.

Maggie sat down and K jumped from her shoulders, sniffing at the worn velvet seat cushions, more curious than afraid. *"Meh,"* he said, looking at Maggie.

"Shhhh," she admonished. "Remember—you're a fur stole."

John sat opposite Maggie, and K turned his attention to him.

When John stretched out his lanky legs in front of him, K marched right up them, like a gangplank, and stared into John's eyes.

John held the cat's gaze. A challenge went back and forth between the two males, then K jumped down and went to curl up beside Maggie. He watched John through narrowed eyes.

"I know you don't get this from the papers," John said, as if they'd never stopped working together, "but the Boss is becoming more and more difficult. I don't care personally, but he's losing support in the House. And I'm also worried about his health."

"Yes, but America's in the war now. That's what he wanted—all he's ever wanted."

"Yes, the American Eagles have come, just in time to save the day," John replied drily. He looked at Maggie, who hadn't taken off her coat or gloves. It was frigid in the compartment. "You must be frozen. Let me get you a cup of something warm."

He went in search of the woman pushing the tea trolley, leaving Maggie with K and her thoughts. She took out her knitting and had made significant progress on a soldier's sock by the time he returned with two cups of weak cocoa, two Lund cakes, and *The Times*. "You're knitting," he said, surprised.

"Your ace powers of deduction are just as impressive as ever, Mr. Sterling." Maggie put down the sock and accepted the cocoa.

"You knit now, Miss Hope?"

"Yes, I knit." Suddenly she realized it didn't hurt quite as much to think about Berlin. It still hurt, and probably always would. But not quite as much.

They were silent as scenery slid by: snowy mountains, the occasional dark tunnel, a *V* of honking geese. There were schoolchildren playing ball, small shaggy ponies, and streams and lacy waterfalls. Maggie watched, stroking K, while John, opposite, read the newspaper.

"Glasgow's not that far," said a man talking outside the compartment, to which his companion answered, "Aye, but it's far enough."

"Would you like the paper?" John asked, folding it and handing it to Maggie.

"Thank you," she said, accepting it. She scanned the articles. "The numbers from Pearl Harbor keep growing." She blinked back tears. "Now they're saying nearly twenty-five hundred Americans killed."

"How many injured?" John asked.

"Oh, I don't know," Maggie said. "Let's see—'One thousand one hundred and seventy-eight injured, both military and civilians.'"

"I always look at the statistics for the wounded," he said. "I always wonder if any of them feel that they would be better off dead."

Maggie looked at John. "Is that how you felt?"

It was now his turn to look out the window.

When Sarah returned to the flat, she noticed that an envelope with her name on it had been slipped under the door:

Dear Miss Sanderson,

Your name has been passed on to me with the suggestion that you possess skills and qualifications that may be of value in a phase of the war effort.

If you are available for an interview, I would be glad to see you at Arisaig House, today, at three p.m.

Yours truly,
Timothy Gordon,
Captain.

———

She walked to the main house at the assigned time, gave her name for Captain Gordon, and then waited downstairs in the vestibule until Gwen at the reception desk called her name.

An officer walked her up the thistle-carved stairs and ushered her into an office, formerly the master bedroom suite, full of desks and file cabinets and stacks of papers.

"Come in, sit down," a man said. Seated at one of the desks, he had a long face, with a long nose and long ears as well. There were deep furrows between his eyebrows. "Would you give us a few minutes?" he said to the other men.

When they had left, Sarah took a seat opposite. "Thank you for coming, Miss Sanderson. I'm Captain Gordon. Miss Hope let me know you are fluent in French, and know Paris well. And that, while you're recovering from an illness, you're quite athletic."

"Yes," Sarah replied. "And I'd like to do my bit for the war effort."

Captain Gordon leaned forward and made a steeple of his hands. "Well, Miss Sanderson, how do you feel about this German business?"

Sarah took a moment to think. "I—I suppose I feel that—for the second time—the Germans have bamboozled their way into war—and that's two wars too many. As Maggie—Miss Hope—may have mentioned, my grandmother was murdered by the Nazis in Paris recently."

"Ah—so you're looking for revenge."

"No," Sarah answered. "Well, maybe. A bit. But it's not personal. I don't hate the Germans, per se, but I do hate the Nazis. *They're* the ones who've perverted everything. For the Germans, oddly enough, I have pity."

"I was hoping you might separate the Nazis and the Germans."

"I hate the Nazis. But I'm a woman, and there's not much I can do about it. If I were a man, I'd already be in the armed forces."

Captain Gordon considered the slight young woman in front of him. "Yes, that must be frustrating."

Then, as if he'd made up his mind: "Miss Sanderson—how would you like to go to France and make things a bit uncomfortable for those who would invade other people's cities—and kill their grandmothers?"

Sarah snorted. "Me? Go to France? How can *anyone* go to France?" She laughed. "You may or may not be aware that the Channel boats are no longer running. What sort of game are you having at my expense, Captain?"

"There are ways of going to France other than the Golden Arrow, Miss Sanderson."

She frowned. "You mean the War Office can send people to France? Despite the Germans?"

"The War Office?" He gave a dry laugh. "No, the War Office is far too respectable to do any such thing. Never mind how it's done, but a trip to France could be arranged. Let's call *our* office—the one that could send you to France—The Firm. Tell me what you think."

Sarah looked him straight in the eye. "I think you're absolutely bonkers."

"Miss Sanderson, you have no husband, no children. You are fluent in French. You have dark hair and dark eyes and look, if I may, Gallic. You know and love Paris. You could move around and not be spotted."

"And then what?"

"We're sending what we call hush-hush troops to the Continent to 'set Europe ablaze,' as our esteemed Prime Minister put it. One of our goals is to organize and train a secret army in France, supply them with British weapons, and teach them how to use them against the Nazis. How to carry out sabotage, to make things difficult, keep them off-balance." He made a note on a pad of paper. "I must interject here, if you haven't figured it out already, that the job is quite dangerous. Some people, as they say, 'fail to return.' However, with your particular skill set, you could be of great value to us."

Sarah's eyes were wide. "Look, Captain Gordon, I'm just a girl from Liverpool, with very little formal education. I don't know much about politics or governments—or secret armies, for that matter."

Captain Gordon stood and turned to face the window. Outside, the sun was beginning to set, glowing blood-red over the water. "Twice in your lifetime, your country has been gutted like a fish by Germany. But this war is not just one country against another—it's the fight for freedom against the powers of darkness. You have the drive and the discipline and the strength from dance to succeed, as well as the language and geographic knowledge. Now we just need to know—do you have the stomach for it?" Sarah was silent.

He turned back to face her. "Tell you what. Come to us for a period of training."

"Here? At Arisaig House?"

"Here, and a few other places in Scotland. Then you, I, and The Firm will know for sure if you're right for the job. You could still leave at any time, gracefully. We only take volunteers, you know. We believe in free choice."

He took his seat again. "Now, it would be silly to talk to you about security and what that means in this business, but for every person involved in The Firm it is as secret as can be. For God's sake—and I never take the name of God lightly—keep it so."

"This is what Maggie—Miss Hope—does, isn't it?" Sarah said, realizing. "Oh my God, Maggie's a spy!"

"You know I can't possibly comment, Miss Sanderson."

Sarah stood and shook his hand. "Thank you, Captain Gordon." She walked to the door, then, merrily, called, *"Au revoir,"* over her shoulder.

After Sarah Sanderson had left, Captain Gordon took out a sheet of paper and studied it. It had a surprising number of personal details about Sarah Sanderson. The date and place of her birth, family tree, where she'd been educated, where she'd lived, where she'd toured with the Vic-Wells. At the top left-hand corner of the sheet was a small hieroglyph—the symbol that the integrity of the person questioned had been investigated and determined to be sound.

Captain Gordon wrote at the bottom of the typed sheet, *Found Sarah Sanderson to be direct-minded & courageous. God help the Nazis if she gets near them.*

Maggie and John changed trains at Glasgow, and headed south to London. The sun had set, and the blackout curtains had been pulled. They could barely make out each other's faces by the blue bulbs. After sandwiches and coffee, they began a discussion of *That Hamilton Woman.* "The Boss is obsessed with it. I can't tell you how many evenings we watched it at Chequers."

"Well, I've seen it, too, of course," Maggie said. " *'Has it ever occurred to you that a woman can sometimes be of more help than a man?'* Although it seems a shame that Lord Nelson had a hero's death, while Lady Hamilton had to die alone, an alcoholic, in prison."

" *'You must please excuse these souvenirs . . .'* " John said, looking at her.

" *'I had no idea,'* " she quoted back. " *'They told us of your victories, but not of the price you had paid.'* "

They sat in silence, until John stood and switched seats so he could be next to Maggie. *"Meh,"* K protested, jumping up and wedging himself between them.

"We should probably get some sleep," John said.

"Yes. We probably should."

In the darkness, they closed their eyes, then reached for the other's hand.

Snow was falling on the city of London, covering it in white, like a bandage, as their taxi made its way past bombed-out blocks, next to those left curiously intact. Barrage balloons still stood guard.

"Wait," said Maggie. "I want to see how much damage there is to my house. Driver, may we please go by Portland Place?"

"Your grandmother's house was bombed?" John asked.

Maggie nodded. "The tenants escaped, but they tell me it's uninhabitable now. I just need to see for myself."

When they reached Portland Place, there were already signs of damage from explosions on the street—broken windows boarded up, burned trees, craters in the street marked off with hastily built fencing.

"It's—it's still standing, at least," Maggie said finally, as they reached the address. It was true: A bomb had flattened what had been the upper story of the house, leaving nothing but charred remains. The first floor was burned and the windows were cracked.

Maggie looked from the window of the taxi. "Damn," she said, taking it in.

"Yes," John said.

Maggie bit her lip, hard. "All right, no need to gawk," she said finally, tasting blood. "Let's get to David's."

———

At David and Freddie's flat in Knightsbridge, they were able to freshen up and change.

"You're just in time for the *bon voyage* party tonight," David exclaimed, clapping his hands. "At Number Ten. Everyone will be there, oh, you must come!"

Maggie nodded. She had a few things she wanted to say to Mr. Churchill before committing to go to the United States with his entourage. "Will you be joining us at the party, Freddie?"

Freddie shook his head. "Only for staff, I'm afraid." He sneezed, then pulled out a cambric handkerchief and blew his nose.

"Oh no," Maggie said, suddenly piecing it together. "Are you allergic to cats?" She'd put K in her old room, for the time being, letting him get used to his new home.

"Afraid so," Freddie said. "More of a dog person, really."

David was not one to wait on ceremony. Once John and Freddie went into the library to work, he pounced. "So, are you and John back together?"

"No." *Oh, David . . .* Maggie felt a warm wave of affection wash over her. He might be somewhat tactless when it came to matters of the heart, but he always meant well. "It's complicated."

"Doesn't have to be." David leaned back in his chair. "Oh, suffering Sukra, I don't see why you two don't just tear each other's clothes off and have at it. I don't understand all the angst, all the drama. Pansies, I'll have you know, don't waste so much time."

"David!" Maggie exclaimed.

"We pansies are quite efficient, it's true." David nodded. "Pocket squares and whatnot. Men and women could take a page, you know. Stop wasting so much time. *Carpe diem.* Or *noctem*, as the case may be."

"Well," Maggie retorted, "I can assure you that everyone's

clothes are staying on, thank you very much. I had the bullet removed. I quit smoking. I adopted a cat—or I guess he adopted me.
Humpty Dumpy has been put back together again—and I'd like to
make sure that glue holds before any rending of garments occurs."

"Fair enough. And, speaking of the king's horses . . ."

John entered the room and sat at the table with them. David
poured him a cup of tea.

Maggie, eager to change the subject, looked to David. "What
am I going to do with K? Obviously, he can't stay here. Poor Freddie will die sneezing."

"Well," he said, pushing up his silver-framed glasses. "You
could bring him to Downing Street. He could stay with Nelson
and the resident Number Ten cat."

"K? At Number Ten?" Maggie was surprised. "Would that be
tolerated?"

"Please," David said, "we're British—we adore animals. It's
children we can't stand. That's why we invented boarding schools.
More tea?"

The cocktail party at Number 10 was being held in the Blue Draw-
ing Room. There was the hum of conversation and, in the background, the tinkle of a piano.

"May I fetch you a drink?" David asked Maggie once their
coats were taken care of. K had been dropped off in the kitchen,
and was busy trying to make friends with Mr. Churchill's cat Nelson, who was not at all interested. The Number 10 cat glared down
from a high perch.

"Thank you, that would be lovely."

She looked around, disconcerted by being back. Here she'd
once taken dictation and typed while bombs rained down outside
and Mr. Churchill had smoked and shouted and kicked the waste-

basket. So much time had passed. So many things had changed. But it still looked the same—an enormous and empty room. The grand oil paintings had been taken away for safekeeping, leaving vacant frames. And the huge Persian carpet had also been rolled up and put into storage. The chairs and sofas ringing the walls remained, though, and a cheerful orange-and-blue fire burned behind the fireplace's grate.

In the crowd, she spotted Miss Stewart, Mr. Snodgrass, and Mrs. Tinsley. Maggie immediately went to the older woman, Mr. Churchill's longtime typist and her first supervisor at Number 10. "Miss Hope, you look much better than the last time you were here," the older woman said. "Not so sallow and sickly. Why, I do believe there's even a touch of pink in your cheeks now. Scotland must have agreed with you."

And some things never change. "Thank you, Mrs. Tinsley," Maggie said, putting a hand on the woman's arm. "I'm so sorry for your loss. I remember your photograph of your son in uniform, by his RAF plane."

Mrs. Tinsley blinked, hard. "Thank you, Miss Hope."

The crowd parted, and Mrs. Churchill came forth in a cloud of lavender chiffon and gray pearls. "Miss Hope, so glad to see you back," said Mrs. Churchill, shaking Maggie's hand warmly. "Please take good care of Mr. Churchill on this trip, won't you, dear? America seems a bit . . . unpredictable. Like the Wild West."

"I—" Maggie began, not wanting to talk about it with Mrs. Churchill before talking to the Prime Minister himself.

David appeared and handed Maggie a coupe of Champagne. The three of them clinked glasses. "And take care of yourselves over there."

"We'll try our best, Ma'am."

There was the sound of a crash, then a yowl, then the shadow of a cat running from the Prime Minister's office, tail low.

"No one named Nelson *ever* runs from a fight!" Mr. Churchill shouted, holding on to a squirming K. He addressed the party. "And who is this rascal? To whom does he belong?"

"He belongs to me, sir," Maggie said. "His name is K—Mr. K, on more formal occasions."

"K, hmmm? Is he in espionage? You know, some of my best top-secret agents have just one-letter code names."

"He's extremely good about sneaking about, sir, and gathering intelligence—about food sources especially."

David interposed. "Sir, it's all my fault—I told Miss Hope that the cat could stay here, just during our trip to Washington."

Mr. Churchill walked over to the group, scratching K under the chin. "Found him in Scotland, did you?" he asked Maggie.

"He, well, he sort of found me, sir."

"Well, he can't come to America with us. Not even my beloved brood can."

"No, sir."

"But he's welcome to stay at Number Ten for the duration."

"Yes, sir. Thank you, sir!"

"Come with me to my office, Miss Hope," Mr. Churchill said, still cradling K in his arms. "We must talk."

Inside, with the thick door of his study closed, the P.M. dropped down into a leather chair and motioned for her to take the one opposite. "Sit! Sit!" he admonished, reaching for a cigar from his breast pocket. He looked older now, stouter but at the same time weaker than when he dictated the Battle of Britain speech to her. His blue eyes were weary. Maggie did as she was bid and sat.

"I'm terribly sorry, sir. But I can't go with you. To Washington." It was a lie. She knew that the best way to get what she wanted, Elise's rescue, was to be coy.

Churchill regarded her with dark-blue eyes and chewed on his cigar. "But I must have Hope!" Then, "Are you afraid?" he asked. "The ocean voyage alone, with all those Nazi ships and submarines, would put most men off. And according to the Geneva Conventions we're not technically supposed to bring women—there's a loophole, though, because you'll be going as the Prime Minister's agent. Plus, I don't want to hire a new typist over there. Some Yank who'll probably spell all of our noble British words wrong."

"I'm not afraid, sir," Maggie said, twisting her hands in her lap. "After being sent blind to Berlin. After learning about the anthrax that you're developing . . ."

"Ah," the P.M. said, leaning back in his chair. Having mutilated his cigar long enough, he took out a monogrammed gold lighter and touched the flame to its end, sucking in. The tip turned crimson. "Not going with me, eh? Your sense of morality has been punctured?"

Maggie didn't know where to rest her eyes, but they kept returning to the unwavering blue ones on her. "I don't question the necessity of the war, sir. I don't question that it's a just war. But I do have reservations about how we're going about fighting it."

"What are your specific issues, Miss Hope?"

"First, I was hired to work as your secretary under false pretenses. You used me for my family connections—connections I wasn't even aware of—without informing me.

"Next, I was trained as a spy and sent to Berlin. Again, I was used for my family connections and sent under false pretenses.

"And then there's the anthrax. One of my dearest friends—a patriot, who risked her life to capture Claire Kelly—nearly died as 'collateral damage' to your anthrax experiment."

Maggie took a deep breath. "You must understand that—with all due respect, sir—I do not trust you."

Churchill smoked impassively, a wreath of blue smoke drifting above his head. The fire crackled in the hearth.

"Miss Hope, we've been discussing theoretical moral problems in our highest circles. Let me pose to you one of our most frequently discussed scenarios. Suppose Hitler has given orders for the Luftwaffe to obliterate a city—a city that is not London. A nonmilitary target. An undefended city of civilians. Hitler wants to demonstrate his power—that he can flatten any target he chooses in Britain and get away with it. We know of this because our cryptographers at Bletchley Park have unscrambled some of that secret Nazi code. There's no mistake, it's been checked and cross-checked."

He kept the full intensity of his gaze upon her. "Now, what would you do?"

Maggie thought before replying. "Could the attack be stopped with an all-out effort by the RAF, sir?"

"Yes, of course. But there's a catch—the Germans will know we had prior knowledge of the raid. They'll know we broke their code. It comes down to the code, or the city."

"Well, surely we could evacuate the children . . ."

"No! To do so would betray the secret. And the city would be bombed anyway and we'd still have lost the advantage of breaking the code. Think, Miss Hope! *Think!*"

"Just to clarify, sir, we are talking about letting innocent civilians die. Without warning."

"Yes. Now let's make it more complicated—because life often is. This city that will be bombed—it's a city near Bletchley, and many of the people working at Bletchley have relocated their families there. So it's not random and anonymous families who will die, but families of the people who broke the code in the first place."

Maggie's forehead creased. "There are only two possible moves, sir—either defend the city in an all-out battle, or—"

"Or what, Miss Hope?"

"Or . . ." Her heart sank as she realized the only other option. ". . . sacrifice the city and keep the secret. Lose the battle, in order to win the war."

The Prime Minister rested his cigar in a cut-glass ashtray. "And what would *you* do, Miss Hope?"

"I would—" Maggie stared into the dancing flames. "But it's—it's an impossible choice, sir."

"Yes, but as Prime Minister: You. Must. Decide."

"I would sacrifice the city," Maggie said finally. "I would sacrifice the city to win the war."

"And now, Miss Hope, you know how impossibly hard my job is. And how impossibly hard it was, with you, in regard to your past. But we had an advantage and I pressed it. I used you to press it."

"You used me."

"I did. And I'm deeply remorseful, Miss Hope, for any mental anguish I've caused you. But you've furthered our cause more than you know."

Maggie took his words in. "Thank you, sir. I accept your apology. But what about the anthrax? With all due respect, how could you possibly approve the development of such a monstrous thing, sir?"

"You yourself have used a gun, Miss Hope, have you not?"

"Yes, I have," Maggie answered, voice steady. "I took a man's life in Berlin. And I take full responsibility for my actions—and will until my own dying day. But biotoxins—they're indiscriminate. They're shameful. They're—for want of a better word—*dirty.*"

"Dirty, you say? And you prefer *clean* weapons, like guns."

"At least you look your enemy in the eye. And it's better to die by gunshot than by a long, slow, festering illness."

"You're talking again about your friend. The one who nearly died."

"Yes, and two women who did die. Innocent women, who were simply in the wrong place at the wrong time. Doctors, whose edict is to 'first, do no harm,' are making poisons to be used as weapons. It turns civilization on its very head."

"Do you think we are alone in our potion making? We received all of our information from France before she fell. Germany has its own wizards and warlocks, making their own bubbling cauldrons of poison. Surely we would be remiss not to act to protect ourselves against our adversaries?"

He sighed gustily. "Sometimes I miss the Battle of Britain. Everything seemed so clear back then. Right and wrong. Good and evil. Black and white. Freedom and slavery. But we're fighting against humans who have been infected with an inhuman germ. And so we must fight. With broken bottles and pitchforks if we must. And even with mustard gas and anthrax."

He rose and walked to a credenza arrayed with various cut-crystal bottles and glasses. "Oh, my dear Miss Hope, things are going to become much darker before the dawn." He poured two fingers of Johnnie Walker Black into one of the glasses and added a tiny splash of water. "And people wonder why I drink," he muttered.

"That's why it's important to differentiate the Germans versus the Nazis. The Nazis are a humorless creed, and a damned creed, carrying misery and fear where they go. In addition, they're dreary sentimentalists. The kind who go to a whorehouse, and then, after it's over, show the whore pictures of their wife and children back home and cry. They're not terrible, and they're not even all that interesting when all is said and done. Crashing bores, really.

"Miss Hope, you don't have much family, do you?"

Maggie tried not to guffaw in the presence of the Prime Minister. *That's an understatement.* "No, sir."

"I didn't, either, you know. In that way we are alike."

"Sir?"

"Like you, I was an only child. My father was absent more than he was present—was absent even when he was present. And my mother—well, she was like a movie star to me, just as glamorous and just as real as an image on the silver screen. We moved so much, when I was young, and then I went to boarding school . . . and then she died . . ."

He shook himself from his reverie. "That's why I married Clemmie, why we built Chartwell, why we had children. Family, Miss Hope, family is what's important!" he roared, raising his glass. "And while we can't choose the one we come from, we *can* create our own."

"Yes, sir."

"Think you'll settle down, get married?"

Maggie blushed. "Maybe after the war is over, sir."

"My advice is—don't wait too long. Get married and have children. Four, if possible—one for Mother, one for Father, one for Accidents, one for Increase."

Maggie cleared her throat. "Mr. Churchill, your mentioning family brings me to another thing I wanted to ask."

"What? Speak up, Miss Hope!"

"I'm actually not an only child. In Berlin, I learned that I have a half-sister, Elise Hess." Maggie chose her words carefully. "If you promise to do everything in your power to get Elise Hess out of Germany, then I will come with you to Washington, DC."

The Prime Minister sat down and pondered his drink for a moment. Then he looked up. "You think I have time to locate and save one German girl—the daughter of a high-ranking Nazi, no less?"

"She's on our side, sir. She's a nurse and an aspiring nun, and she put herself in great danger to help John Sterling and a Jew named Ernst Klein, who's now patching up the British army in the Mideast. And she's my sister."

The P.M. smoked, then took another swig of his drink. Ash fell on his vest. "Well played, Miss Hope, well played. And so I say to you—I will do everything in my power to rescue your sister, if you agree to come to Washington with me. We leave tomorrow."

"Tomorrow? Sir?"

"Tomorrow. Get your things in order and return bright and shiny in the morning."

"Yes, sir. Thank you, sir."

He waved his cigar at her. "Go. Go away now."

Maggie stood. She had won. She would save Elise. "Yes, sir."

Back at the party, David was waiting. "How did it go with the Boss?"

Maggie smiled. "Looks like I'll be coming to DC with you."

"Wizard!" David exclaimed, clapping her on the back. "We're going to have an excellent time. No rationing there, remember?"

Maggie lowered her voice. "I'm worried about Mr. Churchill."

David's smile faded. "The pressures are starting to get to the P.M., I'm afraid. It's a horrible thing to say, but the attack on Pearl Harbor couldn't have come at a better time. Things were quite grim for a while there. Grimmer than most people knew."

The pianist segued into "There Will Always Be an England." People stood to sing.

As voices drew out, "Britons, awake!," the P.M. burst into the room. "We're going to watch *That Hamilton Woman*," Churchill declared, "in honor of our voyage to America! We have moved into a new phase of this war, and while it might not be the beginning of the end, I do believe—now that we stand side by side with the United States—that it just may be the end of the beginning, the part where Britain stood alone.

"The film's been set up. Move along, then, move along!"

"Again?" someone whispered.

David mouthed to Maggie, "He's obsessed."

"So I've heard."

The assembled guests found seats in the long Pillared Room. The lights were dimmed, the projector began to roll, and the film started.

The Prime Minister mouthed the words Laurence Olivier and Vivien Leigh spoke as Lord Nelson and Lady Hamilton along with them in the darkness. "*'Tell him we're not the guardian angels of every country too lazy to look after itself. You've got to do something too! At the battle of the Nile, we cleared them off the seas, but as long as those madmen had their armies on land no country in Europe is free, they want to get hold of the whole world. If you believe in freedom, stir yourselves! Prepare and help drive them off the land! . . . You cannot make peace with dictators! You have to destroy them, wipe them out!'*"

In the dimness, Maggie thought of the next generation and, God willing, the next. She thought of Chuck and Nigel's baby— his cuddly roundness and the way his head smelled like shortbread, warm from the oven. *If our generation doesn't do something, what will the world be like for the next? I may physically die. I may morally die. I may lose my soul. But it's a sacrifice I'm willing to make. Take me, use me. I'm ready.*

She noticed that, a row away, John was watching her. He made a little walking motion with his fingers and she nodded. They left the room together. John found their coats, and they went up to the roof, where the P.M. used to watch the Blitz, to the deep consternation of his private detective and Mrs. Churchill. The edges were lined with walls of sandbags.

"London doesn't look so bad," Maggie remarked, "at least, covered in snow. I was thinking about that earlier. It hides a lot. Although all the damage is still there, underneath." Her hand went to her own bandage. But her wound—her wounds—were healing now.

"At least the bombing's stopped—for the moment—while Hitler turns all of his attention to Russia."

"Oh, Lord," Maggie said, looking at the devastation below, realizing. "While I was gone, they took out the Admiralty. Mr. Churchill must have been disconsolate."

"Actually, what he said was, 'Now I can see Nelson on his column more clearly.' "

"Yes, that sounds like him." Maggie smiled.

"So," John began, "how was your time in Scotland? I picture you like Artemis, running the moors of Scotland with a bow and arrow."

"Artemis has a gun these days. I suppose David can be my Apollo."

John ran his hands through his hair. "Well, please don't turn me into a deer, like poor what's-his-name."

"Actaeon. No, you're more like Orion, I suppose."

"Not Adonis?" John said, with an arched eyebrow.

"Oh, you'd like that, would you?" She laughed. "But these days I'm sure I'll end up alone. Like Artemis. Or Athena. Or even Bastet, the cat goddess."

They stood for a moment in silence, as large lacy snowflakes began to fall. Then John said, "I wonder what everyone's doing downstairs now. Probably breaking out the Champagne. The *good* Champagne." He looked down at Maggie. "Sorry you're missing it. And you must be cold. Shall we go downstairs now?"

"Well," Maggie said with a grimace, remembering the last time she'd been drunk, and had made herself a fool in front of John,

"I've more or less sworn off liquor these days. Besides, I know exactly what's happening. Mr. Churchill will swear. Then Mrs. Churchill will say, 'Oh, darling, please don't use that word in front of the ladies!' And Mr. Churchill will say, 'Oh, bother, Clemmie. Lady Hamilton never chided Lord Nelson for *his* language . . .' And then David will offer them both drinks and smooth everything over."

"He does love that film."

"I love it, too. I thought of you tonight, while I was watching it. Especially when Lady Hamilton mocks Lord Nelson. *"'And there sits John Sterling, exhibiting his various moods, one by one. John Sterling in a bad mood. John Sterling in a good mood. John Sterling in an exuberant mood . . .'"*

"Yes, well . . ." John looked at Maggie and took her gloved hand in his. "What mood is this?"

She remembered the film enough to remember the line was "in love," but didn't want to say it. "John Sterling—allowing himself to be just a wee bit happy?"

"It will be Christmas soon, and then New Year's—1942. How strange it sounds . . ."

He raised her hand to his lips and kissed it gently, like a chivalrous knight.

"This doesn't change anything, you know," Maggie managed.

"No, of course not," John said, tucking her hand under his arm.

"In Washington, our relationship will be strictly platonic," she insisted. "We shall be consummate professionals."

He smiled. "Consummate," he agreed.

As they headed back down to the party, Maggie said, "I like what Mr. Churchill said about beginnings and ends tonight—'This might not be the beginning of the end, but it may be the end of the beginning.'"

Chapter Twenty-four

Clara Hess was ready to die.

Like German spy Josef Jakobs before her, she had been court-martialed in front of a military tribunal at Duke of York's Head-quarters in Chelsea. Because of her unwillingness to participate in the Double Cross system, she'd been convicted after a one-day trial and sentenced to death.

Like Jakobs's execution, Clara's was to take place in the East Casements Rifle Range, on the grounds of the Tower of London. Eight soldiers from the Holding Battalion of the Scots Guards, armed with .303 Lee-Enfields, were waiting to fire in unison at her heart.

"Clara." It was Frain, along with a Catholic priest, an older man with a long, drooping face, only emphasized by an even lon-ger, drooping mustache.

She looked up at Frain, face hard. "Is Margaret here?" she asked. "Edmund?"

"I'm sorry, Clara," Frain answered gently. "They're not." They had not come to the trial, either.

"Do you have any last words?" the priest said, face as white as his collar.

"No," Clara managed, standing. He face was bare of makeup and her natural light brown hair, streaked with gray, was begin-ning to grow in, leaving a contrast between her real hair and the bleached platinum blonde she had sported in Berlin. But instead of looking older, she looked younger and more vulnerable. Except for the set of her mouth.

"We're going to blindfold you now." Frain stepped behind her, taking a black cloth from inside his suit's breast pocket. As he placed it around her eyes and tied it tightly, he leaned in to smell her hair.

"Peter," she said in a small voice, unable to see, her hands reaching out in vain in front of her.

"I'm here," he said, taking one of her hands and pulling it through his arm as if they were about to enter a dinner party. "I'll be with you."

"Thank you," she whispered.

They made their way out of her cell and down the staircase of the Queen's House and out the door. Clara's nostrils twitched as she smelled the frosty air. "I'll take it from here, Father," Frain said to the priest.

Together they walked, arm in arm, as though out for nothing more than a Sunday stroll. Then Clara heard a car engine start and Frain dropped her arm as he went to open a car door.

"Peter?" she said, reaching out her hands, clawing the empty air. "Peter? Don't leave me!"

Frain grabbed Clara around the waist and, careful to protect her head, helped her into the backseat of the waiting car, slid in beside her. "Go!" he snapped at the driver, who shifted into first gear and pulled out, leaving a shower of gravel and snow behind.

"Peter?" Clara asked. She began to pull at her blindfold.

"Keep it on," he said, taking her hand in his. "It's better for both of us if you don't know where we're going."

———

An hour or so later, the car pulled to a stop. Frain untied Clara's blindfold; it fell to her lap. She blinked at the light, and at the sight in front of her.

They were at the gate of a stately manor home, encircled by barbed-wire fences. Frain gave his identity papers to the Coldstream Guard on duty. The guard looked them over, then handed them back to Frain. "Our newest guest?"

Frain nodded. The driver pulled around the circular drive, stopping at the grand entrance. The double doors opened and a man stepped out. He opened the car door for Clara and offered his hand. "Welcome, Frau Hess." He gave a stiff bow. "We are delighted to have you with us."

"Clara, this is Lord Murdoch," Frain said. "He's your host here."

Clara blinked, then found her voice. "And what sort of place is this?"

"This is to be your home now, Frau Hess." Lord Murdoch was smiling. "We hope you'll be very happy here."

Clara looked up, taking in the soaring grand architecture. A chill wind ruffled her hair. She looked at Frain. "Thank you," she said, and lifted herself on tiptoes to kiss him on the cheek.

"You really do have nine lives, Clara."

"Well, at this point, I'm probably on my eighth."

She turned back to Lord Murdoch and offered her gloved hand. "This will do," she said. He bent and kissed it.

Clara gave one of her dazzling smiles, the one that used to bring audiences to their feet at the Berlin Opera House back when she was a prima donna. "Yes, this will do quite nicely."

Historical Notes

This is where we get to that part of the book where I always say this a work of fiction. My goal is to entertain, and if a reader here or there decides to do further research on what "really" happened (as some have written to tell me), I'm delighted.

Let's start with the SOE training camp in Arisaig, Scotland. Yes, Czechs and Slovaks, Norwegians, as well as all the agents who were sent to France, trained there. Arisaig House still exists and is now a bed-and-breakfast, where I'm honored to have stayed. The present owners still have the original plans to the house, marked up by British officers, remaking the manor house into a workable administrative hub, making the servants' dining room the officers' lounge, and even creating a small barbershop in the basement, near the wine cellar.

And yes (a lot of people questioned this!) the laundry was sent to a convent in Glasgow. Also, there really was a Japanese-American man on staff to teach martial arts, although his name seems lost to the ages.

The grounds really were the SOE's training grounds and even the present-day gardener, Richard Lamont, says that he's careful when he digs, "because you may hit the odd unexploded grenade."

There is a plaque commemorating SOE agents at Arisaig House, most of whom were dropped behind enemy lines in France. There is also a memorial to Slovak Jozef Gabčík and Czech Jan

Kubiš—who assassinated Nazi Reinhard Heydrich—in the town of Arisaig, where there is also the Museum of Sea and Isles, with a section dedicated to SOE.

For more information, I recommend the book at the Museum of Sea and Isles and also at Arisaig's Land, Sea, and Islands Centre, titled *Special Operations Executive: Para-Military Training in Scotland During World War II* by David Harrison. It contains amazing details about life in the Arisaig area and the instructors and trainees of SOE. I am indebted to it.

And yes, for those history scholars among you, the date of Special Envoy Kurusu's arrival to Washington, DC, and Hitler's declaration of war against the United States are both a bit early (artistic license).

In researching Pearl Harbor, I relied on many sources, but especially *At Dawn We Slept* and *The Broken Seal: "Operation Magic" and the Secret Road to Pearl Harbor*. Both are fascinating. So many of the characters in this book were real people, especially Mrs. Dorothy Edgars, Lieutenant Kramer's secretary, who translated the decrypt revealing the upcoming attack on Pearl Harbor on Friday, December 5, 1941, and was told by Kramer, "it could wait until Monday." (Of *course* a secretary called it, was all I could think . . .) Alas, *The Broken Seal* is out of print now, but the odd copy still exists, and, who knows, maybe it will come back as an e-book?

I had the privilege of visiting the Pearl Harbor Memorial and USS *Arizona*, and also the USS *Missouri*, the USS *Bowfin*, the Aviation Museum, the Royal Hawaiian Hotel, and the Manoa Hotel. The Army Museum on Waikiki is not as well publicized as some of the others, but it's a gem of a museum, and well worth going to.

———

In terms of information on spies and spycraft in World War II, I relied on many books, including *Beaulieu: The Finishing School for Secret Agents*, by Cyril Cunningham; *Churchill's War Lab: Code Breakers, Boffins and Innovators: The Mavericks Who Brought Britain Victory*, by Taylor Downing; *The Spies Who Never Were: The True Story of the Nazi Spies Who Were Actually Allied Double Agents*, by Hervie Haufler; *The Master Spy: The Story of Kim Philby*, by Phillip Knightly; *Young Philby*, by Robert Littell; *Ian Fleming*, by Andrew Lycett; *One Girl's War*, by Joan Miller; *Codename Tricycle: The True Story of the Second World War's Most Extraordinary Double Agent*, by Russell Miller; *Spy/Counterspy: The Autobiography of Dušan Popov*, by Dušan Popov; *My Silent War: The Autobiography of a Spy*, by Kim Philby; and *Odette*, by Jerrard Tickell.

There are many conspiracy theories about Pearl Harbor. Did President Franklin Delano Roosevelt know and still allow the attack to take place? Did Winston Churchill know? I don't believe FDR knew, after speaking to any number of scholars and doing extensive reading. However, I've chosen to have my fictional Mr. Churchill know about the impending attack and say nothing. First because I do believe the intelligence gathered at Bletchley Park was equal, if not superior, to the intel gathered by the United States' "Magic" machines and Purple code, but also because the British were much more organized than the Americans in terms of intelligence, with less petty bickering and infighting among the branches of service.

Second, the Abwehr gave Popov a map, which the British knew about, breaking down Pearl Harbor into sections, which Popov took to J. Edgar Hoover. Popov, in a later television interview, said that Hoover dismissed his concerns about Pearl Harbor because he

disliked him personally, and threatened to have him arrested and
thrown out of the United States under the Mann Act. In addition,
the British noted the Japanese Fleet off the coast of Formosa (now
Taiwan) and informed the Americans of the ship movement. They
must have believed that the fleet's movements posed a danger to
Pearl Harbor.

Whether it's true or not, for the purposes of this novel, I made
it so. Why? Because I believe *if* Churchill had known, he would
have done anything—anything—to save Britain. And so, his fictional actions here are completely in character.

Many books on the people, places, and institutions mentioned were
extremely helpful, specifically: *The Royal Ballet: 75 Years,* by Zoe
Anderson; *Daily Mail's Britain at War: Unseen Archives,* by Mau-
reen Hill; *Chequers: The House and Its History,* by Norma Major;
*The Last Lion 3: Winston Spencer Churchill: Defender of the Realm,
1940–65,* by William Raymond Manchester; *Honolulu: Then and
Now,* by Sheila Sarhagni; and *Dinner with Churchill: Policy-Making
at the Dinner Table,* by Cita Stelzer.

Yes, the British really did have mustard gas stockpiled for use during World War II, and were also developing anthrax. The research
did take place in Scotland, but on Gruinard Island, geographically
much farther to the north of Arisaig than where I fictionally placed
it. (It's ironic that at the time this was written, the use of chemical
weapons is still in the news with Syria.) For a fascinating look at
British research, and to watch actual footage of the experiments
on sheep, see "Gruinard Island Anthrax Biological Warfare Experiment Great Britain 1942" at www.youtube.com/watch?v=
TIpB2gVliyk (warning: not for the tenderhearted).

———

In dealing with the making and stockpiling of chemical and biological weapons in World War II and the history of chemical and biological warfare, as well as the concept of "just war," important books included: *Human Smoke: The Beginnings of World War II, the End of Civilization*, by Nicholson Baker; *The M Room: Secret Listeners Who Bugged the Nazis in World War II*, by Helen Fry; *Just War: The Just War Tradition, Ethics in Modern Warfare*, by Charles Guthrie and Michael Quinlan; *A Higher Form of Killing: The Secret History of Chemical and Biological Warfare*, by Robert Harris and Jeremy Paxman; *The Art of War*, by Niccolò Machiavelli and Ellis Farneworth; *The Horrors We Bless: Rethinking the Just-War Legacy*, by Daniel C. Maguire; *The Most Controversial Decision: Truman, the Atomic Bombs, and the Defeat of Japan*, by Wilson D. Miscamble CSC; *The Art of War*, by Sun Tzu; *War Is a Lie*, by David Swanson; *On War*, by Carl von Clausewitz; and *Just and Unjust Wars: A Moral Argument*, by Michael Walzer.

Japan in World War II and the attack on Pearl Harbor specifically was a fascinating topic to research. Again, I'd like to thank Ronald Granieri, PhD, and Michael Feeley for some of the book recommendations: *The Reluctant Admiral: Yamamoto and the Imperial Navy*, by Hiroyuki Agawa; *Hitler's Japanese Confidant*, by Carl Boyd; *The Man Who Broke Purple: The Life of Colonel William F. Friedman*, by Ronald William Clark; *Pearl Harbor: Final Judgement*, by Henry C. Clausen; *Codebreakers' Victory: How the Allied Cryptographers Won World War II*, by Hervie Haufler; *The Broken Seal*, by Ladislas Farago; *Pearl Harbor: FDR Leads the Nation into War*, by Steven M. Gillon; *Fateful Choices: Ten Decisions That Changed the World, 1940–1941*, by Ian Kershaw; *Marching Orders*, by Bruce Lee; and *At Dawn We Slept: The Untold Story of Pearl Harbor*, by Gordon W. Prange.

For information on floriography, I'm indebted to: *The Language of Flowers*, by Kate Greenaway; *Flora's Interpreter and Fortuna Flora (Classic Reprint)*, by Sarah Josepha Buell Hale; and *The Language of Flowers; With Illustrative Poetry; to Which Are Now Added the Calendar of Flowers and the Dial of Flowers*, by Frederic Shoberl.

A final book, which must be placed under the category of "other," was used for the basis of Clara Hess's story. It's classified as nonfiction—whether you believe that or not is up to you. Regardless, it's fascinating reading: *The CIA's Control of Candy Jones*, by Donald Bain. I'm not sure I believe it, but it's fascinating (and disturbing) to contemplate, and the origins of making such Manchurian Candidate–like spies allegedly has Nazi-era roots.

I relied on many films, as well, including: *Diary of War: Road to Pearl Harbor; Ken Burns: The War; Great Blunders of World War II; History of World War II: Japanese Paranoia; Japan's War: In Color; J. Edgar Hoover; John Ford's December 7th; Pearl Harbor: Before and After; Pearl Harbor: Dawn of Death; Pearl Harbor: Legacy of Attack; Pearl Harbor: The View from Japan;* and *War in the Pacific with Walter Cronkite. War in the Pacific* is particularly fascinating because it shows real-life spy Takeo Yoshikawa discussing his espionage work on Oahu, as well as his relationship with Consul Kita.

Acknowledgments

Thank you to Kate Miciak and Victoria Skurnick, Maggie Hope's fairy godmothers—tussy-mussies of pink roses, snapdragons, and violets to each.

And thanks to the usual suspects, Noel MacNeal and Idria Barone Knecht. For Noel, a bouquet of pink peonies. And for Idria, a vase of irises—purple and one yellow.

Pots of chrysanthemums to Lindsey Kennedy, Maggie Oberrander, Priyanka Krishnan, and Laura Jorstad, for all they do.

Dozens of lavender roses to Gina Wachtel, Susan Corcoran, Vincent La Scala, Kim Hovey, Dana Blanchette, and Sophia Wiedeman at Random House. And the Random House sales team deserves an extra special thank-you and an armful of camellias for believing in Maggie Hope from the beginning.

Bunches of bluebells to new friends in Scotland, including Sarah Winnington-Ingram at Arisaig House; her son, Archie Winnington-Ingram; husband, Peter Winnington-Ingram; and lovely golden labs Midge, Tarka, and Riska. As well as Richard Lamont and his lovely wife, Ann Lamont. Staying on the actual property where SOE agents trained and being able to explore the nearby land was invaluable. Being able to see the original floor plans the SOE officers wrote over when they appropriated the house gave me goose bumps.

In addition, a special thank-you and stalks of birds-of-paradise to Richard and Ann Lamont, who also took the time to speak with me and answer my questions. I'm humbled by your warmth and generosity to the lone Yank wandering around the Western Islands in winter—in questionable footwear, no less.

Branches of holly berries to Alison Stewart, who runs The Land, Sea & Islands Visitor Centre, and also to David M. Harrison, author of *Special Operations Executive: Para-Military Training in Scotland During World War II.*

Nasturtiums for Officer Rick McMahan in the United States, and Officers Lee Loftland and Paul Beecroft in the UK, who looked things over from the police and coroner's point of view.

Thanks and pink cherry blossom petals in cups of sake to friends from Japan: Taka Tsurutani, Yasushi Yagashita, Manabu Nagaoka, Mizuka Kamijo, Satoshi Tsuruoka (aka "Samurai Big Bird"), as well as Canadian Karen Fowler, and U.S.A.'s Michelle Hickey and Scott Cameron. I was privileged to be able to visit Tokyo while my husband was working on the Japanese production of *Sesame Street,* auditioning and training their Big Bird. It was during Sakura Matsuri season, and I completely, absolutely, and utterly fell in love with all things Japanese. Thank you for your hospitality in showing my husband and me around Tokyo, and sharing your vast knowledge of all things Japanese. Domo arigatou gozaimasu andどうも 有難う 御座います.

Thank you and a bunch of shamrocks to Michael T. Feeley, for both the book recommendations and good cheer.

A boutonniere of verbena and special thanks to historian Ronald J. Granieri, PhD, for suggestions for books, articles, films, and endless history-nerd chats about World War II (including enough conversations about anthrax and bioweapons that I'm sure we've landed on a government watch list).

Leis of hibiscus flowers to dear Kimmerie H. O. Jones and her mother, Valerie Jones, for the spirit of *aloha,* help in Honolulu, and stories of the attack on Pearl Harbor from the Hawaiian civilian point of view.

Delphiniums to Wendy Alden, BScN, for medical advice; Claire M. Busse, for flower symbolism; Scott Cameron; Camille Capozzi Carino and Jerry Carino; Edna MacNeal; and Caitlin Sims for their help and support.

A nosegay of magnolia blossoms to Professor Phyllis Brooks Schafer—Londoner, Blitz survivor, UC Berkeley lecturer, and all-around lovely person.

Gorgeous gladiolus to the inspiring Dr. Meredith Norris, for answering medical and anthrax-related questions.

And, as always, thank you to Matthew MacNeal—who would undoubtedly prefer chocolate to the cactus flowers I'd offer.

And, lastly, red poppies for the brave SOE operatives who trained at Arisaig House and elsewhere.

If you enjoyed *The Prime Minister's Secret Agent*, read on for an exciting early look at *Mrs. Roosevelt's Confidante*, the next ingenious suspense novel in the Maggie Hope series by *New York Times* bestselling author Susan Elia MacNeal!

PUBLISHED BY BANTAM BOOKS TRADE PAPERBACKS

Chapter One

Elise Hess was back in Berlin.

She'd been arrested as soon as she'd arrived back on German soil, as she knew she would be, and taken to Spandau Prison on Wilhelmstrasse—a fortress of shadows, battlements, and thick smokestacks.

"What is your position on Operation Compassionate Death?" they asked her. "Did you know Clara Hess was going to betray Germany? Who were those with her, and how were they hidden on the train from Berlin to Zurich?"

They were being polite this time, Elise noted. The superintendent of Spandau, acting as primary interrogator, offered her coffee and cigarettes, and kept the lights out of her eyes.

He was a tall man, thin, but with a paunch that gave him the ominous appearance of a spider.

"We have your friend Frieda in custody here, too," he said confidentially, getting up and walking around her, putting a hand on her shoulder. He leaned in, speaking in a confiding way. "We know you helped her husband, a Jew, escape. But how? And how was your mother involved?"

Elise remained silent. Frieda had betrayed her, but that didn't mean she would betray Frieda.

"Look," the superintendent said, finishing his circle around the table and sitting opposite her again, "I was raised Catholic, too. Do you know what the priests used to say? 'Give me a boy for seven years and I will give you a Catholic for life.' I understand how it works. And I understand you're a nurse and you want to be a nun? So admirable . . . But you're covering for a Jew-lover and a traitor—they've set you up to take the blame. And you know"—he pressed a hand to his heart—"it hurts me to see them do it, a lovely Aryan girl like you. If you could just tell me something, a little something, I'll see if I can help you, in return . . ."

Elise was sleep-deprived and hungry. She was confused and grieving. Her head hurt, her body hurt, her heart hurt.

"I'm not going to tell you anything," she said slowly, "so why don't you just do what you're going to do to me and get it over with."

An ugly look shadowed the supervisor's face. He pushed back his chair and regarded her with cold eyes. "What is your position on Operation Compassionate Death?"

Elise felt light-headed, but she held her ground, her eyes shining with conviction. "I believe that so-called Operation Compassionate Death isn't euthanasia—but murder. Dr. Brandt and the rest are murderers of innocent children."

"That is hearsay."

"I wish it were—but I've seen the gassing of children from Charité Hospital with my own eyes, at Hadamar."

The superintendent had lost patience. "That's enough. Guards!" Two men in gray uniforms grabbed Elise, one at each arm, and led her away.

"You're being moved, Fraulein Hess," he called after her.

Elise didn't answer. She knew where she was going. All the prisoners whispered about it, dreading the trip and the destination.

"I hope you will enjoy your stay at Ravensbrück. *Auf Wiedersehen, gnädiges Fräulein.*"

PHOTO: © LESLEY SEMMELHACK

SUSAN ELIA MACNEAL is the *New York Times* and *USA Today* bestselling author of the Maggie Hope mystery series, including *Mr. Churchill's Secretary*, *Princess Elizabeth's Spy*, and *His Majesty's Hope*. She is the winner of the Barry Award and was shortlisted for the Edgar, Macavity, Dilys, Bruce Alexander Memorial Historical Mystery, and Sue Federer Historical Fiction awards. She lives in Park Slope, Brooklyn, with her husband and son.

www.susaneliamacneal.com
Facebook.com/maggiehopefans
@SusanMacNeal